DECONSTRUCTION ACRES

by

Tim W. Brown

Tim Brown (signature)

III Publishing
P.O. Box 1581
Gualala, CA 95445

First Printing: October 1997

Cover Design by Michele Mach

for Audrey B. Pass

Portions of this novel have appeared in *Chicago Quarterly Review.*

ISBN 1-886625-03-4

ONE

Underdog became a townie during the second week he lived in Jasper. His purpose for coming to town was to begin his freshman year at Jasper College. He and his parents arrived on campus in an overloaded Oldsmobile, squeezed into and wriggling amongst all the possessions required to appoint a comfortable dorm room: suitcases filled with brand-new clothes bought from Underdog's high school graduation money; a black-and-white portable TV; a stereo system whose components were split into five boxes; toiletries contained in a plastic bucket for carting to and from the communal bathroom; a few of Underdog's favorite books; a box filled with school supplies; another box whose sides bulged from holding a football, basketball, baseball glove and frisbee; backgammon, chess and Monopoly games; posters rolled up and rubber-banded together; and a Norfolk pine tree, a gift from his high school sweetheart, which Underdog held in his lap, its branches slapping his face the entire trip due to the breeze blowing in open windows.

They parked in front of Barrett Hall, Underdog's new home, a dormitory he chose, despite its distance from most classrooms, because he wanted to try life in a high-rise after living all his life in a one-story ranch house. At check-in, the resident assistant informed him that his room would be on the second floor, not on the higher floors, much to Underdog's disappointment. Jostling with a hundred other students and their attendant families, Underdog and his dad managed to move his things into Room 212. As usual, his dad complained the whole time, about the line of people waiting for the elevators, and of the heat. Obese from a sit-down insurance agency job and a two-gallon-a-week ice cream habit, his dad sweat a lot; Underdog noticed that with each ride up the elevator, sweat stains on his dad's shirt became more pronounced, as did his chili pepper smell. Sick of his dad's complaints, he suggested that they take the stairs, since it was only one flight up. His dad said to hell with that idea, he had "to get up and go to work tomorrow and pay for all this."

Underdog's mom stayed in the room, busying herself by exploring its storage capacity; she pulled open all the desk and bureau drawers and felt around inside them, opened up the closet and peered inside, and crouched on her knees to assess whether Underdog's empty stereo boxes would fit under his bed. By the time Underdog and his dad finished bringing everything up from the car, his mom had an efficient storage system figured out and directed where each item should be put. Once all of Underdog's things were stowed to his mom's satisfaction, his dad announced that he and his mom had to leave, so they would get home before it got dark. Never mind, thought both Underdog and his mom, that it was only three o'clock, that it wouldn't be dark for another four or five hours, and that his parents' house was up in Peru, a half-hour drive north. "Let's go," his dad insisted as his mom hastily kissed Underdog on the cheek and wiped her eyes, fighting off tears welling up. Before walking through the heavy, self-locking doors that led to the elevator lobby, his mom sniffled and turned to wave pitifully, and his father accusingly pointed his finger and said, "Make sure to call your mother."

Leave it to his dad, thought Underdog, sitting on his bed and looking over the dorm room, to rush him and his mom through a big event in their lives. It reminded him of past occasions, like when his dad wanted to skip the reception after Underdog's induction into the National Honor Society, or when he was irritated by the little brothers and sisters of Underdog's classmates running around the park during the band's family picnic, then demanded that they leave right after they ate, causing Underdog to miss out on all the fun and games afterward.

At least his mother acted like she would miss him; she even sat him down at the kitchen table several weeks before his move to Jasper and told him how she was glad to see him grow up, but sorry to see him move out of the house. Sensing that her son suspected that his father was glad for him to go, she added that his dad would miss him, too.

"But he keeps telling me how he can't wait for me to move out so he can turn my bedroom into a TV room," Underdog said.

"You know it's hard for your dad to show how he feels."

"Well, he sure yells a lot. He doesn't have any trouble showing when he's mad at me. Which he's been all the time lately."

"That's a sign he's torn about the idea of you going off to college. Deep down, he knows he'll be sorry when you're gone."

"Has he told you that?" Underdog asked.

"No, but I can tell he'll miss you."

"I wish I could tell," he responded, then left his mom, who cried softly into a pot holder. He wanted to tell her that he'd miss her, too.

But instead he shut himself in his room, put on headphones, and turned his stereo up loud to drown all of the sad thoughts suddenly swimming around inside his head.

The sound of the door to his dorm room opening interrupted Underdog's reverie. In came a gangly individual wearing a seed corn baseball cap who was carrying a laundry basket full of folded shirts and blue jeans. He set the basket down on the other bed in the room, then introduced himself as John Schmutzer. Immediately after shaking Underdog's hand, he took off his shirt, saying, "It's hotter than a pig barn inside here." The hat, the pig barn crack and the classic farmer tan revealed to Underdog indicated that he had acquired a farm boy for a roommate.

To get a feel for his new roommate, hoping he was of the cool farm boy variety — like his friend Jeff, who threw beer and bonfire parties on his parents' farm outside Peru, and not the sick type that picked up kids who lived in town, beat them up and dumped them in corn fields far away from home — he said, "Yeah. I wish I had a beer right now to cool me off."

To Underdog's great relief, John said, "Me too," and then they talked about kicking in on a small refrigerator where they would store all their beer. That issue settled, John left to move the rest of his things into the room, and Underdog walked down the hall to take in his new surroundings. Hovering outside ten or twelve doorways there were his new floor mates, each looking him over expectantly, hoping to make a new friend. Underdog politely nodded to each, but saw nobody that he thought he could relate to, since nearly everybody, in their sleeveless Forty-Niner and Cowboy tee shirts, had that brawny, macho look of the jocks at his high school, whom he couldn't stand. To prevent any unwanted conversation, he ducked into the bathroom. Inside the bathroom, he was glad to find that there were a number of shower stalls, all of which had its own shower curtain to ensure privacy as residents washed. The thing that Underdog most hated about high school was showering in gym class; there were parts of his body that he simply didn't like washing in front of people.

Upon his return to the room, he found a note taped to the door from John. It said that he was going out to buy books at the campus bookstore and promised that he would stop over at the home of a buddy, who was old enough to buy beer. At that moment, the door across the hall opened and out stepped a shaggy-haired guy wearing a faded Aerosmith tee shirt. To Underdog, this looked like a person he could maybe relate to.

"Mark Reid," said the guy.

"You can call me Underdog."

"What are you, some kind of cartoon?" asked Reid.

"Everybody calls me that. Ever since my second grade Halloween party, when I wore an Underdog costume."

Seeing that his beer approach worked once already in breaking the ice, and hoping that Reid might himself have some beer to share while he waited for his roommate's return, Underdog said, "I wish I had a beer right now to cool me off."

"That'd be good," said Reid. "But you know what I could really go for? A joint."

Underdog laughed, for unbeknownst to his parents, he also had packed among his things a plastic baggie full of marijuana. "I've got some," he said.

"I'll get my papers. Plus I've got a couple of beers." Reid went to his room and returned a moment later with a sweaty paper sack. Both of them furtively glanced up and down the hall, then slipped into Underdog's room. Underdog dug the baggie of weed from out of his school supply box, while Reid pulled a couple of cans of Budweiser from out of the paper sack. He also pulled out a can of spray deodorant.

"What's that for?" asked Underdog, watching Reid open the door to the hall again.

"Throws the R.A. off the scent," answered Reid, spraying a big, white cloud of deodorant into the hallway. When he shut the door, he said, "Best to put a towel under the door, too."

"Is it safe to smoke in here?"

"Well, you can get kicked out of the dorm if they catch you. But if you take a couple of precautions, you won't get caught."

"Sounds like you're an old pro at this."

"I'm a sophomore now. I guess that gives me pro status."

After Underdog stuffed a towel from his toiletries bucket under the door and Reid rolled up a joint, they pulled chairs over to the window and proceeded to pass the joint back and forth. They took long drags, then blew the smoke through the screen, watching it disperse over a basketball court. As they smoked, they got acquainted. Reid was a sociology major from Iowa; he listened to bands like Aerosmith and Guns 'n Roses. Underdog informed Reid that he planned to pursue a program in business administration, and he preferred more straight-ahead rock and roll, but he could still appreciate the head-banger stuff.

After they had smoked about three-quarters of the joint, the door swung open, and John walked in the room juggling a plastic shopping bag filled with books, a twelve pack of Miller beer, and a ten-pound bag of ice. "Join us?" asked Underdog, motioning John to hurry up and shut the door.

"No, but you go ahead and start the beers without me," said John, a little startled. "I'll be back," he said, laying down his load on his desk, then exiting again.

"You didn't tell me you got stuck with Schmutzer," said Reid. "We better put this out before he gets back."

"He doesn't approve?"

"No, man, he disapproves. Real bad." Underdog hastily put out the joint on the window ledge and pocketed the roach. For several minutes they both sat silently, anticipating John's return and feeling swarms of ants crawl up their legs, a paranoid sensation made doubly bad by marijuana. Then they heard a knock at the door, knuckles rapping hard and insistent.

"I think we're busted," said Reid. "They know we're in here, so you better open up."

Underdog opened the door, and there stood the resident assistant who checked him into the dorm earlier that afternoon. The R.A. spied around the room, raised his eyebrows in acknowledgment of Reid, sniffed the air a few times, then asked Underdog to follow him to his room. There he explained to Underdog that John had complained of his marijuana smoking, that as R.A. he must respond to the complaint by filling out an "incident report," and that Underdog would have to appear at a hearing before a college disciplinary board to determine if he should be removed from the dorm.

What followed was a week where Underdog felt adrift in a river full of white water rapids. The routine of attending class buoyed him, giving him the impression that things were floating along nicely, that his head was still above water. But below the surface he sensed a nasty undertow which threatened to pull him under for good, with nothing, not a rock or branch, to cling to. The only lifeline anybody offered to throw was when the disciplinary board assigned his case to the school's ombudsman, a woman who would represent him at the board's hearing.

She was not a lawyer like he hoped, however, but a math professor who, it was plain, would rather have been teaching class than serving her turn as ombudsman in the rotating system the school had devised. As Underdog sat in her office in the Sciences Building, explaining his side of the story, she barely listened; instead, she stared out the window at the twisted metal sculptures that dotted the college square, and twirled her bangs in her fingers, acting like all the bored girls he observed in high school study hall. All his experiences with her before the hearing pointed to the fact that they might as well have thrown him a sack of lead to catch, so he could sink to the river bottom and be done with it.

At the hearing itself, Underdog felt certain he would be railroaded right out of the dorm when he looked over the three persons making up the disciplinary board. The first, the Director of Residence Halls, whose pained expression made Underdog think he hadn't had a bowel movement in weeks, declared his intention to "make this case send a clear signal at the start of the school term" about his policy of zero tolerance concerning drugs. The second, a senior business major who wore a navy blue three-piece suit with an American flag in its lapel, testified how drug parties prevented him from studying for final exams the previous semester. The third, a weasly-looking professor of ethics, expounded on how Jasper College had a mission to steer its students away from the "immoral fog of drugs" so that they could assume their places in society.

Also present was John Schmutzer, whom Underdog had succeeded in having the entire dorm floor refer to by the nickname "Schmuckster" in response to his tattling on him. Underdog explained to everyone who inquired that he would have been perfectly happy to stop smoking pot if John had asked. Although many of the guys he talked to did not do drugs themselves, they nonetheless sympathized with Underdog, for John had violated an ancient schoolboy code by tattling. John recounted for the board how he walked in on Underdog, embellishing his story with out-and-out lies, like how the room was so thick with marijuana smoke he left coughing and choking. Absent was Underdog's partner in crime, Reid, who honorably refused to speak at the hearing.

Earlier in the week, during one of those rare moments when he had the ombudsman's attention, he asked her why Reid was not facing the disciplinary board. She answered by saying that it was "a situation analogous to drunk driving." Only the drunk driver is held responsible, not his passengers, she explained; the offense in question occurred in Underdog's room, so Reid would not be held accountable.

Since he was caught red-handed, Underdog's only defense was that he did not know that smoking marijuana resulted in getting kicked out of the dorm. Professor Morality responded by saying that "in all judicial systems, ignorance is not an excuse in breaking the law," adding that the towel under the door which tripped up John Schmutzer when he entered the room was evidence that Underdog knew he was committing an illegal act. After deliberating for only four minutes, the board ruled that Underdog had twenty-four hours to vacate his room, and the college would refund his room and board money less one week's stay.

There was more bad news for Underdog, however. The constipated Director of Housing announced that he would also be expelled from the college. He admitted that he had no jurisdiction over off-campus housing, saying, "If students who live off-campus want to smoke dope and zone out on MTV, that's their business." But then he brought to everyone's attention the *in loco parentis* rule that required all freshman-level students who were registered at Jasper College to live on campus. Underdog could probably get away with attending class for another few weeks, but the Registrar's Office would eventually catch up with him. He advised Underdog to withdraw from school right then, so the college would refund more of his tuition than if he waited to be dropped from their records. Thus, a few hits of marijuana effectively ended Underdog's college career before it started.

Until the final decision was made, Underdog did not inform his parents of the goings-on. But once the hearing before the board was over, he returned to the dorm to place the phone call. Ever since being turned in by Schmuckster, he spent a minimal amount of time in the room. Reid and his roommate were nice enough to let Underdog drag a mattress into the center of their room and sleep on the floor, and he spent most of his time outside of class in their room, fretting over his troubles and drinking beer in an effort to dilute them. He was sure that they wouldn't mind if he called long distance from their phone, but he decided to call from Schmuckster's phone and stick him with the cost. Upon Schmuckster's leaving for his Friday three o'clock class, Underdog entered the room to get on with the dirty deed.

As could be understood, his parents were shocked that in a matter of a week their son was kicked out of both dorm and school; they were doubly shocked as to why, because, with the help of breath mints and eye drops, Underdog had succeeded in hiding his smoking habit from them for three years. They had never caught him smoking marijuana, they probably didn't even know what it smelled like. So when he proposed moving home and attending Peru Community College, his father refused. "You had your chance, young man, and you muffed it. I'll be goddamned if I have a drug addict living under my roof," he said. Moreover, he refused to have any further dealings with his son, telling Underdog before hanging up the phone that he was on his own and not to bother calling home again.

Feeling sorry as a misbehaving dog abandoned miles from home, Underdog began to pack up his things. While fumbling with his cassette player and box, the phone rang. He decided to answer, hoping it was his father calling back after he had a half-hour to cool off. Instead, his mother was on the line. Her voice breaking, she told him that she and his father had talked it over and decided to let him keep the refunded tuition and room and board money to tide him over until he found a job. She would have loved for him to return home, she explained, but she couldn't go against his father's wishes. Then she hung up in a hurry, leaving Underdog only to imagine how tear-soaked the pot holders in her kitchen must be.

TWO

After his dismissal from Jasper College, Underdog searched for housing in the student ghetto, a part of town nestled between the college and "Suds City," what Jasperites nicknamed a two-block stretch of bars straddling Highway 17. There he found a third-floor room to rent in a boarding house. Sticking out from the rest of the homes on the block, which all were dressed in paler hues, the exterior of the house where he lived was painted mustard-brown, what Underdog called "puke" when directing friends who wanted to stop by. "I live in the puke-colored house on Elm Street," he would say to them, alluding to a color that his friends, mostly over-imbibers at the bars of Suds City, could readily identify.

Underdog's landlady, Mona Baine, would surely be upset if she heard him describe her house that way, for the upkeep of the three-story Victorian home had become her mission in life. Originally from Terre Haute, Indiana, Mona Baine became a townie when she moved to Jasper with her husband, Jack Baine, an instructor of physical education and golf coach at the college. She met Jack in Terre Haute at a golf tournament that he was playing in. Smitten, he called her "Teeth," an apt description of her constant smile, and also a play on "Tee," in honor of her exaggerated eye teeth, pointy like white golf tees growing out of the roof of her mouth. (Understandably, he kept this private joke to himself.) After meeting, they kept in touch by writing and phoning as he traveled from city to city on the junior P.G.A. tour.

Believing Mona the only girl in the world for him, Jack determined that if he were to marry her, the chance of supporting her was not good if he continued to play golf professionally: he typically shot in the mid-eighties, the second or third worst every round, so his share of the purse was too small to feed himself, let alone a wife or children. Host families housed and fed him on the tour, but his winnings never added up to much more than beer money.

With perfect timing, Jasper College contacted his agent towards the end of that year's tour and proposed a deal that would solve his financial worries and simultaneously supply a golf-related income: they offered to make him coach of their golf team. His only other duty would be to teach one golf class per year, for students whom he called "duffers," who needed to earn an extra hour of elective credit to graduate. Jack leaped at the opportunity; with no regrets whatsoever, he quit the P.G.A., married Mona, bought her a big Victorian house on Elm Street, then twelve months later supplied her with a baby daughter she named Judith, in honor of his mother. For the next several years, life for the Baine family went on as smooth and simple as the game of golf: green by green, each hole attained with a graceful stroke and good follow-through.

That is, until the big thunderstorm in summer of 1976, on an afternoon weathermen had predicted would present a zero percent chance of rain. The storm came over the horizon "with all the speed, surprise and destructive power of Japanese planes attacking Pearl Harbor," reported the *Jasper Weekly Shopper* afterwards. Accuracy, too, when noting with what precision a lightning bolt shot down Jack Baine, who was caught pants down, literally, while he urinated behind the seventh green of the school's nine-hole course. People still disagree whether or not a tornado also hit — some say they saw one, others saw none, and one person claimed to have seen twin tornadoes — whatever the case, the storm uprooted trees, snapped telephone poles in half and scythed a quarter-mile-wide path in corn fields. As for Jack Baine, they found him after the storm, looking like a grilled pork chop, his face charred to a delicate crunchiness, nylon jacket melting around the edges, fatty beer gut sizzling and bubbling underneath.

Within two years of her husband's death, Mona Baine's grief had largely dissipated, thanks to the project of converting the upstairs portion of her house into rooms for boarders, which she pursued with all the enthusiasm of a beaver constructing a dam. Through classified ads run in the Jasper College *Chronicler*, she solicited "quiet, studious young men," whom she affectionately likened to weeds that blew in farm fields, grew for one or two years beside more civilized corn or wheat, then moved on to the next field. Her current crop of young men included Underdog, who, not wanting to repeat his dorm mistake, generally kept to himself in his room, like his two Nigerian roommates on the second floor, graduate students who in their spare time stayed home and chain-smoked unfiltered cigarettes. He mainly listened to his stereo through headphones and saw his depression reflected in the furnished room he rented, which contained myriad shades of blue: navy blue curtains, a sky blue bedspread, a cobalt blue carpet peppered with cigarette burns, and a dresser lacquered blue, the layers of paint so thick that the drawers stuck during humid weather, almost like the paint never dried.

"Bastard better open this time," said Underdog, as he leveraged himself to yank open his underwear drawer, glued shut on account of the rainy September morning. After unsticking the drawer on his third try, he commenced dressing. How appropriate! he thought, reminded that the quiet face he put on for the Baine household, psychological wet paint, prevented females from reaching inside *his* drawers, among other good things that could take place in his room, like maybe a good old-fashioned drunken bout spent bawling and kicking walls.

Outfitted in a black tee-shirt, blue jeans, cloppy work shoes and a denim jacket, he headed downstairs for work. To avoid as much rain as he could, he decided to take the inner stairs rather than the outside ones down the side of the house, which he preferred because he could more easily avoid people he didn't want to see, like Mona or Judy Baine.

But as he swung around the corner onto the second floor landing, there knelt Mona, furiously dipping a rag into a pail full of pine-scented ammonia cleaner and wiping down the maplewood banister. Underdog mentally added this chore to a growing inventory of Mona's manic, round-the-clock activities he had witnessed, which included washing leaded-glass windows, dust-mopping hardwood floors, sponging down plaster walls, scrubbing out porcelain sinks, scouring stainless steel bathroom fixtures, waxing knotty pine paneling, vacuuming cobwebs, beating oriental rugs, polishing Jack's golf trophies, and, depending on the season, raking leaves, shoveling snow or cleaning gutters.

"High-ho, high-ho, it's off to school we go!" sang Mona Baine.

"Going to my job at the print shop," he muttered.

"Oh. Then it's off to work we go!"

"Um, yeah," he said, brushing past her.

"Save your pennies," she called down the stairs after him. "Maybe you'll move into your own house someday, meet a nice girl, settle down."

Once again, Underdog was astounded at the irony: despite bad luck with how marriage turned out for her, Mona Baine remained annoyingly upbeat about the institution, especially since house rules forbade "visiting" with a girl in your room. Exiting the house, he pulled his jacket over his head. Then, like a crab pulled mostly inside his shell, he blundered sideways through blowing rain to Jasper College, where he worked at the college's print shop.

Since Underdog's expulsion from school took place in the days before the Japanese auto plant was built outside town, the only place in Jasper to find a job was at the hated college. Swallowing his pride, which went down like handful of broken glass, he made an appointment at the Placement Office, where he discovered a woman with a higher sympathy quotient than the math professor Ombudsman. Although she stated that she preferred registered students to "civilians" when filling jobs, she went ahead and inflated a part time work study slot into a full time "Bindery Assistant" job at the campus print shop. The work largely consisted of collating, stapling, saddle-stitching and shrink-wrapping printed matter for various college departments.

Stationing his soggy self at the bindery table, he began to fasten plastic spiral binders onto booklets roughly twenty pages thick, putting a job marked "no hurry" first to allow his clothes to dry before beginning his other important duty, delivering finished print jobs to offices all over the college. By eleven o'clock, however, the rain still had not let up. He couldn't delay his morning rounds any longer, so he gathered a load into an empty paper carton and departed for the first stop, the student activities office. Carrying the box occupied both hands; unfortunately, neither hand was available to hold an umbrella to shield himself from rain drops pelting his forehead like bugs smacking into a windshield.

Like everybody, except for farmers nursing fledgling corn or soybean plants outside of town, Underdog hated rain. Bad weather vexed him to no end; an impersonal force to many people, it was something whose effects he took personally. He thought it all so unfair that bad weather happened to him, somebody who possessed a live-and-let-live outlook. After all, he didn't start a water fight with anybody, he wasn't spraying anyone with a garden hose; why was he getting sprayed? Perhaps what bothered him most was that there was no recourse, nobody to complain to who could do something about bad weather, make it stop. If it were truly God controlling the weather, then he was not the merciful supreme being that his reputation boasted of, but instead the supreme bureaucrat, sitting atop the great chain of being, nose in his ledger, deaf to a dissatisfied customer's legitimate gripes.

In a futile effort to dodge the rain, he revised his normal route so he cut through as many buildings as he could. He bypassed altogether one of his favorite sites, the alumni garden, still bursting with late-blooming flowers. Instead, he found himself trudging down the main hall of the biology building, where he smelled formaldehyde, a smell not unlike strong-scented marigold. Then he ducked into the Art Building; strolling through the halls, he viewed impromptu gallery walls hung with charcoal drawings depicting the same flower and vase, each one more lopsided than the next and autographed illegibly by freshman art majors.

Hearing a steady commotion coming from a door left ajar, he decided to investigate. He peeked into a studio full of students sitting at tables scribbling on big sheets of paper. Looking toward the front of the room, he spied a beautiful woman reclined on her back, posing nude. He stood for a second, hypnotized by the sight, until he noticed saliva gathering at the corners of his mouth, whereupon he lowered his eyes in embarrassment. Not daring to look a second time, at least not yet, he snuck glances at the drawings of her materializing on paper.

The female students appeared to eye her critically, a few of them drawing her breasts too small, not giving her full credit, or cattily drawing her hips too wide. The males gaped at her upturned, red-haired sex, trying their best to accurately and lovingly draw each fold. Underdog wished he had pencil and paper, too, wished he had the skill to capture the essence of this woman, who, coated with light freckles, drew to mind a leopardess. Most of all, he wished for her to train her eyes on him to let him puzzle the source of her distant, haunted gaze. With her image etched onto his retinas, like photographic ghosts on offset printing plates back at the shop, he moved on to his next destination, a fitting one given his sudden urge to mate, Animal Husbandry.

* * *

During lunch the rain stopped, which made Underdog grateful. He was less grateful for what he ate, a bagel bought out of a vending machine in the student center. After heating too long in the school-maintained, industrial-strength microwave oven, it tasted like a lawn mower wheel. Still chewing the last of it, after popping it in his mouth a thousand yards before, he approached the Castle to resume his work day. He wondered if passers by noticed him leering at the image in his head of the naked art woman.

The Castle — Castle Hall — was originally the entire sum total of Jasper College. Three stories tall, not counting the turrets and towers, it loomed menacingly over everything in the central campus area. Constructed of rough-hewn limestone, it was a panoply of towers, turrets, parapets, massive arched doorways, gargoyles and dark, skinny windows, from where you expected to be shot in the gut with an archer's arrow if you got too close. Each time Underdog entered the structure he was reminded that in nineteenth century America, like in the late twentieth, architects who graduated at the bottom of their classes designed wacky-looking college buildings, not stately banks or grand museums.

The Castle's first floor contained three things: a large meeting room sometimes booked for conferences (bug scientists most recently); the "Little Theater," an auditorium where plays were produced or small-time rock bands performed (a play about the Lindbergh baby kidnapping the most recent show); and a gymnasium, which had been renovated to serve as the college print shop. The gym, which probably held no more than several dozen spectators in its heyday in 1910, was long ago supplanted by a quonset hut-looking thing, where Jasper's Division III basketball and volleyball teams played before audiences numbering in the low hundreds.

Underdog entered the print shop office, a tiny room perched above the gym where radio announcers and official scorers sat in times of yore. "Make sure you mark your time card that you're back from lunch," said Ron Sullivan, for the two hundred and fifty-ninth work day in a row. Feet up, he sat at his desk, peering menacingly over the top of a *Soldier of Fortune* magazine. On the magazine's cover, a shirtless, flat-topped man posed proudly with cartridge belts crossing his heart. Above and to the right of Ron's chair, a dusty, scraggly boar's head hung on the beige canvas-covered wall, a "troublesome kill" that often served as visual aid for the personal hunting dramas Ron narrated for anyone who gave him more than a minute of his time. Nearly everybody in the office, including Underdog, was bothered by the boar's head, but couldn't complain about it since Ron was boss.

"I will," answered Underdog, signing in, then darting back out, feigning a brusque, diligent air. He tried to spend as little time as possible with Ron, whom Underdog expected some day to come to work armed with a semiautomatic rifle and blast to bits the old noisy collator, which he promised "to do something about someday."

On the gymnasium floor there still could be seen faint basketball court striping, the circles, lane markings and out-of-bounds lines that past players wore off in their long-forgotten games. At one end of the court there were five offset presses of varying sizes and capacities, set in a 2-3 defensive pattern, the biggest press where a basketball center usually is positioned, under the backboard. At the other end, a 3-2 defensive set was seen, with a rotary collator, paper cutter, saddle stitcher, folder and shrink-wrap machine.

As Underdog proceeded to the paper cutter, a machine that resembled an electric guillotine, he purposefully shuffled his feet, scuffing the hardwood floor with his steel-toed work shoes, how he got back at every crabby gym teacher and lunch monitor who ever yelled at him for wearing street shoes on gym floors of schools he attended during his life. The only requisition sheet he found taped to the paper cutter directed him to cut glossy paper in poster sizes, which he did. Then he assembled a load for his afternoon delivery run.

He walked upstairs to the third floor of Castle Hall, where each room was exactly the same tiny size, because the third floor served as the original student dormitory, with doors spaced out regular as a soldier's pace. Presently, these rooms were being used as administrative offices of different sorts. Three and four-person departments like the accounting office were stuffed into them, the same as one-person operations like Latino Student Outreach. His only stop on three was the payroll office, where Mildred, the secretary, greeted him with oatmeal cookies she baked the night before. This was a fringe benefit of his job: he always walked in on birthday celebrations or bon voyage parties and partook of cake, brownies or cookies baked for the occasion. Underdog helped himself to a cookie and thanked her; she thanked him in return for the letterhead he brought her, then by way of saying good-bye, jokingly cautioned him to "stay out of trouble."

"Always do," he responded, suddenly embarrassed in front of the grandmotherly Mildred by the lust he felt for the naked art woman.

He headed downstairs to the second floor of Castle Hall, which housed the college's bread-and-butter offices: records, admissions, financial aid and the credit union, which is where he stopped next. He plopped his box on the counter, prompting a red-haired woman, whose back was to him, to swivel around in her chair and face him. "May I help you?" she asked.

Underdog was dumbfounded: it was the naked art woman. He shut his eyes and shook his head in an Etch-A-Sketch effort to erase the cruel hallucination, because it certainly could not really be her. But when he opened his eyes again, she was still there, now fully clothed in a low-cut, leopard-print top and tight stirrup pants. Drawing all of his attention were freckles sprinkled across her chest and down her cleavage.

"Do you need some help?" she asked again, looking at him like someone looking at a mentally disturbed individual, polite yet quizzical.

"I, um, didn't recognize you with your clothes on," was all Underdog managed to mumble.

"Excuse me?"

"I mean, you're new. Haven't seen you in here before."

"No, you probably haven't — it's only my third week working here. But it sounds like you've seen plenty of me in the Monday-Wednesday life drawing class."

"Me? Um, no."

"Then what was that 'didn't recognize me' comment?"

"I was delivering something this morning. Passed by the studio. The door was open. I looked in."

She fixed her gaze on him. "You were spying on me? Because I've had men do that before, and if you are . . . ."

"No, no, nothing like that. It was a there-at-the-right-time-and-place thing."

"Did you like what you saw?" she asked, leaning back in her chair and mocking her art class pose. Apparently he said the right thing, because her mood improved immediately. It was like making a mistake when writing: you explode in anger, wad up a piece of paper, and toss it into the trash. Then you start anew, muse forgiven.

Underdog swallowed hard. "Very much," he said.

"I'm Ione." She directed his attention to the brass name plate on her desk. Her last name was Twayblade.

"You can call me Underdog."

"What the hell kind of name is that?"

"Been called that since I was a kid."

"Is that how you view yourself in life?"

"Never really thought about it."

"I tend to go for underdogs. Take me out on a date."

Underdog pondered the idea for a moment. He couldn't believe how smooth their interaction was going now. "I've got nothing going on Thursday," he said.

"Then pick me up at Taylorville E-9 at six-thirty. And remember — I'm expecting you to sweep me off my feet."

"Sure," he said. He picked up his box and turned for the door.

"Underdog?"

He turned back again.

"Did you have something for me in the box?"

"Um, yeah," he said. As he pulled off the lid, he bobbled the box, almost spilling its contents onto the floor. After recovering control, he reached inside, pulled out two rubber-banded bundles, and handed them across the counter. "Your deposit slips, ma'am," he said, bowing respectfully.

"That will be all, Underdog," she responded, then waved him out of her office with a flourish.

As he left Castle Hall to finish the rest of his run, he thanked everybody he could think of for his good fortune, trying not to leave anyone out — God, Jesus, Allah, Buddha, Zeus, and the puffy, cumulus clouds floating in the now-clear sky — because he managed to meet, talk to and make a date with the mysterious nude female he only beheld from afar earlier that day. Hugging his box, he quite literally skipped between the afternoon's remaining delivery locations, every so often chanting the words "Ione Ione Ione" as his soles clapped the sidewalk, not caring a good goddamn how silly he might look to passers by.

THREE

Judy Baine had a crush on Underdog. She wanted to see what lay beneath the underwear of Underdog. She knew she liked everywhere else on him. She liked especially his forearms, how veins curled around them. And she liked his shoulders, how broad they were, like he carried sheep on them, rugged shepherd character that he was. Underdog fit the type of man she liked best, one whose body only hinted of athleticism, unlike the jock weight lifters at the college who looked manufactured, with biceps bigger than her head and stomachs that were hard and ribbed as washboards.

Though he didn't devote whole evenings to lifting weights, or spend money on powdered protein additives, or ask around the weight room about steroid connections, he still was concerned with his physique. So on slow days at the print shop, he'd step onto the storage dock in back and work out with paper cartons taken off tall stacks. He slipped his fingers under the fiberglass straps, then muscled them up and down in various routines, counting to ten and choo-chooing like a loco.

Underdog knew full well that he piqued Judy's interest; he sensed her lurking upstairs in the boarders' portion of the house, off-limits to her, which she frequented anyway. He felt her eyes on him, peeking around a corner, or looking up from the bottom of the stairs, or timing things so she walked past the bathroom as he exited. So he made a point of accidentally-on-purpose allowing her glimpses of himself, traveling between his room and the bathroom wearing only briefs. When he really felt full of the dickens, he put on his favorite pair of underwear: black and orange bengal-striped bikinis, which he believed flattered his bulge.

Lately, their peek-a-boo sessions had come to resemble a dramatic farce, with characters opening and slamming doors, tip-toeing between rooms, hiding behind curtains, jumping inside closets. All of this led Underdog to think that she might reach out soon and touch what hitherto she had only looked upon.

Born a townie, Judy Baine lived at home with her mother, Mona. The classic underachiever, she dropped out of Jasper College after only one semester, despite free tuition owing to her deceased father's faculty position. Not the bookish type, she must have inherited her mother's farmer genes — she could pretty near make anything grow. Hence, when she turned eighteen, she started her own business with her small inheritance, a landscaping operation. Actually, "landscaping" was too fancy a term considering that what she mostly did was lawn mowing, weed pulling and hedge trimming. Regardless, she worked wonders with yards — turning a lot choked with dandelions or crab grass into a uniform green lawn growing the finest Kentucky blue combed stiff as Astroturf.

She advertised in the *Jasper Weekly Shopper*, and word of her skill had spread by mouth so far and wide that lawn work kept her busy sixty hours a week during spring, summer and fall. And her clients paid her well; she charged a set monthly maintenance fee that covered weekly mowing, weeding, edging and applying fertilizer or seed, if necessary. She also contracted for additional projects like planting flower beds and tilling vegetable gardens. Her expanding client list included the Taylorville Mobile Home Development; the First National Bank of Jasper; East End Medical Park; Jasper College President Milton Flaghorn; and just-added celebrity Professor William Fletcher.

She made good money three seasons out of the year. But when the last fallen leaf was raked up and bagged in autumn, the lean times commenced as winter gusted into Jasper. Apart from some cleaning she did for her mother around the boarding house, she had much leisure time on her hands, which afforded her the opportunity to pursue indoor activities. Outdoors, she worked miracles growing grass, flowers and tomato plants, but her favorite indoor things to make grow were the penises of her mother's boarders. And for that particular fall and winter she had decided to make Underdog's her pet project.

Indeed, Underdog noticed that her advances had grown bolder in just the past few days. Two nights before, he stopped home to eat and change before he went out to see what was shaking — maybe something, probably nothing — at Roger's Bar. Aware that he stuck to this schedule five nights of every seven, Judy concocted a Garden Mistress scenario where she lay in wait for him.

Appetite dulled by the faint smell of ammonia that trailed Mona Baine everywhere, Underdog threw out the canned minestrone soup he had warmed on the stove and proceeded from the basement boarders' kitchen to the bathroom upstairs to wash his hands. When he flipped on the light switch, there sat Judy on the toilet, stark naked, a potted shrub between her spread legs. "Like my bush?" she asked, looking up at him.

Underdog quickly looked her up and down. No doubt whatsoever that she was lean and fit, a woman sculpted from solid, corn-fed material. He certainly liked what he saw, which was everything, felt himself strain against his fly. But instead of seizing upon her, he muttered, "Excuse me," and turned away, flicking off the light and leaving the bathroom for the safety of his bedroom, where he dove under the covers and rocked slowly back and forth, counting backwards from one thousand, until his erection subsided. He tried to convince himself that he made the right decision in not having sex with Judy — after all, laying the daughter of your landlady, someone akin to your mother, was like doing your own sister. Sure, it would be convenient having a live-in lover to scratch you when and where you itched, but what if either party lost the itch, salved by someone else's calamine? Worse, what if Mona found them out?

These and other questions echoed in Underdog's head, keeping him from sleep and distracting him for two whole days from safe operation of the paper cutter and hole puncher.

That is, until he met Ione, when a whole new set of questions came to mind. Ione had jump-started his genitals, which had gone cold from months of disuse. To keep his cells fully charged until his date with her later in the week, he decided after all to plug into Judy, about whom he had dropped all doubts by the time he rounded the corner on his walk home from work, and the puke-colored boarding house came into sight.

The first place he searched for Judy was in the bathroom, the scene of their crime two nights before. Upon flipping on the light the only person he saw was himself, reflected in the mirror that was bolted onto the wall. Next, he descended two flights of stairs to the boarders' kitchen; all he found there was his Nigerian roommate Ndeka, clasping a Pall Mall in one hand and laying out turkey legs in a baking pan with the other. "Ah, Underdog," he said, exhaling smoke.

"Ndeka! You seen Judy?" asked Underdog.

"Not yet tonight, no. Shall I put on a turkey leg for you? I make them up very tasty."

"No thanks. But maybe some other time."

"Your loss then," said Ndeka, zestfully peppering his turkey legs.

Underdog decided to take his search outside. He threw open the boarders' outside door, which exited onto the cement driveway running alongside the house to the garage in back. Each way he turned he saw signs of Judy: beside the house there were evergreens exactingly trimmed and shaped into cubes, and in cracks of the driveway there were crumpled brown weeds, which she must have recently squirted with weed killer. Noticing that the overhead garage door was open, he hurried back to investigate.

Judy was not inside. For a clue to her whereabouts, he inventoried Judy's implements: hanging from nails pounded into studs were garden and grass rakes, sidewalk edger, shovel, spade and hoe; lying against the wall were twenty-pound bags of garden soil, peat moss and fertilizer; and parked along the back wall were the push mower, wheel barrow and fertilizer cart. Conspicuously absent were the riding mower and weed eater, indicating that she was still out on a job. But since it was fall, and daylight hours were getting shorter and shorter, he thought it would not be long until she got home. He decided to wait for her in the garage.

He studied its main occupant, Mona's 1991 Jupiter car, one of the first thousand to roll off the Jasper assembly line. Jupiters always looked front-heavy to him, with chopped-off, hatchback rear ends, and low-slung front bumpers scooping the road for better aerodynamics. He remembered the time she caught him once and babbled about her car for twenty minutes. "Since 1910, my family drove strictly Buicks or Oldsmobiles. Big, sensible cars," she said. "I broke farm tradition buying Jap crap. But I didn't fit with the farm wife set, did I? I married a golf pro and moved into town."

He decided it might be a longer wait than he first suspected, so he helped himself to one of the lawn chairs that hung from hooks on the wall opposite Judy's garden tools. He unfolded it and sat.

It was around seven o'clock when Mona Baine appeared in the shadows just outside the reach of the garage light. The rectangular doorway framed her in a striking pose, looking as though a color slide of a sunset were superimposed behind her, with trees and housetops bathed in rich, orange-red light. She held up her hand to shield the garage's bare bulb from her eyes, which scanned the interior from the left side to the right side.

"Oh, it's you," she said, eyes landing on Underdog. "I came out to yell at Judy for leaving the light on and running up my electric bill. May I ask what you're doing out here?"

"Waiting for Judy," he answered. "I, uh, know somebody who needs her services. Something that should be taken care of right away. I know how you hate us guys knocking on your door at night, so I decided to grab her here." Unable to look Mona in the face while engaging in this deception, he looked down at the cement floor in front of him and scraped his right shoe a few times across gravel sprinkled on an oil spot.

"That's nice. I'm sure she'll appreciate the tip." She smiled approvingly.

"I hope so."

"Well, it's silly of you to wait out in the garage for her. I imagine she'll be home before too long. When she gets in, I'll send her up to your room."

"That would work." Sure would, he thought.

Mona turned around and headed back up the driveway to the house. "Don't forget to turn out the light," she called out as she faded into darkness, which had fallen during their brief conversation. As she walked away, she whispered to herself about what a nice, quiet boy that Underdog was; how responsible he was in paying his rent by the first of every month; how he worked hard at school or at the print trade, whatever he did, she could never remember. Her thoughts proceeded to how he might be a good match for Judy. Entering the house, she resolved to sound out Judy on the subject of Underdog; if there were any interest, she planned to hint that he ask Judy out on a date or something.

Upon hearing the storm door slap shut, Underdog extinguished the light, bumbled his way out of the dark garage, and tip-toed to the house back down the dark driveway. As he considered his imminent rendezvous with Judy, an erection rose inside his pants. When it got too insistent, he slapped his lap a couple times in hopes of taming it. At the same moment the stoop light flicked on, prompting him to freeze mid-slap. Noticing Mona looking down on him from her kitchen window, he brushed off his lap and tops of thighs, like his clothes were dusty. Before opening the door, he gave her the thumbs up sign; she nodded and gave it back.

Upstairs, Underdog readied himself for the upcoming seduction. He undressed, then slipped on his bengal-striped underwear. He reapplied some Old Spice roll-on deodorant. He put on his robe and thongs. He tuned his radio to the college's public radio station, which was broadcasting a Debussy piano piece that sounded romantic to him, like gently falling rain. Stage set, he sat in his chair and waited for Judy's arrival.

A few minutes later he heard the putt-putt-putt of her lawn tractor as it pulled up the drive. In another five minutes, he heard her steps on the stairs, the familiar creaking of a floorboard outside his room, and at last a knock on the door, which he opened wide.

"My mom said you had a job for me," said Judy, looking sheepishly down and away from him, no doubt because of the episode two nights before. She hadn't yet changed out of her work clothes, a soiled halter top, cutoff blue jeans and grass-stained tennis shoes. Without saying a word, he took her hand in his, and with a single motion slammed the door, twirled her around jitterbug style, and flung her on his bed, where she landed in a sitting position.

Still bouncing slightly on the buoyant mattress springs, she looked up at him expectantly. He sat alongside her, leaned over and began lightly kissing her shoulder. "What's the deal?" she asked, shrinking away.

"Shhh." He pulled the halter strap off her shoulder and kissed some more.

"How come you didn't want me Monday night? I was ready to give myself to you. Gift-wrapped. And you turned me down. Very cold of you." Her breathing quickened, her concentration weakened, her sentences broke up into phrases.

"To be honest, I was scared. But now."

She pushed him away, pulled her top over her head, and reached around her back to unhook her bra, which she let drop to the floor. Then she rose from the bed, kicked off her shoes, peeled off her ankle socks, and shimmied out of her shorts.

Most striking about Judy was the sun's effect. Her sun-bleached hair lit up the room almost incandescently. And her face, shoulders and chest were deeply tanned, calling attention all the more to her contrasting white breasts, which were round and heavy, with large brown nipples, concentric shades of dark and light reminding him of targets. Her tan ended at her ankles; Underdog noticed her feet were so white that, even when barefoot, she looked like she still wore spanking-clean tennis shoes.

They traded places; he stood to take off his robe, while she lay backward on the bed. The position she settled into was remarkably close to the pose Ione struck in the art class earlier that day. Thoughts of the two women started to alternate in Underdog's head, like rapidly switching back and forth between two radio stations at opposite ends of the dial — Ione the classical, Judy the rock and roll.

Ione had a thinner build — slimmer arms and legs, waist and hips, and smaller, conical breasts. She also didn't have the chiseled muscles of Judy, whom Underdog inspected, noting her taut biceps, firm abdomen, and solid thighs and calves, developed from ten to twelve hours of daily physical labor. No, Ione was more supple than Judy, and he guessed more vulnerable, too. Also, she was much paler; if

Judy were a sunflower, lifting her broad, tawny face to the light, then Ione was a white orchid, thriving in the shade, a more subtle zone.

"Are you going to stare at me or jump me?" she asked, snapping Underdog out of his reverie.

"Jump," he said, leaping on her and straddling her waist with his legs. As he nosed her breasts, thoughts of her and Ione continued to compete in his brain. Ione would likely smell cleaner than Judy — before they made love she would have taken a bubble bath and sprayed on floral-scented perfume. Yet he could not deny the effect of Judy's scent on his olfactory nerves. Sweat, lawn mower exhaust and grass combined to form a sweet and sour smell. Indeed, while kissing his way down her belly, he noticed blades of cut grass had stuck to her skin, seasoning her like herbs.

While burying his face in Judy's crotch, he thought how he had never been so lucky to have caught the interest of two women, each of whom was a worthy version of the feminine ideal: Ione was Athena or Aphrodite depicted in ancient Greek statues, and Judy was the sun-worshipping ski bunny pictured in girlie magazines.

"I've got to get up for a second," she said, slipping into Underdog's robe. She left the room briefly and returned with a condom. "Have to use this, with AIDS and everything."

"Agreed," he said. "Where did you get that from?"

"The bathroom. I stashed it in the cabinet the other night, when you rejected me."

"I'm sorry about the other night. I'm not rejecting you now."

After tearing open the foil package with her teeth, a cinnamon smell enveloped the room. "It's flavored," she said, putting it on him.

"Smells like Dentine gum," he said.

"Tastes like Big Red," she said.

FOUR

One thing that made Underdog's job less of a drudge than it might sound was regular access to every office on the Jasper College campus. Hearing of his ready access to exams the print shop printed, people regularly offered to broker copies to actual test-taking students, relieving Underdog of almost all risk. As well, budding muckrakers from the *Chronicler* asked him to forward any dirt involving the college administration. Passing up profit in favor of principle, he chose not to betray those trusting him.

Yet, though Underdog made an earnest display of averting his eyes from confidential documents, like servants at the fringes of royal plots, he sometimes stole glances and even read juicy stuff word-for-word. True, his role was spectator and not participant, but he still enjoyed the insider information for its own literary sake — the characters involved, the moral battles fought — and not for monetary reward or leak value to the college newspaper. Thus, he reserved time during the day to sneak off and read such material in places like the library, where he hid in stacks farthest from the entrance; or supply closets he knew were unlocked; or his favorite place, the Music Building, where he ducked into private practice rooms.

Which is where he found himself after lunch with his friend Reid at Sweet Gherkin Delicatessen, a busy spot in the center of town, where the two chowed on all-beef hot dogs, potato chips and cherry Cokes. Reid, now a graduate student of sociology, spoke of his abnormal psychology class, where that morning he watched a movie narrating the story of a woman who had undergone radical sex change surgery, discovered she wanted to be a man again, so had reconstructive surgery to restore male genitalia. Underdog, normally one to find such oddities interesting, all but ignored Reid during their meal, periodically sighing and moaning involuntarily at thoughts of Judy or Ione.

Underdog shut himself inside the soundproof practice room, gratefully away from the noise of a French horn player who practiced her scales, attacking each confidently, then muffing it by the end. The document he couldn't wait to read, which he was transporting from the president's office to the print shop, consisted of minutes taken at a recent Board of Trustees meeting. What caught his eye was mention of William Fletcher, a name he had heard a number of times in past weeks, causing him to wonder who this man was. He removed the carbonless print requisition sheet, placed the document in front of him on a music stand, and began to read.

Bored with financial gobbledygook, he turned ahead a few pages and read through the material regarding William Fletcher. That section also sounded like it was written in bureaucratese; President Flaghorn was, after all, known to many in town by the name "Blowhorn." Nonetheless, when he added the information found in the minutes to various news items that appeared earlier that fall in the *Jasper Weekly Shopper*, he thought he had a pretty good picture of who this character William Fletcher was.

William "Race" Fletcher moved to Jasper when he accepted an offer to fill the Edward Abbey Chair in American Civilization at Jasper College. Not without controversy, the college created this position upon the death of Osa Wallace, the sole remaining heir to the Wallace barbed wire fortune. Although the endowment Mr. Wallace bestowed amounted to three million dollars, part for capital improvements and part to endow the Abbey Chair, the school's Board of Trustees declined to accept any monies from the estate, at least initially.

Jasper College president, Milton Flaghorn, objected to "endowing a chair named for a radical who inflames our youth, whose writings advocate the destruction of property in a dubious and misguided fight to protect the environment." To argue his position, he cited Edward Abbey urging "gangs of saboteurs" to sneak onto government land and tamper with nuclear missile silos; as well, he referred to instances where followers of Abbey's "monkey-wrenching" philosophy hammered nails into trees to prevent loggers from sawing them down. "When a power saw cuts into a tree thus doctored," he explained, "nails can rip through a human body with the same devastating effect of shrapnel from a hand grenade." In short, Milton Flaghorn steadfastly opposed any relationship between the college and "a man who during his lifetime adopted a philosophy of violence, intimidation and disrespect for the law."

Other members of the Board recognized the serious contradiction in the college's mission of training young adults to become responsible members of society, while at the same time acknowledging the work of a man who labored to undermine the structures of that same society. Moreover, all of them, at one time or another, had witnessed the antics of their benefactor, Osa Wallace, and wondered what sort of example he himself would set. In particular, they discussed an incident the winter before when Mr. Wallace was apprehended by sheriff's deputies at the end of a high-speed chase over half the county, after someone witnessed him tossing a Molotov cocktail from atop his three-wheeled motorcycle through the window of a fast food restaurant under construction on Highway 17. Finally cornered, ironically enough, against a barbed wire fence by squad cars closing in, the old man, his beard caked with icicles, looking like a scarecrow stuffed with yellow leaves from corn stalks he cut a swathe through, surrendered. Later, while giving his statement at the sheriff's office, he complained of "all the damn burger joints and strip malls cropping up and spoiling the view from my farm."

The fire he started quickly burned out, and damage to the restaurant was limited to a broken window and a handful of melted floor tiles, but the sheriff, vowing to prosecute whom everyone knew to be the richest man living in Jasper County, charged Mr. Wallace with a total of fourteen violations, most of which involved breaking traffic laws. Being rich, Osa Wallace easily bailed himself out of jail, handing over one thousand dollars culled from various zippered pockets on his motorcycle jacket. Before his case came to trial in the Jasper County Courthouse, however, he came to an untimely end through rounding a blind curve and ramming his motorcycle into the back of a tractor pulling a trailer full of shelled corn.

Nevertheless, despite their reservations about the characters of both Edward Abbey and Osa Wallace, certain members of the Board saw their opportunity to retire some debts incurred when adding on to the library several years before. They could tolerate the new chair if it meant putting the college's finances back into the black. Thus emerged a split in the Board, pitting the pragmatists, led by Ephraim Zimmer, against the rejectionists, led by President Flaghorn. Counting Mr. Flaghorn's vote as the tie breaker in determining whether or not to accept the money, the pragmatists lobbied hard to add an at-large member, drawn from faculty ranks. After a bitter, six-month-long battle, the pragmatists prevailed in seating a professor of Russian history on the Board, and they persuaded one other Board member, who previously sided with Mr. Flaghorn, to vote for accepting the money. Blaming his loss on the recruitment of what he called a "Marxist dupe," President Flaghorn saw himself out-maneuvered and out-voted.

In order to water down the message of the man for whom the chair was named, while at the same time retaining a little of the spirit, the Board began to solicit candidates who held populist, agrarian beliefs, scholars along the lines of writer Wendell Berry. Among the mountains of curriculum vitae they received, there appeared one from William Fletcher. Despite his youth (born June 15, 1954) and his relative inexperience (never held a full-time teaching position), his application unquestionably looked the strongest: Ph.D. in American studies from New York University; undergraduate work at a small, private college in the rural Midwest (which presumably inculcated values desirable for this particular position); and close to a dozen articles published in professional journals pertaining to American civilization, including *Popular Culture* and *American Quarterly*. Where William Fletcher really stood out, however, was in the title of his first published book, *Deconstruction Acres: Imploding the Myth of Rural Simplicity*.

When questioning the English and history faculty about the applicants, the Board found that if they were to hire Race Fletcher, they would catch themselves one of the biggest fish swimming around the academic pond, for *Deconstruction Acres* was quickly revamping the way scholars studied American culture. The book effectively shattered the bumpkin image traditionally attached to inhabitants of rural America by showing how American characteristics like self reliance, shrewdness and common sense had survived the onslaught of urban culture insinuating itself, via the mass media, into the vast, underpopulated portions of the continent. Indeed, through depicting displaced urbanites clashing with country folk, the television show *Green Acres* revealed city dwellers to be the true provincials.

In addition to being a critical success, attested to by favorable reviews in such high-profile publications as *The New York Review of Books* and *Harper's Magazine*, the book was a popular success, too. Originally written as a Ph.D. dissertation, it was first published by a university press. After three printings numbering two thousand each, a mass market publishing house bought the rights. With the addition of thirty-two stills from the *Green Acres* TV show, the book was published under the title *The Green Acres Story* and promptly became a surprise hit with the reading public, surging as high as number four on the *New York Times* Bestseller List. Sales from the book had thus far earned Race Fletcher royalties of over nine hundred thousand dollars. Fletcher looked doubly attractive to the Board, since the college had a rule that stated a small percentage of any publishing profits earned by individual faculty members would be paid to the university to further its collective mission.

For Race Fletcher's part, he wanted to live a life consistent with the themes expressed in his book and was happy to relocate to Jasper. More than anything, he wanted to escape New York City, his home since he began graduate school in 1977. In this, he resembled the main character on the *Green Acres* show, Oliver Wendell Douglas, who sings during the opening credits, "Keep Manhattan, just give me that countryside."

The word "countryside" perhaps is a stretch; Race Fletcher didn't buy a farm, he bought a place in town. But compared to his Greenwich Village residence, a walk-up building with apartments so small it seemingly was built of several dozen stacked telephone booths, his spacious new house and one full acre of grounds appeared positively manor-like, in the old English sense. Indeed, the design of his home fed this comparison, as it was built in the Tudor style around 1890 by barbed wire baron Dempster Wallace, Osa's grandfather.

Referred to still as the "Wallace House," it had not belonged to anyone in the Wallace family since the 1970s, when the dilapidated structure, vacant since the 1940s, was sold by Osa Wallace to a couple who renovated it into a bed and breakfast. They replastered the crumbling walls, resealed the warped hardwood floors, restained the sun-faded interior woodwork, repainted the peeling exterior siding, and replaced the drafty windows. They furnished the house with antique beds, dressers, sofas, ottomans, chairs, lamps, rugs and knick-knacks dating back to the turn of the century. They installed new plumbing fixtures, including a whirlpool bath in the bridal suite. Unfortunately, they lost their shirts; despite aggressive advertising in tourist publications and a feature article in *B&B Magazine*, there was nothing to draw visitors, since, apart from the college, Jasper County possessed little in the way of tourist attractions, like historic settlements, caves or fishable lakes.

Once his position was finalized, Race Fletcher purchased himself a fully appointed home for a quarter-million in cash. Soon thereafter, he captured the entire town's attention for two reasons: his Range Rover, the only one most Jasperites had ever seen, and a rumor, whose source was a secretary in the English Department named Janet, which engulfed the town like a prairie fire, prompting everyone to ask each other for an entire week if they had heard about Race Fletcher's collection of two hundred animal skulls displayed in every corner of his home.

When he finished with the board of directors document, Underdog brought it to the print shop, where he handed it to Ron Sullivan for check-in, who returned it to Underdog to photocopy immediately and take back in a special trip, because when the President said jump, you jumped. The task was a simple matter of punching in a few numbers; entering a collate command; then pushing the big green Start button. He waited as the photocopier kicked out stapled sets of minutes, although he made sure to look away from the bursts of light that clicked forty times a minute, because he recently noticed nasty purple blotches in his peripheral vision. He hoped exposure to Xerographic rays wasn't robbing him of his eyesight.

After a few minutes, he looked at the gauge and noticed it was approaching 480, the total count. Hardly anything could tire this machine out; until it stopped it huffed and puffed rhythmically, performing its calisthenics without exhaustion. Like pulling dried clothes off a line, he gathered paper stacks out of the rotary collator and boxed them.

At the direction of Sharon, Milton Flaghorn's secretary, he placed the booklets on a walnut counter outside the president's office. "Interesting reading," he said to her.

"You don't mean to say that you read it?" she barked, like she had a loudspeaker sewn inside her throat. Sharon had close-cropped red hair and a face full of red freckles; she was tall and built like a pear. Underdog had the impression that she could beat the shit out of him anytime she chose.

"No, I didn't. Just trying to get your goat," he said, thinking that this was an appropriate remark, given her goat face.

"There better not be any stray marks. You wiped the glass, I hope." She thumbed each booklet, carefully eyeing each page with the expression of a drill sergeant checking how tightly beds were made.

"You know I did," he said, leaving the office and wondering if, at the end of the work day, Sharon changed out of the flats she wore and into combat boots for the journey home.

Before returning to the print shop, he stopped at an out-of-the-way sculpture located in the southeastern corner of the college, where campus gave way to recently harvested cornfield. Constructed of welded steel plates, it was an exact replica of a picnic table. Neatly etched across the table top were two-word phrases, like "Art/Society," "Action/Reaction," "Love/Hate" and "Life/Death." It was accompanied by two young trees with skinny trunks and not much cover, planted there to someday create a park-like setting. He reflected awhile on Judy and Ione, felt spasms of danger, pangs of guilt, aches of lust, waves of sexual relief. All day, he was mindful of Judy's smell wafting up from his chest, remnant of their rendezvous the previous night. As well, he was unsure all day where to take Ione for their upcoming date. He was afraid they would have to settle for either Roger's Bar, where you had to shout over crappy country rock bands, or the Black Angus Restaurant, reputed to serve the best food in Jasper, but where Underdog knew otherwise, from eating mealy shrimp there once.

Cutting through the student union on his way back to the print shop, a flyer tacked to a student activities kiosk caught his attention. It pictured Race Fletcher and the English Department secretary posed like the American Gothic couple. Underdog read the text below the photograph.

GREEN ACRES VIDEO FESTIVAL
Thursday, Sept. 24, 1992, 7:00 p.m.

Little Theater, Jasper College
Three Classic Episodes
Will Be Shown

Introduction by William Fletcher,
Abbey Chair Prof. of Amer. Civ.

Reception Sponsored
by Art Department

"Bingo!" thought Underdog, pleased that an event where he could take Ione finally presented itself, scheduled on the correct day and everything. She might think it awfully corny, and it probably was, but it was something different than what passed for fun in Jasper, like a hay ride sponsored by the Elks Club. Besides, he wanted to meet this William Fletcher. He sounded like a cool guy.

FIVE

Ione lived in Trailerville, the disparaging nickname of a mobile home development outside Jasper, across the train tracks at the west edge of town. The name was the logical result of two circumstances: it was a trailer park, and it was located within the boundaries of the school township including Taylorville, an unincorporated village four miles down the highway. In times past, Taylorville would have been called a "one-horse town"; in the present, it still had very little going for it. Aside from lights inside the windows of a few dozen homes clustered along the highway, the only signs of life were farm boys in seed corn caps loitering outside a gas station mini-mart or unchained dogs dodging traffic as they crossed the road. Not even signs posting lower speeds caught the attention of drivers of vehicles traveling through at sixty-plus miles an hour.

Like urban housing projects, where a large percentage of residents are unwed mothers, Trailerville was in large part populated by single and divorced women heading families of rowdy kids. Many lived off food stamps and other trappings of the welfare state, because the farm economy went bust, leaving their estranged husbands and boyfriends unemployed and unable to pay alimony or child support. Nevertheless, despite their poverty, nearly everybody owned her own mobile home and felt a certain amount of dignity from that fact. Plus, in recent months satellite dishes cropped up on a few roofs, signifying that the Japanese auto plant had helped to improve the lots of people living there.

Before meeting Ione, Underdog had never visited Trailerville. The place had a white trash reputation; whenever the newspaper reported that a fight broke out in Jasper High School, or a burglar was apprehended, or a drug ring had been broken up, the perpetrators inevitably came from Trailerville. When drinking at Roger's Bar, he studiously avoided customers who hailed from there, generally fat, red-bearded men and chubby, overly made-up women. Also marking a resident of Trailerville were tattoos.

Once, in a barroom incident that involved tattoos, Underdog nearly provoked a fight with a Trailerville man, who grabbed a pool cue and faced him in a batter's stance because he was gazing a little too intently at the man's girlfriend. Never mind that the woman was wearing a halter top, which revealed below an elaborate tattoo depicting flowers and leaves growing on vines that curlicued completely around her waist and dipped under her belt. Indeed, she stuck her hands into her back pockets and gently pushed her jeans down onto her hips, evidently to show off as much of the tattoo as possible. Naturally, Underdog couldn't tell the man that, far from looking at his girlfriend longingly, he was instead grossed out by the sight of her, though fascinated, too. So to keep his teeth he settled for apologizing and promising not to look anymore.

Given her apparent class, it was curious that Ione would live in such an environment, Underdog was thinking, as he walked through the gateway to Trailerville, indicated by a sign arching over the driveway which read, if you filled in the letters bleached out by sun, "Taylorville Mobile Home Development." Planted around the signposts were flower beds bursting with red and yellow mums and decorative boulders freshly painted blue. Underdog was struck by the contrast between grounds keeper Judy Baine's loving attention to the landscaping of Trailerville, and the sorry-assed state of the rest of the development, which was manifest in crumbling roadway, rust streaks trickling down fronts of trailers, cinderblock steps leading up to doors, and plywood nailed over broken windows.

He crossed an asphalt playground overgrown with weeds growing through zig-zagging cracks; at either end were netless, rimless basketball backboards suspended from poles. As he watched gangs of unsupervised children throw rocks or punches at one another, he felt momentarily sad that these were very mean little kids, none of whom were living the happy-go-lucky childhood that they deserved.

Confused by the layout at first, Underdog found, as he walked deeper inside, that trailers radiated from the main entrance. Trying to pick out number E-9, it struck him that Trailerville resembled a fanned-out deck of dysfunctional pinochle cards containing only Queens and Jacks, no Kings.

Underdog finally found Ione's mobile home, the cleanest, best-kept trailer in row E. In one of the few decorative touches he noticed in Trailerville, a three-foot evergreen shrub grew out of a large terra cotta pot beside her front door. Reminded of his bathroom encounter with Judy Baine earlier in the week, he suddenly felt guilty for so nakedly betraying her. Before knocking, he looked around him furtively, feeling the same as in dreams, when you discover everyone is staring at you for leaving the house wearing only underwear. Seeing nobody, he took a long, deep breath and rapped on the storm door with his knuckles.

Immediately after Underdog turned his head away from the main aisle through the trailer park, Judy Baine crossed row E, weed eater slung over her shoulder. Noticing Underdog at the door of a trailer, she stopped and was about to holler his name — maybe she could prod him into screwing her in the nearby corn field. But then a woman opened the door and let him in. Deflated as a wind sock on a dead-still day, she staggered back to her tractor, which was parked behind a hedge by the Trailerville front gate, bewildered that a pale, skinny, flat-chested bitch with no ass could have caught the attention of Underdog, when only last night her own voluptuous body lay next to his.

Meantime, Ione asked if Underdog wanted a "cocktail" as he sat on her black leather couch.

"What have you got?" he asked.

"Everything you could possibly want." To demonstrate, she opened a heavy-looking, natural pine cabinet across the room, revealing on the top inside shelf bottles of scotch, bourbon, rum, vodka, gin and tequila, and on the bottom shelf amaretto, Irish cream, Kahlua, schnapps, cognac and several varieties of red wine. "I've got white wine and beer in the fridge, too, if you prefer."

"I'll have a beer."

"Bud, Miller, Heineken, Coors or Lite?"

"Uh, Budweiser."

"Coming right up."

While she was in the kitchen, he stood up and took stock of his surroundings. He walked over to the television and examined his reflection, making sure his hair was reasonably well-combed. Then he looked over her stereo system, noting that she had an impressive array of stereo equipment: five-CD changer, along with turntable, receiver and tape player. On shelves beside the stereo there were dozens of CDs, consisting mainly of re-mastered recordings by pop songstresses like Bessie Smith, Billie Holliday, Marlene Dietrich, Ella Fitzgerald, Judy Garland, Sarah Vaughn and Peggy Lee. On shelves below these, there were hundreds of record albums, ranging from rock to jazz and from country to classical. Especially well-represented in her collection were Broadway soundtracks like *Pal Joey, Guys and Dolls, West Side Story, Cabaret, Phantom of the Opera* and *Miss Saigon.*

Turning around to return to his seat, he noticed what he missed when he first sat down: a wall filled with Liza Minnelli pictures hanging above the couch. In the middle of the arrangement was a framed *Cabaret* movie poster. Surrounding this were another ten black and white photographs: several of Liza as Sally Bowles, posing in derby, bustier, garters and fishnet stockings; one with Liza embracing Joel Grey; one of a very young Liza with Judy Garland; and a couple more of Liza singing on various stages, wearing sequined evening gowns.

"I've been told many times I look like Liza Minnelli," Ione said, re-entering the room. "Do you think I look like her?"

"Maybe a little bit," he said, making an exaggerated display of looking her over, then looking at the pictures. The bobbed hair, slinky frame, nervous manner, and big, brown eyes were all similar. "But you've got a nicer nose. It's not so buttony as hers."

"You're too kind," she said, handing him a pilsner glass full of beer. She raised her goblet of white wine. "To Liza."

"Cheers," said Underdog, then took a big gulp of beer. "What's that you're drinking," he asked.

"Sauvignon blanc. Do you know wine?"

"I can't tell the difference between wine and grape juice."

"I'll teach you."

"I've got the idea you're going to teach me a lot of things." He sat on the couch.

"I'll teach you how to be deliciously decadent. Like Sally Bowles." She, too, sat on the couch and scooted close to him.

"Inside here it's like an oasis. That is, compared to the rest of Trailerville."

"I like to surround myself with nice things. I couldn't afford them if I bought a house in town. Even a small one."

"This your ex?" he asked, picking up off the coffee table a copper frame oxidized green. The photograph was of a man with a handsome, chiseled face and long, black hair pulled back into a pony tail.

Ione grabbed the frame from him and slapped it face-down on the table. "My husband."

"Your husband? I had no idea you were married before."

"He's dead."

"Dead? Jeez, I'm sorry. Was it an accident? I mean, he must've been so young."

"I don't want to talk about it." She scooped up their empty glasses and escaped into the kitchen. When she returned, she was chewing her thumbnail. Then she stopped when she saw him watching.

"We ought to go," he said, standing. "The lecture starts at seven o'clock."

"We'll take my car," she said, fishing a long time inside her hand bag for keys. Once found, they left the trailer and got into her yellow Volkswagen Beetle parked out front.

"Haven't seen one of these cars for a long time. They're a rarity these days," he said, fastening his seat belt.

Distracted, she didn't respond the entire ten-minute drive to Jasper College.

* * *

Underdog genuinely liked the program, although William Fletcher's opening remarks were tough to take. For fifteen whole minutes he took off on several rhetorical detours, discussing what he called the "deconstructive aspects" of the TV show *Green Acres*:

> Repudiating his native New York, Oliver Douglas desires to live the pastoral ideal. He speechifies on the innate common sense and nobility of the farmer, with patriotic fife and drum music accompanying him on the soundtrack, much to the annoyance of residents of Hooterville. However, though he fancies himself an expert on rural values, he never truly integrates into the surrounding society. The more he tries to put into practice the values he preaches, the less successful he is in farming the old Haney place. Therein lies the irony (and humor) of the show: Douglas is undermined by purporting to understand more of the farmer's life than the farmer himself.

After the talk portion, the Audio-Visual Department rolled three consecutive episodes of the *Green Acres* show itself. In the first, residents of Hooterville started a Pentagon-funded barn operation to build a World War One Jenny airplane. In the second, Oliver Douglas joined the volunteer fire department, which required him to play an instrument in the town's marching band. The third, complete with subtitles, involved the pig Arnold Ziffel, and his efforts in courting a female beagle that only understood French. Underdog laughed out loud several times, impressing those in seats around him with how hip he was; as the night wore on he found himself agreeing with William Fletcher that *Green Acres* was the best show ever to appear on television.

After the show, Underdog and Ione went into the foyer outside the Little Theater for the reception. It was Underdog's experience that he liked receptions better than the paintings on the walls at art openings or the string quartets played at recitals. For one, you could drink and eat for free. For another, you could shoot the breeze with people, rather than sitting completely still and quiet all night in Yawnsville. Both were just rewards for all the boring things he endured in the name of giving himself a little culture.

For her part, Ione was bored silly. First off, she thought that efforts to read all manner of deep, significant meanings into the *Green Acres* show was the height of folly. Second, the show was really stupid. Students at Jasper College would laugh at just about anything: talking pigs, cheap slapstick, corny doublespeak, you name it. She had her doubts about this Underdog guy she came with — he actually thought such things were funny. She also had her doubts about Race Fletcher's sanity.

But she had no doubt that she was physically attracted to Race Fletcher. He had a very dashing air about him; he exuded the confidence only rich, urbane people exhibited. He wore a sharp, double-breasted suit, complemented by a splashy, hand-painted necktie; his hair was wavy, and a curl or two fell Clark Gable-fashion across his forehead. She even begrudged him wit; she may have thought his research into *Green Acres* was a dumb pursuit, but his commentary, particularly certain asides, were funny and charming, like when he called *Green Acres* "the golden egg, laid by the golden goose *Beverly Hillbillies*, in the golden age of television."

In the foyer a movie premiere atmosphere quickly developed. Flashbulbs popped and video camera spotlights glared from a press contingent, consisting of the *Jasper Weekly Shopper*, the *Jasper College Chronicler* and *Strobe Magazine*, a trendy rock and roll monthly published in New York, which earlier that week had named Race Fletcher regular columnist. Quite a large number of people jostled in the receiving line that formed to fawn over him. There were many students, each of whom told him how much they loved his lecture. There were professors who complimented Race Fletcher, although each had to regurgitate a specific point he found compelling. And there were a couple of silent, but interested townies, impressed by this smarty-pants city slicker.

Then there was Ione, who curtsied as she extended her hand to Race Fletcher when it was her turn to greet him. Of everyone present, only she had the guts to tell Race Fletcher to his face that she thought *Green Acres* was a stupid, not deep, TV show.

"So basically you think my project is a lot of cow pie," he said.

"Bull pie," she responded.

The laughter she drew from Race Fletcher echoed sharply off the marble foyer walls, and the general din grew noticeably louder. After one or two final paroxysms, he turned his attention to Underdog, who introduced himself. When Race Fletcher asked what he did, Underdog told him that he was a townie.

"Rhymes with 'Pawnee,'" Race Fletcher said, then reached around him to shake hands with the woman next in line. It appeared that Race Fletcher was ignoring everyone except those who had the gumption to argue with him. Underdog figured that Race Fletcher was accustomed to praise, so accustomed that he practically ignored it, saying "thank you" blankly to those who dished it out. When the evening was over and everyone had gone home, he forgot them.

What lit him up were the rare individuals who talked back to him; these were the people he remembered. No doubt he would remember Ione later in the evening when everybody went home. And that was the problem. She seemed to be making too good an impression on Race Fletcher, and he was making too good of one on her. She remained at his side, caught up in the glamour of the event — the swarm of fans and reporters, the scent of money and manly musk, and her honored spot beside him, where she joined him in shaking everyone's hand.

It was plain to Underdog that he had lost Ione for the evening. She clung to Race Fletcher like velcro. He observed their knowing glances, saw them brushing hands. Underdog quickly sized up the scene: Ione was an attractive female, the most interesting Race Fletcher had met all night, so he fastened onto her, even though she called his work stupid to his face. Surrendering to the situation, Underdog decided to leave. He saw no point in announcing his departure to Ione.

Underdog left Castle Hall, stooped and dejected. He decided to take his customary route home, heading how the crow flew.

On many nights he returned from campus or the bars of Suds City by avoiding streets, especially the mains, because none went the direction he often needed to go — diagonally — but east and west and north and south. This meant lurking in Jasper backyards, which he leapfrogged until he arrived at the puke-colored boarding house on Elm Street.

Regularly spending time in backyards familiarized Underdog with how Jasper townies lived. Most prominent was evidence of kids: yards full of pull toys and riding toys; luckier kids with swingsets or playhouses, the luckiest with treehouses perched in the forks of gigantic oaks; and sports equipment, including the trickiest things of all to negotiate when dark, badminton nets, croquet wickets and jarts stuck in the ground. Also, there were tool sheds where dad's toys were stored, the lawn mowers, rotor tillers and wheel barrows. And there were Mom's contributions to the back yard, her attempts at beautification, the flower beds, bird baths and Dutch windmills pumping furiously in strong wind.

Aside from risk involved in cutting across yards in the first place — for example, if the cops were called on him for peeping, or if he drew gunfire from territorial homeowners — there were physical hazards to think about. It being night, visibility was severely reduced. He could break a toe kicking a garbage can or, like the previous week, trip over a barbecue grill and burn his elbows landing in smoldering coals. One of the worst dangers he confronted was dogs. Some yards indicated their presence with dog houses, but most times dogs ran loose barking, or they snuck around silently, guilty of digging up flowers or peeing on the above-ground swimming pool, but aiming to get in good with their masters by barking at intruders or biting them in the ass.

In the backyard of the Slartman's, he paused beside an elaborate Virgin Mary shrine. The Virgin herself, a three-foot molded ceramic statuette, was positioned in a circular bed of sparkling white feldspar and surrounded by neatly trimmed rose bushes. She was draped in blue robes, and painted on her face was an expression of supreme understanding. It wasn't fair for Ione to drop him, thought Underdog, sharing his opinions telepathically with Mary. After all, he asked her to the lecture in the first place; she wouldn't have met Race Fletcher if it weren't for that. He didn't like this Race Fletcher guy, either, didn't appreciate his "Pawnee" crack. He didn't quite know what was meant by it, but he knew it wasn't good. Noticing in the yard next door a black jockey statue caused him to wonder if it might be racist, like he was some second-class citizen, part of the region's indigenous peoples to whom the more enlightened Race Fletcher was introducing civilization. Whatever his intentions, the appellation clearly was made to impress Ione with his superiority over townies. If he learned anything tonight, it was that Race Fletcher condescended to small-town life. Just like Oliver Wendell Douglas in *Green Acres*, who presumed he knew everything but in reality knew nothing.

Much as Underdog was angry at Ione, however, he forgave her, though, partly because the Virgin, not the icon but the idea of her, prompted him, and partly on account of that haunted look Ione got in her eyes. He had seen it twice so far, when he glimpsed her posing nude in art class and when she alluded to her dead husband. He understood now its source was early widowhood, and he wanted to protect her from all the sad feelings assaulting her. More, he wanted to protect her from Race Fletcher, who, given the opportunity, might take advantage of her injury, exactly like an ambulance-chasing lawyer. Underdog decided that he would simply try his luck again the next time he saw her, probably the following week during a delivery. Only he wouldn't take her anywhere within twenty miles of Race Fletcher, if he could help it.

As he climbed over still another fence, safe from cops, dogs or guns, he felt a flush of pride in his skill. But how would he explain this talent, this pursuit, to Ione? His motivation was not voyeuristic — he usually averted his eyes from windows, respectful of the private family dramas unfolding within. In fact, it was essential to keep out of sight and therefore out of trouble. No, more than anything, it was overcoming the challenges fences presented.

Ironically, Jasper made its mark in the 1880s as a center for the manufacture of barbed wire, which ranchers and farmers unreeled across the continent, domesticating everything. And now chain link and redwood blocked Underdog's path, indicating to him that "fence" was just another term for taking freedom away. Indeed, when he was two yards away from home, he began unconsciously to hum the song "Don't Fence Me In."

From the next yard over, he noticed lights were on downstairs in the Baine portion of the house, unusual for after eleven o'clock at night. Hearing a ruckus when he entered the door leading upstairs, he knocked. Mona answered the door; her eyes were red and moist.

"Is everything okay?" he asked.

"No, it's not," she said. "Judy was brought home tonight by the police. They pulled her over for drunk driving. On her lawn tractor! Can you imagine?"

Elaborating further, Mona told him the story. Evidently, Judy was upset by something bad that happened earlier in the day, only she still hadn't said what. To drown her sorrows, she stopped at Roger's Bar and drank five Long Island ice teas. Then she mounted her lawn tractor and attempted to drive it home along the side of the roadway, like normal. Problem was, she was drunk and couldn't steer it properly. A policeman sitting in his parked squad car saw her weaving all over the street, so he followed her, then flagged her down. She failed in walking a straight line or touching her nose with her eyes closed, so she was arrested for driving under the influence.

Contending with Ione business all night, Underdog forgot about Judy. Once he heard Mona's story, he realized that Judy somehow knew about him and Ione. He was reminded of what his father said once, about a month after Underdog was kicked out of Jasper

College, when he began speaking to his son again. "In life," he said, "tomfoolery is punished, sooner or later." Now aware of his assholery, Underdog figured that in treating Judy how he did, he got what he deserved from Ione.

SIX

Underdog awoke the Friday morning after Race Fletcher's reception hungover from drinking cheap champagne, followed by cheap red wine when the champagne ran dry. It felt like a gang of thugs were taking swings at his head with two-by-fours. He pried himself up off the sweat-glued bottom sheet, trudged through his morning bathroom routines, then dressed back in his room, which smelled like a vineyard.

Outside the house, an even stronger smell smacked him in the face like a smelly glove: pigs, giving off a smell ten times worse than the filthiest outhouse or dirtiest gas station restroom he ever had the misfortune of stepping into. It was an all-pervasive stink that drifted into town when the wind came from the southeast. Its source was a massive feed lot operation, a collection point for area hog farmers' stock, where a last-minute dose of grain and vitamins were pumped into doomed pigs before they were trucked off to the slaughterhouse.

Underdog visited there two years before, as part of a side tour you could take from the Jasper County Fair. He and Reid had drunk a few beers, and they had shared a joint, so for entertainment during their high they took seats in the minivan and went. A half-mile away you rounded a bend and saw five navy blue silos towering above the prairie alongside a dozen long, narrow pig parlors. Next, you heard the low rumble of tamping feet and pig talk. Inside the pig parlor itself, hundreds of grumbling pigs jostled around in pens on either side of the corridor. Some jumped up, kicking their forelegs over the fence and sticking their snouts in your face, saying hello like dogs might, and a few piglets that had slipped between wooden fence slats raced up and down the corridor. Gagging from the awful smell, Underdog left before the tour guide ended his talk, to much laughter from Reid.

As he walked to work, Underdog gulped down big breaths and held them for as long as he could, aware this was smell that blanketed many square miles, a smell you could never walk away from. Indeed, it was appropriate that everything smelled like shit, after his exhausting, disappointing night.

He stopped to buy a cup of coffee at the student center. As always, he was amazed that the work/study student who poured his coffee and rang him up was different every morning. Today it was a mousy girl who was kind enough to wipe off a spill down the side of his styrofoam cup with a sponge before handing it to him. Leaving the cafeteria, he scooped up a copy of the Jasper College *Chronicler* to read in the slack times later in the day. He skimmed through the stories on page one, but read one story word-for-word:

Student Struck by Train;
Suicide Suspected

JASPER TOWNSHIP — A Jasper College student was struck and killed yesterday evening by a train outside Jasper. Tsuge Takahashi, 19, was pronounced dead at the scene by Jasper County Coroner Fred Miller. The cause of death listed was multiple injuries.

The engineer of the train, Jeffrey Washington, contacted by radio the Jasper County Sheriff's office at approximately 11 p.m. to report that his train had struck a young man. The site of the accident was about one mile east of the Jasper city limits. Officers arrived on the scene at 11:10 to question the engineer. He claimed that a smiling Takahashi stood on the track facing the approaching train with his arms spread. Washington was unable to stop the train before hitting Takahashi.

Sheriff Thomas Gwynne believes that Takahashi's death was the result of suicide. He plans no further investigation.

Sources report that Takahashi, a sophomore, had been despondent over failing grades in his freshman English class. Dr. Fran Warner, school psychologist, said that Japanese students are very success-minded. "When they fail in school, the shame they feel can sometimes lead to suicidal thoughts," she added.

Takahashi was the son of Mr. and Mrs. Naotaka Takahashi, 1116 Base Line Road. Mr. Takahashi is a manager at the Jupiter Motor Company assembly plant. A private funeral is planned, and a noontime memorial service for students has been scheduled at the Student Center on Monday, Sept. 28th.

For the rest of the morning, Underdog could not shake the image of the smiling kamikaze student lit up brighter and brighter in the beam of the train's headlamp, arms spread to embrace oblivion.

* * *

Wouldn't you know, Underdog thought as the morning progressed, that one of his delivery stops was the credit union. He couldn't avoid Ione, not even for one day. Gathering up his load, he decided to make her office the last stop, in the hope that she would be out eating lunch.

His first stop was Student Publications. He didn't have anything to deliver, never did — the *Chronicler* was printed up in Peru at a newsprint plant — but it was a good place to hear the latest gossip. At the assignment desk sat Chuck, a senior journalism student whom Underdog had gotten acquainted with at Roger's Bar.

"That was some disturbing story, about the Japanese student who got killed," said Underdog.

"I drove out to the accident scene," said Chuck. "There was nothing left of the kid but chili-mac."

"Yuck! I'm going to call you 'Upchuck' from now on." His violent shudder at such a grotesque sight was magnified by a wave of hangover nausea.

"Check out the story in the *Shopper*," said Chuck, picking up a copy of that paper. "Listen to this racist, inflammatory rhetoric: 'A spokesman for the Anti's, the name attached to Jasperites who came out against the Jupiter auto plant before it was built, called the tragedy "another example of what hyper-driven Japanese will do to our town."' That will cause a stir, you watch."

Unable to stall any longer, Underdog stopped in the credit union. To his great relief, Ione was not anywhere sight. An older man, very conservatively dressed in a navy sport coat, white shirt, gray slacks and blue- and red-striped tie, looked up from the desk behind Ione's. Underdog noticed his square, wire-rimmed glasses were salted with dandruff. "I'm the head accountant," he said, extending his hand. "I'll take those. Our office administrator called in sick this morning." Underdog gave him the debit forms and promptly exited.

He spent the remainder of his day fuming with jealousy, as he contemplated what mischief Ione and Race Fletcher could have gotten into overnight. At one point in the afternoon, when Underdog was re-filling the photocopy machine with paper, Ron Sullivan scolded him for slamming shut the paper drawer harder than he needed. "You break that machine, and I'm taking it out of your salary," he yelled over the noise of presses and collators.

When quitting time rolled around, and he saw his unfinished business with Judy Baine looming closer, Underdog realized that going home would be no picnic either. During the walk home, his mounting dread caused him to break into a cold sweat. Fortunately, the only person he ran into at the boarding house was Ndeka, who remarked as they passed on the second floor stair landing, "That was quite a lot of noise last evening. I heard from our landlady that Judy never got out of bed today."

"Yes, it certainly was quite a commotion," said Underdog, who ran the rest of the way upstairs and locked himself in his room. Looking inside the bottom drawer of his desk, he saw he was fairly well-stocked with chips and crackers, a private cache of food kept in his room to prevent its theft from the kitchen, plenty to eat while he hid in his room all night.

He stripped to his undershorts. As he sat on the bed munching Doritos, the telephone outside his door began to ring. After the eleventh ring, he determined nobody else was going to answer, so he opened the door and pulled the phone inside his room. Being a more-or-less permanent fixture at Mona Baine's boarding house, Underdog was in charge of the phone, and when the bill came he collected money from each transient roommate. An extra-long cord ran from a jack in his room, under the door, and out into the hallway, where it connected to a desk phone resting at the top of the stairs, which was available for anybody's use.

"Hello," he answered. There was a moment of silence at the other end of the line, followed by a huge sniffle.

"Hello?"

"Underdog? It's Ione." Another sniffle.

"Are you all right?" he asked.

"Yes," she said, the pitch of her voice rising tentatively, then "No," pitch falling again, denoting the true answer.

"What's the matter?" he asked, hoping that Race Fletcher had broken her heart, and she would be free to lavish her affection on Underdog once again.

"Can I meet you somewhere?"

"How's Roger's Bar?"

"Too public. I need to be alone with you." Some vocal overtone suggested to Underdog that her eyes probably had that haunted look in them again.

"Maybe we could take a walk?"

"Meet me by the ugly picnic table sculpture on campus."

"I'll be there in twenty minutes."

"Make it ten," she said before abruptly hanging up.

* * *

As Underdog read the two-word dichotomies engraved into the picnic table's surface, he thought of another one appropriate for the situation: "Obsession/Frustration." Then a car door slam interrupted his reverie.

"Nice evening for a picnic," said Ione, as she got out of her Volkswagen Bug. She wore the same outfit as the night before, consisting of a black and white, horizontally striped blouse, a black leather jacket, black Levi's, and suede shoes. Crisply dressed previously, she appeared to have slept in her clothes, as they were now rumpled. Adding to her sorrowful aspect was the mascara ringing her eyes, making her look like a raccoon whose mate had run off with another.

"Nice night for a stroll, now that the pig smell has lifted," said Underdog, taking Ione's hand in his. He led her toward the railroad tracks forming the southern boundary of the college. "I have a romantic streak when it comes to trains," he explained.

After a quick look around for campus cops, Underdog and Ione stepped off the pavement and onto the tracks. When Ione hesitated, Underdog assured her they would be safe. He directed her attention to the light on the signal bridge in town, which shone red, and explained that this meant the track was empty for many miles in both directions. If and when the light turned green, they would have to keep alert for a train's hot white headlight bearing down.

They traveled west, in the opposite direction from the school's physical plant, where hopper cars dumped coal that fired boilers heating school buildings. Due to an earlier experience, when workmen chased him off the premises, he tended to stay away, unless he were emboldened from shots of whiskey. Underdog remembered there was another reason for heading west: to avoid the previous night's accident scene. "I don't know if you heard, but a student got killed by a train east of town last night," he said.

"Mmmmm," was all Ione said in response. With the autumn rains the gravel was a little mushy, so they kept to stepping on cross ties to save their shoes. Wary of tripping or twisting an ankle, Ione focused single-mindedly on her footing.

"Seems every year or two, a student gets hit by a train," continued Underdog.

Ione let go of his hand and halted suddenly. Underdog noticed that her shoulders were trembling. Then her entire body began to convulse from the most intense sobbing he ever saw. "My husband was killed by a train," she finally managed to say, clutching Underdog's arms and burying her face in his left shoulder. After five or six minutes, her crying died down, and she began to hiccup. Under control again, she backed away and looked at him intently. The mascara previously ringing her eyes now ran down her cheeks in rivulets, creating the striped face of a cheetah. "That's why I called you. What happened to that poor Japanese boy reminded me of what happened to Geoffrey. I was so sad today, I couldn't even go to work."

"I'm sorry for what happened to your husband," said Underdog. "But I'm glad you called me."

After a few heavy sighs, Ione appeared returned to normal, and they continued walking.

"Listen. Are you sure it's safe to walk here?" she asked, directing his attention to a No Trespassing sign along the right-of-way.

"Suicides are one thing, accidents are another," he answered. "Even if you're plowed, you should be able to jump off the tracks in time. Unless, of course, there's fog, and you don't see or hear the train coming."

"Geoffrey's car got hit in the fog."

"That must have been awful. For him and you both." He braced himself for another onslaught of tears.

"It happened so suddenly that I'm sure he didn't feel a thing. They told me his skull was crushed like an egg, and his legs snapped in half like pretzels. But I was spared from the sight. It was a closed-casket funeral." She said this with a surprising lack of emotion.

"We're dredging up bad memories. Maybe we ought to turn off at the next grade crossing," he suggested.

"No. I find it therapeutic."

"I've always considered train tracks the best place in the world to clear your head," said Underdog. Then he told Ione how he spent all his life in awe of trains, from the time he was three or four, living in his parents' first house, located next to the Milwaukee Road in Peru. The yard was fenced in, so there was never the opportunity to wander out of the yard and onto the tracks, but he poked his nose through the pickets when a train passed. From an early age, he enjoyed the delicious vibrations coming from the ground, the same sort of vibrations he felt from his mother, trembly feelings like love.

Later, he dreamt of how far away the train could take him. He read about hoboes riding the rails; he wanted to grow up to be one, to travel to cities like Chicago, New York or Los Angeles, big, teeming places that offered excitement, bright lights, girls. As he grew older, he snuck out from his parents' house, and took walks along the tracks, collecting thoughts and other oddball things, like shiny lumps of coal or track spikes.

They soon found themselves in downtown Jasper; facing them were the dimly lit back doors of bars and stores, the open maws of dumpsters, and chest-high weeds clogged with crushed paper cups and crumpled handbills. Consistent with the season, the weeds were turning brown, as were the skinny leaves of ash trees which grew in every possible spot, even in cracked cement pavement.

As they crossed Fourth Street, about one and a half miles from the college, a full view of the nighttime sky opened up. Looking south, Underdog saw the constellation Orion rising. The old warrior, light-years tall, with infinitely broad shoulders, loomed threateningly over the horizon, as if meaning to say to Underdog, "Ask her."

Before he could, however, Ione asked him first. "What happened to you last night?"

He laughed. "I was just about to ask you that same question."

"You left me there. Why do men act like that? Why do they always leave?"

His laughter gave way to choking, as he realized that she did not appreciate the humor of this coincidence. "You looked like you found a new date for the evening," he said gravely.

"It's you who have to explain. I didn't leave."

"Once you met that Race Fletcher, I felt like a third wheel."

"I came with you, and I'll leave with you," she said, almost shouting.

"Okay!" he bellowed, louder, then put his index finger to his lips and shooshed, afraid their angry words echoing off back alley walls might attract unwelcome attention.

Downtown Jasper now behind them, they walked past the very large grain elevator near the center of town, the tallest structure in the vicinity, aside from two high-rise dorms at the college. Although it was lit brilliantly, almost blindingly, it was idle for the night, the empty parking lot indicating this fact. Early the next morning, around three or four, hulking grain trucks and their heaping trailers would pull up and park, idling until the grain elevator got full-tilt underway at dawn, whereupon they would unload harvested grain, drive off, and drive back again with another load, repeating this pattern until dusk fell.

Four blocks of residential streets beyond the grain elevator, they were surrounded by Civic Park, so re-named in 1933 from the original Civitas, which nobody could pronounce. Civic Park was a good-sized park engulfing the northwest corner of Jasper. Among its amenities were playgrounds, a softball field, a half-dozen picnic shelters, a band shell, and scores of stately, one hundred-year-old oak trees. Hand-sized oak leaves rustling overhead dimmed the moonlight considerably, but a little light filtered through nonetheless, a light that lazily revolved from the wind's effect upon the leaves. Ione was glad Underdog held her hand, for the light appeared sinister to her, like netting cast by ghosts.

"It's true that every man leaves," said Ione, evidently inspired by the peaceful surroundings to speak. He saw that she had a vacant look on her face, as if she were hypnotized or under some spell.

"I didn't always think like that, growing up in the suburbs of Chicago. Boys never even entered my mind — my first love was theater, and I spent all my time acting in plays. I never won the starring roles — I'm not a pretty blond ingenue, I'm skinny and redheaded — but I got good character parts. I met a boy, an actor — he played Tony in *West Side Story*, I played Consuelo — who soon became my boyfriend. He had a 'bad boy' reputation — like, for example, before coming to school he injected vodka into oranges with a syringe, and we got drunk eating them at lunch. In that period of my life, I fancied myself a rebel — I'm sure you snuck alcohol when you were a teenager and thought 'I'm so cool.' Among other things, I saw the absurdity of where I lived, a sterile cluster of suburbs, each with a bigger water tower than the last, announcing the surrounding town's name to indifferent drivers speeding by on the expressway.

"As we metamorphosed from boys and girls to young adults — I know the cocoon-to-butterfly analogy is cliché, but it fits, don't you think? — we learned certain things useful for the rest of our lives. We learned not to mix different liquors, then chase it all down with beer, because we would throw up. Mainly we learned — or at least I personally learned — not to trust anyone, to believe that there was a plot around every corner — from personal ones involving your boyfriend, to global ones involving scientists putting chemicals into your town's water supply, as part of some weird experiment to make the residents engage in sick, perverse behavior.

"One weekend when my parents were vacationing in Florida, Brad and I made plans for a rendezvous at my house. On the phone beforehand he said he had a big surprise planned for me. When he arrived with two friends in tow, he showed me a pill bottle full of little purple tablets, which he claimed was microdot LSD. All three chimed in at once how much fun it would be to trip as a group. So we went into my brother's basement room, which he left behind when he moved out for college. It was a dump — with awful black light posters taped on the walls, and a mildewy, red shag carpet underfoot — but at least it gave us privacy, allowing Brad and me to fool around with a watchful dad upstairs. After a short while, my LSD trip commenced, and I felt increasingly sucked into my brother's waterbed. My head heavy with thoughts and pictures, I lay completely down and floated blissfully on the waterbed.

"All of a sudden my psychedelic bubble burst — I felt three sets of hands on me, unbuttoning my blouse, unzipping my jeans, untying my shoes. 'Check out her tits,' Brad said, unsnapping my bra. 'You told us straight. They're fine,' responded one of his friends, as he and the other boy started pinching my nipples. Soon a mouth was pressing onto mine, and fingers were probing inside me. Then they took turns fucking me, Brad first. I couldn't resist; I felt immobilized by the LSD. After they finished raping me, Brad said, 'Putting PCP in her dose was a great idea, huh boys?' In response, they all let rip a rebel yell, and gave each other high fives.

"I never told my parents, never reported it to the police, never went to the hospital. In one of the few strokes of luck I've had in my life, I didn't get pregnant — it was the right time of the month, I guess. I didn't even know the other boys' names. I recognized them from school, so I could have fingered them, but I felt so foolish and ashamed. Of course, I never saw Brad again — except for once when we came face-to-face in the hall between class bells. He didn't say a word, he just made a rude, smooching sound with his lips before walking away. My stage career ended after that — there was no way I could put myself on display with animals like Brad and his friends hooting and clapping in the audience — and I just bided my time until graduation, when I could finally escape the suburbs.

"Don't worry about the trauma I suffered, though, because I received several months of counseling from the mental health center right here at Jasper College — which is where I landed that fall. The next boy I let touch me, Tommy, promptly made me pregnant halfway through my freshman year — I knew better than to have sex without a rubber, but we talked about getting married, and to show my trust I didn't make Tommy wear one. He always pulled out in time — but it only takes one little sperm to reach its target. When I told him I was pregnant, he said he wanted to take a semester off and move home — which was a town in the southeast corner of the state — to save money by working for his dad at the family store. Then he would return to marry me, re-enroll in school, and live honorably in poverty as we raised our child and finished our degrees. Just as you'd suspect, I lost contact with him two months after he moved away, had an abortion — a royal ordeal in how they vacuum a bloody mess out of you and flush it down the drain — and I went back to counseling, where my therapist and I discussed *ad nauseum* my deep-seated fear of abandonment.

"When I graduated, with a B.S. in marketing — appropriate initials, given the industry — I returned to the suburbs, if you can believe that. I figured all men are assholes — that it didn't really matter if you're in a small town, a suburb or a big city. I got a receptionist job at an advertising firm in a skyscraper overlooking Michigan Avenue, and I lived the life of a commuter — push your way onto the train, push your way into the elevator, push your way up the corporate ladder. I lived for weekends, when I went out to rock clubs with girlfriends — God! some of those nights were horrid, with creepy men wooing you to the warmed-over sounds Beatles or Led Zeppelin tribute bands. It was at a club called McGreevy's where I met Geoffrey. He played electric bass in a rock band called The Jutes — he was their leader and chief songwriter, the intellectual of the group. He dedicated a number of songs he wrote to me, including "Red Hair on My Mind," which caught the interest of a record label. A demo tape of his songs was forwarded to I.R.S. Records by some guy who knew a guy who was the friend of a drummer who did studio work for Elvis Costello. Before he died, it looked as though Geoffrey was on the verge of signing a record contract.

"To make a very long story short, I decided that I needed fresh surroundings to overcome my grief, so I ended up moving back to Jasper in August, intending to put a tragic phase of my life behind me."

Far outside of town now, probably more than two miles, Ione ended her monologue. Underdog, mesmerized, finally said, "I'm frankly at a loss to say anything."

"Just don't leave me again," said Ione. "No matter what I say or do, I need a man like you, Underdog, someone who listens to my stories and understands."

Faint red light from the distant signal bridge colored the rails an eerie red hue, illuminating their path like miles-long neon tubing. The hum of transformers on telephone poles strung beside the track added to the general effect, one of atoms in the air stirred up by light, electricity, danger. A little further down the track, the sound of running water drifted into earshot, and all of a sudden Underdog came to a stop. Sensing he was spooked by something, and feeling spooked by that, Ione clutched him from behind and asked, "What is it?"

"Trestle." Her eyes followed his in looking over the edge of a stone retaining wall supporting the bridge over Hackberry Creek.

"What if a train comes?"

"It won't be a problem, as long as you start when the signal's still red." Both looked to assure themselves that the light hadn't yet changed.

They began to cross the bridge. Underdog stepped along the ties without looking at his feet, while Ione stepped carefully, not as sure-footed. Soon, however, she found that crossing the bridge was not anywhere near as perilous as she first expected. Moonlight reflecting off water lit gaps between ties, indicating where not to step.

"Step lively!" said Underdog, already across the bridge, directing her attention to the signal behind her, which had switched to green. A moment later the headlight of a train came into view.

Ione quickened her pace. Without panicking in the least, she finished crossing, and they clambered down the embankment to wait for the train. They listened to the faraway, out-of-tune warning honks as the train chugged through town. "A diesel horn makes a real sad sound," commented Underdog, gazing at her wondrously. "It's the second saddest sound I've ever heard. Next to the sound of the stories you told me tonight."

"Make love to me, Underdog," urged Ione, peeling off her jeans. Following her lead, he pulled off his pants, too, and they grappled, lips locking like puzzle pieces. Without breaking their embrace, they fell onto the road bed, heads landing a mere six feet from the rails. As they rolled over several times, feet tangled up in pants around their ankles, Underdog felt gravel scraping his backside, and Ione felt drops of blood on hers. The closer the train approached, the harder the ground quaked, jarring hormones loose and shaking nerves awake. After hauling from his pocket a condom and donning it, he entered her, just as the locomotives roared mightily by, blotting out their screams of terror and pleasure. After about half the train had passed, they each climaxed, and by the time the caboose signaled the end of the train, their pulses had slowed to near-normal rates.

Asses numb from the pounding they took from gravel, the couple helped each other up and dressed. "I think my butt is dented," said Ione, rubbing herself in hopes of regaining some feeling back there.

"Mine too," he said.

"No nude modeling for this kid till I heal," she said.

"The lights about a half-mile off in that direction are from Trailerville. We should go to your place to recover."

"We could dab each other with rubbing alcohol. To disinfect our butts!" she joked.

"Kinky," said Underdog, arm around her waist en route to her mobile home.

SEVEN

Ione and Underdog left a trail of inside-out clothes through her trailer as they bounded from back door to bedroom, where they jumped on the bed to the sounds of squeaky springs and smacking lips. As they grappled, she told him he would find a condom in her bathroom if he wasn't packing another. Inside her medicine cabinet, he located a clear plastic baggie filled with several different brands of prophylactics in a myriad of varieties. There were plain, lubricated, spermicidal, ribbed, slim, flavored (reminding him of Judy Baine momentarily), extra-strength, and even glow-in-the-dark.

"That's quite a cornucopia of condoms," he said, returning to her side. "It reminds me of your refrigerator stocked with every kind of beer."

"Bet you think I must've done it with a bunch of guys to collect so many different kinds," she said.

"It crossed my mind. You'd have to go through several boxes to come up with what's left over in that bag."

"Actually, it's a grab bag from the Rubber Tree that I bought the other day, before our date. They put samples of their most popular styles in each bag. I hope you found a rubber to suit your taste."

"I hope I chose one that you like, too," responded Underdog, pointing to the word "ribbed" on the foil package.

"Remember when you didn't need a rubber?" she asked.

"That was before my time, I'm afraid," he said.

"How old are you?"

"Twenty-three."

"I guess it *was* before your time. I'm twenty-nine, so I remember those days. It's funny how everything completely chilled in the eighties — from direct heat to heat conducted through a layer of latex."

During their next lovemaking session, Underdog noticed for the first time that Ione had an asterisk-shaped scar on the left side of her abdomen. Afterward, as she lay on her back while he gently blew on her belly to dry the beads of sweat collected there, he asked, "Did you get your appendix taken out?"

"Wrong side. Appendix scars are on the right. No, that's from the time I was thrown in jail. I got arrested at an anti-Apartheid demonstration when I was a student, and I spent a night in the Jasper County Jail."

"You spent a night in jail?" he asked, incredulous.

"Really, about seven hours. Until I got stabbed."

"Stabbed?"

"We were blockading the student center, and the campus cops had to call the sheriff for help. A pair of deputies dragged me off to jail. Later on, they brought in a Trailerville woman who tried pushing me off the bunk I was sitting on. I shoved her back — I was there first, after all — and she stabbed me with a paring knife she had hidden in her hose. How she got it in the cell with her, I don't know. They took me to the hospital, stitched me up, and left me with this ugly scar."

"It gives you character," commented Underdog, seeing further evidence of her wounded nature.

"For future reference, it tickles erotically when kissed."

Ione's stabbing story led her to another incident that took place three years before, when a man from her suburban apartment complex murdered his girlfriend with a carrot peeler. He stabbed her one hundred and thirty times and carved a nine- by twelve-inch rectangle of skin out of her thigh. "The carpet was covered with little slivers of skin, like carrot peels," she said in conclusion, then commenced another story, followed by another.

All night long, as he listened to Ione recite her autobiography, Underdog gradually became aware of wanting to possess her past. He wanted to reach back in time and grab onto the good times she told him of, then squirrel them away for later, continued enjoyment: high school graduation, which released her from the suburbs' grip, or her trip to France at age twenty-two, when she spent a week in Paris cafés and museums, followed by a week luxuriating on nude beaches in the south. Or her eighth birthday party, the first Underdog had heard of that truly featured pony rides. Or a 1987 performance by the Joffrey Ballet, when the choreographer signed the poster which hung in a silver frame over her bed.

Likewise, he felt an urge to enter history and set things straight. He yearned to track down every boy or man who hurt her, each of the three who raped her especially, and beat the living crap out of him. He longed to slow the cancer which claimed the life of her grandmother the week before her fiftieth wedding anniversary. He wanted to offer up his shoulder for her to cry on at her dead husband's funeral. Most of all, he wished he were able to pluck

Geoffrey from his seat before the train pulverized his car, so he could compete for Ione's attentions, fair and square, with a man and not a memory.

During one of several pregnant pauses, Ione feverishly picked her nails and tore bits of skin off her finger tips. Then she stared at her raw, purple-red digits, looking pleased at her handiwork, no doubt feeling the same pride one feels when slicing an apple peel off in one piece. For his part, Underdog marveled at how deeply grooved this habit left her fingerprints, so pronounced with the top layer of skin gone, offering still another example of how pain was ingrained in her identity.

Noticing Underdog's attention drawn to her fingers, she said, "I started picking my fingers the night of the murder at my apartment complex," she said. "I picked them till they bled as I sat and listened to the commotion upstairs, completely afraid for my life, praying for the police to come and put a stop to it."

"You give new meaning to the phrase 'rosy-fingered dawn,'" he joked, pointing to first light emerging through her windows. He vaguely understood the impulse to flay your wife or girlfriend; he didn't understand why one peeled off a fair-sized area of one's own finger skin. Searching for a reason, he asked, "What's bugging you?"

Scooting closer to him, she said that she had something to confess. "After the reception ended last night, I went for a ride with Race in his Corvette. We drove all over the countryside, guzzling champagne from the bottle, singing along to the oldies radio station, and generally carrying on like high school hellions."

Underdog felt a sharp pain, like a long surgical needle was injecting a big dose of adrenaline into his gut, causing his heart to gallop and his temples to thunder. As if vying with a dead guy didn't challenge him enough, there remained a live threat, Race Fletcher.

"But I didn't sleep with him, never came close."

"Whew," sighed Underdog.

"He asked me to fly with him to New York next Wednesday night, however. He has to attend a meeting — 'my hardcover publisher is handing me off to the paperback people,' he told me — then he wants to paint the town red for the rest of the weekend. Uh, with me as his date. We're going to an art opening in Soho, a poetry reading 'by an old friend' at the 92nd Street Y, dinner at Tavern on the Green, and a jazz show at his favorite nightclub right now, the Knitting Factory. If I lived in a big city, those are exactly the sorts of things I would do. I'm sure you can see I have to go."

"Where does that leave me?" he asked.

"In Jasper," she said.

How cruel that the truth was so *true*, he thought, suddenly feeling hollow as a warehouse. Much as he hated to admit it, she was absolutely correct — she must take advantage of a generous offer and go to New York City.

It was all so tentative, he thought as he absorbed this latest disclosure, how most couples got together: immediately upon their meeting, they want to be part of their mates' plans, promote as much as possible their staying, and prevent by the same token their straying. But it was very hard to fully possess another person, and still more difficult to command the future, which was a total abstraction and as volatile as corn or soybean options. At least the past was solid and measurable, like gold and silver. However, much as he longed to possess Ione's past and control her future, he realized that both were equally unobtainable, both were beyond his means. And this fact depressed the shit out of Underdog.

He looked at his wrist watch, but was unable to make out the time through the frosted crystal. "Damn, I must've scraped up the face when we fucked by the train tracks last night," he said, jiggling his wrist as if this might shake off the scratches.

"It's about seven o'clock," said Ione, raising her head off the pillow and peeking at her alarm clock over a mountain of tangled blankets and sheets. Underdog threw on his clothes, then stepped into the bathroom in order to wash his face and tame his wild hair with a wet comb. With the faucet still running to cover the sound, he opened the creaky mirrored door to her medicine cabinet, pulled out the baggie of condoms, and counted the contents. The number was eleven, supporting her claim that she did not sleep with Race Fletcher, at least not using her own equipment. Knowing this provided him with some measure of relief.

When Underdog emerged from the bathroom, Ione was fast asleep. Shafts of light entered her room between vertical blinds, reminding him of rays that emanated from ghosts. Watching her kick and twitch, he understood that even in her dreams she was haunted. She didn't snore exactly, but a noise erupted from her throat every few seconds, sounding to him like she was gargling blood. He kissed her on the shoulder, pulled the covers over her, and on the magnetized note pad hanging on her refrigerator door scribbled the following:

Ione: Call me next week, because I can't wait to hear the stories about your trip to New York. Signed the best listener in the world, Underdog

Passing through downtown on his walk home, he studied Jasper's Saturday morning routine. He walked by Mott's, a popular breakfast and lunch place on Main Street between Second and Third. Looking in the window, he saw a curious mixture of townies, fully rested and freshly scrubbed in their plaid shirts and overalls, and students, still awake after carousing all night, cross-eyed from drink and hunched over coffee. He considered stopping in for breakfast, but decided he was too tired. Besides, the restaurant usually ran out of his favorite breakfast dish, sausage gravy and biscuits, by six-thirty or seven on Saturdays. Entering Suds City, he slalomed through a flock of burly men whose job it was to clean up after a long and profitable Friday night, sweeping, bagging rubbish and hosing off sidewalks. Each man wore a tee shirt that was color-coordinated to his respective bar's paint job: gold for Home Run Sports Bar, red for Buffalo Bill's Wild West Saloon, green for MacKelly's Irish Pub, and ultramarine for Club Paradise.

Nestled among the bars of Suds City was the Rubber Tree, a store which appeared one day in place of a newsstand notorious in Jasper for stocking girlie magazines, a few of which bordered on the pornographic. For years, outraged Jasperites lobbied for its closure, mainly two groups that would never find themselves in bed together normally, the Jasper College Womyn's Club, a radical feminist organization, and CHAS, acronym for Churches that Hate All Sin, an association of evangelical Christians. With the appearance of the Rubber Tree, a more diabolic foe than the newsstand arose, provoking picketing by these two groups. According to CHAS, the Rubber Tree encouraged promiscuity, adultery and perversion; according to the Womyn's Club, the store promoted rape, because it sold a product connected with sexual penetration, always an act of violation in their philosophy, even in cases of consensual sex.

He crossed the street to look in the darkened front window of the Rubber Tree. Behind the sales counter along the back wall he saw the store's namesake: a green, Christmas tree shape painted on the wall, where condom packages hung from pegs like ornaments. Mounted on the west wall were two posters, the first of basketball great Magic Johnson telling youngsters to practice safe sex, the second saying "Ask for instructions on the proper use of a condom." Part of the uproar concerning the Rubber Tree had to do with this message, for it was common knowledge in town that the clerk, if asked, would retrieve from under the counter a dildo used to demonstrate how to put on a condom.

Tacked up on the east, or opposite, wall, there were two more posters. One pictured a serious-looking woman in a business suit warning women not to rely on men for protection, the other advertising Rubber Tree Grab Bags for sale at six dollars apiece. At the bottom appeared these words: "Baker's Dozen — Buy Twelve, Get One Free."

Sitting in his room after arriving home, Underdog was practically gagging, like he swallowed a large spoon stirring organ soup. Heart, liver, lungs and stomach stewed, as he dwelled upon the fate of the thirteenth condom. Clearly, Ione must have lied about not screwing Race Fletcher. There could be no other explanation, except an outside chance the Rubber Tree miscounted when they assembled the Grab Bag she bought. Or maybe a third party he wasn't aware of was involved.

Aggravating Underdog further, the smell of Pine Sol wafted up from lower floors and entered his room by way of the cold air return duct. Never one to sleep after eight, even on Saturday or Sunday, Mona Baine made certain to wake the rest of the house good and early, too, by putting on her yellow rubber gloves and cleaning the public areas of the boarding house, her weekend ritual.

The last thing he needed to disturb his self pity was a light knock at the door. Ignoring the sound did not make it go away, only louder and more insistent. Caving in, he opened the door. Standing in the hall was Judy Baine in her robe; her considerable bosom nearly spilled out the top, and the short length barely covered the tops of her thighs.

"Aren't you going to invite me in?" she asked in a low voice.

"It's been a rough night, Judy. Can I look you up later?" he suggested.

She looked him up and down, taking note of his wrinkled clothes. "You were out last night with that pale, flat-chested bitch with the skinny ass," she surmised.

"Who?" he asked, faking innocence.

"Don't think I don't know. How can you like that girl and her nasty ironing board body compared to this." She untied her robe and let it fall open.

"Let's talk about this later this afternoon. I've got to get some sleep," he said, knowing he needed to be well-rested to have the presence of mind required to face this controversy.

"Mom's finished cleaning and gone to the Piggly Wiggly. She ought to be away about an hour. Ask me in," she pleaded, reaching down the front of his jeans and cupping his testicles in her hand.

Her surprise move triggered a protective reflex in Underdog. Grabbing by the wrist, he yanked her hand out of his pants and flung it away from him. The force of this action made her lose her balance, and she toppled down the stairs. He watched as she turned two backward somersaults before landing with a thud on the second floor landing.

"Judy!" he called, running down the stairs after her. "Are you okay? I'm sorry. It was an accident. Can I do anything?" he asked, lifting her by the arm. He saw on her knee a bruise growing more purple by the second and a small cut above her left eye that trickled blood.

"You've done enough for today, thank you very much," she sputtered, dazed and wobbly as she limped down the remaining stairs to the Baine portion of the house on the ground floor.

* * *

At four in the afternoon Underdog awoke with a big appetite. An hour later, he could not stave off hunger any longer; he had to go grocery shopping, for he knew his cupboard in the downstairs boarders' kitchen was bare. This meant leaving his room, the only refuge from all the trouble which had blown up around him in recent days. Tip-toeing down the stairs, trying to be quiet as a guerrilla commando who just got done planting bombs, Underdog made it as far as the driveway, where Mona Baine seized upon him. She was waving a broom; he cringed, afraid she might whack him for injuring her daughter.

"I didn't mean to startle you," she said. "I was sweeping rocks off the driveway. Did you know that I had to take Judy to the emergency room this morning?"

"Uh, no," he said, backing away from her.

"Three stitches it took to sew up a cut on her forehead. She said it happened in the garage. She knocked a shovel off its hook and it fell on her face."

"That's terrible," he said, feeling a leaden cloak of guilt around his shoulders.

"Thursday, she gets pulled over on her lawn mower for drunk driving, and today this. You know, she's twenty-one now. An awkward age when children give their parents fits. I hope a man comes into her life soon and takes her off my hands."

"Will she be okay?" he asked.

"She's tough. Always been a tomboy."

"That's good," he said, then dismissed himself. Walking through long autumn shadows on his way to the Piggly Wiggly, Underdog thought hard about the monster he created, Judy Baine, Bride of Frankenstein, complete with crooked scar on her forehead.

EIGHT

Every moment his hands were free in the next several days, Underdog crossed his fingers, literally, in the superstitious hope that it would prevent any phone calls to the print shop from the credit union. By Tuesday, the day before Ione's departure to New York with Race Fletcher, his luck had held: no one in her office had requested that he come pick up any print jobs. During this interval, cumulative instances of dread wound him tighter than a time bomb clock. Seeking any sort of relief from stress, he welcomed Reid's invitation to play in the sociology department's weekly basketball game.

After their Tuesday afternoon classes, a bunch of guys, either sociology department faculty or grad students, referring to themselves as the "Indian Summer League," gathered at one of the campus's outdoor basketball courts to play basketball. None was especially good at the game, yet they gave each other nicknames appropriated from their favorite NBA stars, past and present.

They called the guy who recruited everyone into these games, a full professor pushing middle age, "Dr. J." And although he was white, he still looked like the real Dr. J in a curious way: he had a goatee, plus he had a knack for finger-rolling the ball into the hoop. There was "Moses Malone," who, though he didn't resemble that player physically, resembled him attitudinally, in that he provided a stubborn barrier whichever way you wanted to drive with the ball. They had a "Larry Bird," so named on account of his reddish hair and menacing outside shot. Also on the court was a retired big city cop studying criminology; a tall black guy with a beer belly and big butt, he was dubbed "Shaquille O'Neal." Playing center against Shaquille was the other big man, a gawky grad student they called "Kareem," because he was the tallest guy there, and he wore strap-on glasses. Reid, the most accurate and graceful shooter of the group, took the name "Michael Jordan." They called Underdog "Rookie" at the outset, since nobody had seen him play.

To warm up, they shot free throws, passed the ball around, and tried some fancy dribbling. Then, after a few minutes of missing the hoop, overthrowing passes and dribbling the ball off their feet, at the fringe of the asphalt there stood Race Fletcher, wearing wraparound sunglasses, a gray "Property of NYU Dance Department" tee shirt and gray sweat pants. "Fashionably late," he said, arms spread and hands open in an exaggerated, almost vaudevillian gesture of contriteness.

Everybody stopped. Three or four of the guys, whom Underdog remembered seeing at the *Green Acres* reception the week before, glowered at Race Fletcher, not in the least trying to bury their contempt. Mirrored in their poisonous stares was recognition that Race Fletcher had stolen all the celebrity at a college with very little to go around to begin with. Somebody hummed the opening bars of the *Green Acres* theme song, nasally imitating the twangy guitar; somebody else asked under his breath the question everybody wanted to know: "Who invited this prima donna?" (Dr. J later admitted to inviting Race Fletcher to their game. It seemed that he had something of a reputation as a basketball fiend, and wherever he traveled to lecture, he tried to organize a game with the locals in the yokel English departments hosting him.)

As they gathered under the basket to choose up sides, they realized that Race Fletcher's arrival upset the even number. To solve the problem, Reid volunteered to rotate with him. Selected as a package, Reid and Race Fletcher ended up on the Skins team. Underdog was picked by Shirts, which suited him just fine, because, since grade school days, he associated the smartest kid on the block, Race Fletcher in this case, with being the least adept at sports. The team who got this kid usually lost. Beforehand, Reid explained to Underdog that nobody wanted anyone too uncoordinated on his team, though less for competitive reasons than for economic: the losers were required to buy the winners a round of beers at Roger's Bar afterwards. Underdog learned that in this particular game, he worried less about winning than sportsmanship or economics should dictate — his only goal was to stuff Race Fletcher for stealing away Ione.

Early on in the game Underdog didn't have much of a chance to carry out his vendetta. There were only four guys to a team, so they played man-to-man defense, since you couldn't effectively cover a zone with fewer than five players. Dr. J guarded Race Fletcher for Underdog's team; Underdog's opponent in the early going was "Isaiah Thomas," a shrimpy, but swift, assistant professor, who dribbled around him a lot. But, though Underdog didn't jump as high as Kareem, or rebound as well as Shaquille, or throw a screen like Dr. J, his teammates passed him the ball often anyway, for he was skilled at feeding the ball to Moses Malone, who drove up the lane and shot easy lay-ups. For his talent in the assists category, Underdog drew the nickname of "John Stockton." Larry Bird remarked on the coincidence in pro basketball, where John Stockton fed another player named Malone: Utah Jazz teammate Karl Malone.

Contrary to Underdog's expectations, Race Fletcher wasn't that bad of a basketball player; what he did best was fake outside, then drive inside with the ball. He was a serious ball hog, however. Assuming the role of playmaker for the Skins team, he spent a lot of time by himself dribbling at the edge of the court, more often than not taking the shot himself, instead of passing off to somebody who had a better shot. Because of his selfish offense and his arrogance bred of superstardom, Race Fletcher quickly earned the nickname "Charles Barkley."

Underdog soon realized that Race Fletcher had it in for him as well as he did for Race. Whenever Underdog held the ball, Race Fletcher would leave his man, run over to him, and, if he didn't get a pass or shot off in time, try to tie him up, even if Isaiah Thomas stood there holding his own with him. In the spirit of Charles Barkley, Race Fletcher played aggressive, almost malicious, defense, slapping at the ball, but usually missing and smacking the tops of Underdog's hands instead. Of course, in any organized game this was a blatant foul, but in their weekly games, the sociologists tended to overlook such things. Underdog could have yelled "Foul!" and the rest of the players would probably have backed him up, but he didn't want to appear a crybaby, especially in front of Race Fletcher, who seemed to enjoy tormenting him.

Underdog got his licks in, too, however. Younger, taller, with a twenty-pound weight advantage, Underdog easily blocked him out in rebounding free-for-alls that broke out under the basket, when he managed to knock Race Fletcher off his feet several times. At one point, Underdog was in position to reach over Isaiah's shoulder and block one of Race Fletcher's shots. Watching the ball roll harmlessly out-of-bounds, Dr. J crowed, "There's no need to fear, Underdog is here," a refrain that followed him for the rest of the afternoon, more in praise now than previously in life, like one week in second grade, when, learning of the nickname, his classmates taunted him unmercifully by singing out these words in the morning at the bus stop, in the cafeteria throughout lunch, on the playground during recess, and on the big yellow school bus home.

Near the end of the game, the Shirts team was up by two, 48 to 46, only two points away from 50, the score you had to reach first to win. Dr. J launched a shot from far to the left side, but the ball clanged off the rim. Between the hoop and Underdog was a jockeying

Race Fletcher, who backed into Underdog, trying to prevent him from reaching the ball. Seeing his opportunity, Underdog jumped over Race Fletcher's shoulders, snatched the ball, and, accidentally on purpose, came crashing down on him, elbow cracking him square on top of his skull. Race Fletcher collapsed to the pavement, and Underdog shot an easy lay-up to win the game. "Deconstructed you," he hissed above the prone body of his foe.

After crawling to the edge of the court, shaking his head and spitting the whole way, Race Fletcher lay down on the grass, looking very woozy. Everybody surrounded him asking, "You okay?" and what not. After a minute or two Underdog joined them, then apologized to Race Fletcher for the unfortunate injury he received at his hands. Deep down Underdog wasn't sorry at all, though; rather, he felt extremely self-satisfied, his chest puffed out from inhaling the winds of war, which, for this battle at least, were blowing in his direction.

As might be expected, Race Fletcher didn't feel up to piling into Dr. J's rusted-out Pontiac station wagon and driving downtown to Roger's Bar for after-game beers.

"Man, he fouled me right and left," complained Dr. J to the others sitting at the large oval table in the corner, which converted from a square table by flipping up rounded leaves at either end.

"Me, too," said Shaquille.

"You guys saw how he went after me," said Underdog.

"What a hot dogger. I was open all the time, and he never passed me the ball once," Larry Bird whined.

"Yeah. If it wasn't for him, you guys would be buying *us* beers, not the other way around," agreed Kareem.

"You sure got him good, though," Moses Malone said to Underdog. "I wanted to cheer when you came down on his head. But fair play, and all that stuff."

"Any more cheap shots like that, and we're gonna' have to call you 'Bill Laimbeer' from now on," chimed in Reid.

"I hope he's all right," Dr. J said. "He drove off in that Range Rover of his complaining of a mighty big headache."

"Some things even rich demographics like his don't protect you from," said Isaiah Thomas, who specialized in tabulating statistical data.

"That four-leaf clover on his chest didn't bring him any luck, either," said Moses Malone, referring to the faded green tattoo on Race Fletcher's left pectoral.

"Tell us. Did you do it on purpose?" Larry Bird asked. "I mean, it was too perfect for it to happen by accident."

"I'll never tell," said Underdog. "But one thing is clear. You guys from the college should know better than to mess with us townies."

To a hail of laughter, Phyllis, the waitress whose left eye perpetually squinted due to the smoke curling up from a cigarette always clenched in her left hand, arrived with two pitchers of beer and eight glasses on her corkboard tray. The guys on Race Fletcher's team fished into their pockets and pulled out crumpled dollar bills to buy Shirts, the winning team, their beers.

"You know what the worst thing about that guy is?" asked Dr. J, referring to Race Fletcher. "He's welching on the beers he owes us."

As a kind of toast to that statement, everyone raised his glass and took a big, welcome slug of beer.

* * *

In the course of her work, not every day, but maybe twice a month or so, Judy Baine ran across some kind of dead animal. Sometimes it was a bird, lying on its back, grounded permanently from the mortal pull of gravity, wings stiffly saluting the sky. Other times she would find the remains of gophers, decapitated from the swirling blades of her power mower. When confronted with Nature taking its course on one of her creatures, Judy picked up the carcass and dropped it in a plastic garbage bag with the other yard refuse, which she later unceremoniously deposited at the town's compost heap.

At approximately the same late-afternoon time Underdog lit into Race Fletcher on the basketball court, Judy found a dead squirrel half-buried among damp, fallen leaves clogging the gutter of the street out front of a doctor's home, a red-brick, colonnaded structure built by a fan of the southern plantation style during the last century's barbed wire boom. As she brushed away fallen leaves soggy as sautéed spinach, an idea suddenly hit:

"I should let the flat, skinny bitch with no ass get rid of you," she said aloud to the squirrel.

She dropped her rake and walked up the driveway to retrieve her shopping cart, appropriated from the Piggly Wiggly's parking lot, containing fertilizer, grass seed, peat moss, hand trowels, grass shears and rubber gloves, which she stuck her hands and forearms into, then tugged upward for a snug fit.

Looking over her shoulder and finding the doctor's neatly rowed windows casting blind eyes to her, she scooped up the squirrel with her spade. She flipped it over on its back and found it remarkably well-preserved; being wrapped in leaves evidently had mummified it.

After stuffing a garbage bag full of leaves from the gutter, she carefully laid the squirrel on top, enshrouding it in plastic like all the dead animals she encountered, then sealed the bag with a twist-tie. After attaching the shopping cart to the back of her lawn tractor by looping a leather strap around a hook behind the seat, then having one final look-see around the doctor's yard for any stray implements of hers, she mounted her machine, fired up the ignition and proceeded to Trailerville at a speed of seven m.p.h., via side streets and the shoulder of Highway 17. "Have to drive cautious," she yelled over the roaring engine, steering the front wheels absolutely straight, mindful of her run-in with the law the week before when she was pulled over.

Pausing at the entrance gate to Trailerville twenty minutes later, she recited the words on the sign she had seen a hundred times before: "Taylorville Mobile Home Development." Then, on a smaller sign below, "These premises are for the use and enjoyment of residents and their guests only. No trespassing." Letting up on the clutch again, she pulled ahead into the trailer park, saying, "I'm allowed. I take care of their grounds work."

Staking out her position at the flower bed nearest to Ione's residence, at the intersection of Taylorville Street, the main artery through the middle of the development, and E Street, one of six gravel roadways designated A through F, she made the motions of raking out dead leaves and dried up stalks of irises and daffodils intertwining more hardy marigolds, still fiery in mid-fall. Looking askance, she studied unit E-9 and plotted her strategy. "Car parked outside. Drapes drawn. Pushing dusk. Wait to strike when it's dark," she muttered between breaths, which came more quickly from exertion and excitement.

When the last orange in the western sky was shouldered aside by a deep shade of blue, Judy felt it safe to strike. In preparation, she slipped on her gloves, a ritual she always saw in movies depicting secret agents or criminals who wanted to avoid leaving fingerprints. Stalking forward, dragging behind her the garbage bag containing the squirrel, she approached Ione's trailer. Briefly, she considered posing the squirrel on Ione's stoop, imagined its joints clicking in place like dolls she played with as a little girl. Then she decided to investigate a spot with potentially greater shock value: Ione's car.

Finding the lock buttons up on both doors to the Volkswagen, she snuck around to the passenger side, fell to hands and knees out of sight of the trailer, and silently opened the unlocked door. She placed the deceased squirrel on the passenger seat, arranging its head so it would greet Ione with its blue, clouded-over eyes as she entered her car. Shutting the door as quietly as she could, she slipped away undetected, but not without first noting the Jasper College parking permit stuck on the lower right corner of the windshield. "Figures," she said to herself, as if mere association with the school confirmed a character defect in Ione which only a true townie like Judy could recognize. To draw as little attention to herself as possible, she decided to forego starting her lawn mower right off. Rather, she released the emergency brake lever, depressed the clutch pedal by hand, shifted gears to neutral, and rolled her tractor to the entrance of the trailer park, whereupon she climbed aboard, switched on the motor and headlights, and drove back into town.

She pulled up to the curb outside Roger's Bar, locked her tractor to a light pole with a bicycle lock and chain, and entered the establishment, where there would be plenty of people to supply her with an alibi (although not Underdog, who left with his basketball buddies an hour before). Unlike your typical practical joker, who liked to be in the immediate vicinity of the object of his prank in order to witness the fun, Judy didn't want to be seen anywhere nearby, understandable given her recent legal troubles. Thus, she missed out on all of Ione's shrieks and screams and gasps the next morning, and her jumping so far off the car seat that her head struck the roof with a metallic thud. Judy also missed two weeks' worth of stories, first in New York and then in Jasper, that Ione was telling everyone about her fright and consequent ordeal — of having the squirrel disposed of and the car's interior professionally cleaned; of filing a complaint with the police department and confronting the rude officer who could barely choke back laughter; and of promising to anyone who listened that she would find the culprit and make him pay.

Sipping from a frosted mug of Lite beer, Judy chuckled devilishly as she imagined Ione's reaction to the surprise in her car. Upon reaching the last of her beverage, she raised her mug and toasted herself, saying, "The skinny, flat-chested bitch with no ass ought to know better than mess with a townie." She drank the remaining beer in one big gulp whose bubbles rose from her throat, popping and fizzing like a private fireworks show inside her celebrating head.

Then, sobered by her tractor ride home, when she scrupulously observed every conceivable traffic law, she shared with her mother a dinner of salad and turkey vegetable soup that simmered all day long in Mona Baine's crock pot, after which she washed, retired to her room, and brooded over Underdog as she lay in bed, periodically fingering the cut on her brow, the stitched and knotted emblem of her longing. "It's funny how I hate Underdog, but I ache inside for him, too," she said softly to herself, during a car commercial flashed amidst late-night sitcom reruns she watched on her portable TV set tuned to Channel Nine, piped in by cable all the way from Chicago, shows like *Cheers, Night Court* and others that her life increasingly resembled, with their improbable plot turns and tempestuous relationships.

NINE

It was the Friday before Halloween, during autumn's final burst of gas, when Jasper's maple, oak and sycamore trees flared up in a brilliant display of orange, red and yellow, then were extinguished, leaving them stark and black as charred skeletons. Inside Roger's Bar, Underdog sat on a stool, sipping from a beer and staring at himself in the mirror behind the walnut bar, oblivious to the noontime background bustle of Progressive Beer Day, when plastic cups of draft beer rose five cents every half-hour from a nickel at eight in the morning to the normal price of one-fifty by six at night. If he were to put on the Cubs cap and prematurely manufactured "1989 National League Champs" tee shirt his father brought him home from a business trip to Chicago a few years back, he would have a ready-made Halloween costume, he thought, for the circles under his eyes were as dark as the greasepaint baseball players wore.

Keeping Underdog awake all night long, and claiming every bit of his attention in the daytime, too, were the words "I want I want I want" throbbing inside his head. Their source was an anxiously beating heart reverberating in his chest like a bass drum pacing a frantic circus march. He first noticed the condition on the day Ione left for New York City with Race Fletcher; since that time, he could not shake the insistent words, no matter how hard he concentrated on something else.

"What's the good word?" asked Reid, suddenly appearing in the mirror behind Underdog.

"The heart is a greedy organ, even greedier than sex organs," said Underdog, poeticizing his self pity. Wanting privacy, he and Reid took their beers to a corner where the jukebox stood, apart from the sudden push of patrons ordering forty-cent beers a few minutes before twelve-thirty, when the price went up to forty-five cents.

"I've been here too long," said Underdog, leaning over Reid, face so close his cigarette spilled ashes down the front of Reid's maroon tee shirt.

"Look, you're making an ash of yourself," Reid complained, backing into the jukebox; jarred from the impact, the music skipped ahead a few bars as the laser beam inside the CD changer skirted across the CD, in turn inspiring the bartender to yell at the pair, though the general hubbub scattered his words into gibberish. "What did you do?" asked Reid, irritated now. "Open the bar and blow off work?"

"Been here since the beers cost a quarter — what's that make it? Two hours now? And yes, I took off today as one of my personal days. But that's not what I meant. I mean I've been hanging around this town too long."

"But you're a townie," said Reid, whose Jasper College ties, if only as a lowly graduate student, conferred on him a higher status in the world's eyes.

"Townie," repeated Underdog. He almost spat the word. Then he took a swipe at a branch of the rubber tree in a terra cotta pot by the jukebox, whacking off two leaves the size of ping-pong paddles. Again, the bartender yelled something bar noise swallowed up. "Remember what we used to say about townies?" he asked, continuing. "They didn't have the guts of a grasshopper smacking into a car windshield, that's why they didn't move someplace bigger and better."

"So what are you going to do?" asked Reid. "Move to Chicago or Minneapolis? There's no way you'll get a decent job in either of those places without finishing your degree."

"I'll get a factory job," said Underdog. "It'd beat staying in this stinking town and slaving away at the print shop."

"Factories in big cities are shutting down and laying off people. They're moving their operations to little towns in the middle of nowhere like Jasper. Try applying at the auto plant again. I hear they pay fifteen bucks an hour. To farmboys who fell off their tractors on their heads once too many times." Reid lowered his voice, then looked around to make sure no farmboys stood around. (A couple of years before, Reid unthinkingly made another comment insulting to farmboys. One who overheard it punched him in the breastbone so hard that his heart sloshed around in his chest for a few hours afterward.) "I know you didn't get hired when they first opened, but they're talking about starting a graveyard shift. I bet you catch on then."

"Maybe, but I can't take the thought of college kids five years down the road pointing at me and whispering about still another guy who came to Jasper College and never left. Look at how many sixties refugees there are wandering around town that you and I make fun of."

"You mean like him?" asked Reid, nudging Underdog to look in the direction of the bar, where a familiar sixties refugee, wearing a white shirt, black vest and stretchable jeans to accommodate his middle age spread, busied himself retying his salt-and-pepper pony tail while waiting for his beer. Known to Reid as "Rotten Fingertips," they became acquainted at a meeting of the school's Anti-Intervention Society, an ordeal of the first magnitude that Reid's old girlfriend had dragged him to. The man's complaints from behind the dais of how handling computer paper at his on-campus job was making his fingertips rot, instead of plotting a campaign to publicize the plight of Nicaragua or El Salvador, reinforced Reid's prejudice against long-haired throwbacks from the sixties.

"Maybe not that bad," said Underdog. "But not very far in the future, I'll look like a relic, too."

"You're so caught up in how you're gonna' look. I figure I'm gonna' look the same whether I'm here in Jasper or anywhere else."

"It's not about how you look. It's about wasting what my granddad called his 'salad days.' Think of all the movies you could see in the big city. All of the bands you could hear. Think about all the women you would meet."

"From what I can tell — and this is mere observation, not the result of any sociological study — big cities are a breeding ground for neurotic women. You have to admit the pickings are pretty good in Jasper, comparatively speaking. A new crop of co-eds to break in every year."

"City women are broken in already."

"Breaking them in is half the fun."

"No argument there," said Underdog, suddenly aware of the irony of his statements in light of recent experience. "Imagine a whole city full of Iones!" he added.

"So that's why you're in such a funk. You want to get away from her."

"It's bad, Reid. I took off today because I know that her dandruff-headed boss at the credit union has their ledger pages printed up the last Friday of every month. Then he bitches when they're not done by the first. It never seems to occur to him to place his order further in advance.

"Anyway," Underdog continued, "I couldn't face seeing her today. I thought I might as well keep my streak going."

"How many days now since you've seen her?"

"Twenty."

"I don't understand why you're all fired up over her," said Reid. "There's something sexy about her, I'll grant you that. But you've got a genuine sex bomb living under your roof, whose only goal in life is to fuck you beyond recognition, and you kick her down the stairs when she comes on to you. To me, there's no comparison. It's like a match versus dynamite."

"Let me make one thing clear: I didn't 'kick' Judy down the stairs. She lost her balance and fell on her own." He wadded up his cup and tossed it underhand into a plastic garbage can stationed by a post, a good twelve feet away. "Without four beers under my belt, I would've missed that," he commented.

"Your aim is always better after a few. Same principle with bowling and shooting pool," Reid shouted to Underdog, who shoved his way to the bar, plunked down ninety cents, then returned to Reid with two fresh beers.

"I hear what you're saying," said Underdog, back on the subject. "You're absolutely correct that Judy is more my type than Ione. We both come from the same place. We both come at the same time, for that matter." He winked at Reid knowingly. "But the fact remains, we don't, I don't know, elevate each other.

"Put it like this," he said, trying to explain. "Most townies would be satisfied clunking around town in an old pickup truck. So what if it's too broken down to take you far outside of town? It's reliable enough to get you everywhere you need to go in your narrow little world. But then a brand new Jaguar pulls into town. Suddenly, you're able to go anywhere the highway takes you, in the utmost style. Your whole universe opens up."

"Excuse me," interrupted Reid. "I have two things to say regarding your comparisons. First of all, Judy cannot be compared to an old, beat-up truck. She's a brand new one, with very shapely fenders I might add. Second, Ione may be classy like a Jaguar, but she's a townie, too. The situation is like storing your Jaguar in the garage and never taking it out for a spin."

"I'm talking about a mental thing," said Underdog. "Even if you never leave your garage, sitting in the front seat puts you in mind of somewhere else — doing a hundred and ten across Nevada, climbing the Rocky Mountains, driving over the Golden Gate Bridge. You know, setting your sights on something beyond the cornstalk-filled horizon."

Reid took a big sip of beer and swished it around his mouth for a few moments; with puffed-out cheeks he mulled over all that Underdog had said. Then he swallowed hard, for courage it seemed to Underdog. "Why don't we go for a drive," said Reid. "I was going to let it pass, but now I think I better take you somewhere that illustrates what a fast crowd you're driving with."

"I might as well, as long as you don't mind missing class this afternoon."

"No classes on Friday," said Reid. "Instead, you and I will do a little field work together. To save you from getting run over in the fast lane."

* * *

Fifteen miles north of Jasper, at the crossroads of State Road 64 and the east-west interstate, a monumental truck stop, the largest in the four-county area, rose from the prairie. Built of whitewashed cement blocks and trimmed with burnished aluminum, it gleamed in the sun, reflecting light and drawing notice from afar as effectively as the marble shrines of Ancient Greece. It resembled nothing so much as a miniature city, an oasis located on a major trade route linking the Atlantic and Pacific: included within the sprawling complex were two restaurants, one serving carry-out burgers and fries, the other offering a more traditional sit-down atmosphere; a gas station with two dozen pumps; a mini-mart where all manner of toiletries and microwave food items could be bought; a video game arcade; a truck wash; a laundromat; public showers; a first aid station staffed by a registered nurse; acres of parking where truckers camped at night; a picnic ground where families ate or walked their dogs; and a bar, destination for Jasper College frat boys seeking prostitutes, or so Underdog had heard.

Within the blinding, fluorescent-lit, white-tiled hallways, a bazaar atmosphere prevailed. Total strangers offered to sell you tires, engine parts, pilfered cigarettes, pictures of Jesus, firecrackers, CB radios, marijuana, pep pills, bootlegged liquor, audio cassettes, VCR tapes, cowboy hats, belt buckles, stuffed animals, gold necklaces, wristwatches, even the shirts off their backs if you looked halfway admiringly. Similar to New York, the "city that never sleeps," the truck stop was a true twenty-four-hour-a-day operation. In fact, it rivaled New York in one notable aspect: towering overhead and visible for miles in every direction was an electronic billboard, supposedly bigger than the one in Times Square, which flashed the time and temperature, gas prices, weather reports, news bulletins, road construction alerts, and warnings to Buckle Up and Drive Safely.

Just before the entrance ramp to the interstate, Reid and Underdog turned off State Road 64 and onto a frontage road, whose complicated yellow striping they followed around to the back of the truck stop until finally they reached the parking lot designated for cars. They exited the car and headed to the entrance of Sally Valentine's, an adult bookstore adjacent to the truck stop, which advertised itself with a neon sign atop a hundred-foot metal pole similar to the Amoco and McDonalds signs one normally sees along the interstate. On the trip from Jasper, Reid explained that he discovered something at Sally Valentine's that Underdog ought to know about. It was during the course of gathering information for his research assistantship. He boasted that his notes would probably be incorporated into a book about the culture of pornography that his faculty advisor was planning to write.

A middle-aged woman, whose make-up coated her face like furniture antiquing, maybe Sally herself, greeted them from behind the counter and collected their fifty-cent browsing fee. She wore a black, low-cut sweater interspersed by a fair amount of gold thread, making her look oddly tarnished. A cumulo-nimbus cloud of perfume swelled around her, smelling to Underdog like she overdid it that morning in spraying Eau de Lysol down her cleavage. Perhaps she needed something strong, he thought, to keep away the smell of urine, whose ammoniac odor hung in the air, crinkling the hairs inside his nose.

On the television monitor above and behind the sales clerk, a woman finished shaving off the last bit of hair from the pubic zone of another woman. After a moment of horizontal lines, a flag flapping in the wind appeared, a lushly orchestrated "America the Beautiful" played in the background, and a topless spokeswoman for the Adult Filmmakers Association of America discussed the First Amendment. This was followed by a video depicting a woman squirting milk out of her nipples into the mouths of two eager men.

"An image like that is gross," said Reid in a low voice, pointing discretely. "Especially when you think of the reality behind it. She has a kid, and then she acts in a porno movie a few months later. To top it off, you see her in a scene where she literally takes milk out of her baby's mouth.

"And yet," he continued, "try to tell me you wouldn't want to be one of those guys right now. Right there is the power of porn: it turns you on in spite of your better nature."

Reid led Underdog towards the back of the store, where the video arcade was located. Along the way, Underdog took in the sights. Above all else, he was impressed by the store's likeness to a zoo; fostering this impression were magazines displayed on the walls in wire racks. Their full-color, glossy covers served as windows into the lives of a whole menagerie: he saw sexual positions that challenged the gymnastic abilities of chimpanzees; heads thrown back in pleasure like those of howling wolves; flicking tongues reaching further than a lizard's; whips subduing the savage lion or lioness; and breasts and penises that put elephants to shame.

After passing through a doorway hung with several strands of beads, they entered a dark passageway lined by a row of private video booths; from under the doors of several, light flickered and low-volume groans seeped out of the cracks, causing Underdog to blush, remembering his own experiences masturbating amidst a similar row of stalls in Jasper College men's rooms, only without the visual aids. "You'll find the video inside here very interesting," said Reid, handing Underdog a bunch of quarters and conducting him to the second booth. Exhibited within, according to a sign over the door of the booth, were "Vintage Loops," featuring "Classic Scenes from Adult Cinema."

"Their puns are truly awful," Reid said, pointing to a smaller sign beside the door that said "Coming Attractions," referring to the current choices, not future ones. Printed in black marker on an index card tacked below the sign were titles of two short films, "Taste of the Orient" and "Putting Out a Fire."

"'Taste of the Orient' is a silent, black and white film," Reid explained. "An Asian woman in full Geisha drag strips off her kimono, drops to her knees and blows a white guy wearing nothing but a blindfold and black socks. I'm guessing it was filmed in Japan during the Korean War, in a bath house with an American soldier. Actually, when you consider the action on the screen, the title's a misnomer. It should be called 'Taste of the Occident.'

"Anyway, it's the other movie, 'Putting Out a Fire,' that I want you to watch." He waved Underdog into the booth and began to close the door behind him.

"You're not going to watch it, too?" asked Underdog.

"Trust me. You don't want me inside there with you," said Reid. The mood suddenly became uncomfortable, and it struck Underdog just how private and embarrassing the whole experience of visiting a dirty book store was.

After brushing off the bench with the flat of his hand, Underdog sat; beside him stood a contraption that was similar to the front of a pinball machine, with two coin slots. He dropped a quarter in the slot marked "Film B," the light cut off, the projector began ticking, and on the screen a countdown to zero indicated that the film was about to start.

For the first minute a naked woman lay face-up on a bed, moaning, writhing, panting, licking her lips, clutching her breasts, pinching her nipples, caressing her belly, rubbing her crotch, massaging her labia. She looked ringing wet from sweat, simulated, Underdog thought likely, by somebody off-screen spraying her with a solution of water and oil. The camera panned along her body from head to toe and back, lingering particularly long on her glistening breasts and frizzy bush. Then the camera panned across the room to a window, whereupon the film stopped, and Underdog fed another coin into the projector.

Next, an ax began hacking at the window, shattering glass and splintering the window frame. Once the glass was cleared, a mustachioed fireman, in full fire-fighting regalia, including red helmet, rubber coat and waterproof boots, leapt through the window and pivoted comically, asking "Where's the fire? Where's the fire?" Again, the booth went dim, prompting Underdog to deposit another quarter.

The scene switched again to the woman. "It's me. I'm on fire!" she cried, still lying on her back and rocking helplessly, like an upended beetle that couldn't right itself. To the sound of clopping boots, the fireman entered the picture; after lewdly wagging his eyes and wiggling his mustache, he threw off his coat, revealing underneath a flower-patterned shirt, wide belt and hip-hugging jeans whose bell bottoms were tucked into boots. After a clumsy, abrupt edit, the man, now naked except for his helmet and pukka-shell necklace, guided his penis inside the woman and began pumping away. Aware that he was supposed to arrive at some realization by watching the film, Underdog concentrated hard on what he saw on the screen.

Judging by the hairstyles, the woman's shag cut and the tight curls of the man's permed hair, and by the man's clothing, especially the silk shirt and the widely flared pant legs, the movie must have been made during the 1970s, far enough in the past to attain classic status. Observing nothing notable in the actors' dress, Underdog next examined the set, trying to find some relevance there. He caught a glimpse of a lava lamp on a nightstand beside the bed where the couple went at it. However, aside from this interesting period piece, examples of which could be found in Jasper's hipper resale shops, there was nothing about the bed or on the walls that meant anything to him.

But when the scene shifted, with the camera now behind the woman's head looking down the length of her body and focusing mainly on the couple's pelvic regions ramming together, the mystery of why Reid brought Underdog to Sally Valentine's was solved: above the man's left nipple there was a tattoo in the shape of a four-leaf clover. When the camera angle broadened, bringing the man's face into view, Underdog recognized a young Race Fletcher underneath the helmet, kinky hair and mustache.

When the film cut off yet again, Underdog dropped his last quarter into the machine. In a jumble of mixed emotions, he both relished and loathed a rare, but weird, opportunity. Before this moment, he had occasionally heard detailed information about the meat or motion of his girlfriends' boyfriends — their cleanliness, their sense of rhythm, their talents for kissing or cunnilingus, their warmth and tenderness, or their lack in any of these categories. Now, for the first time, he was able to see up close and personal the sexual prowess of his main competitor.

Scrutinizing Race Fletcher's large penis diminished Underdog initially, for sadly he did not measure up in the size department. However, he regained a sense of superiority when he examined Race Fletcher's technique, which consisted of the most elemental, back-and-forth stroke. He lacked any sort of fluid hip motion, a slow, circular grind that women, including Ione, had complimented Underdog on. If lovemaking was, as they said, a horizontal dance, then Underdog tangoed, whereas Race Fletcher pogoed. Additionally, Underdog could hardly take Race Fletcher seriously in that silly fireman's helmet, whose red color and pointed crest, coupled with the wearer's arrogance, gave new meaning to the word "coxcomb."

A moment or two later, Race Fletcher grimaced like a bowling ball fell on his foot, then announced he was about to come. "Spray me with your hose! Put out my fire!" the woman responded. Obliging, he withdrew from her and released a torrent of semen which froze in the air, for a millisecond defying gravity like spilled milk inside a space ship, before the image faded to all white as the screen went blank and the viewing booth lit up, game over.

Underdog took a deep breath and sat a moment, trying to take in everything he had witnessed in the previous five minutes. Then he left the booth and quickly hustled Reid out the door, into sorely craved fresh air and sunlight. At the time, Reid was stooped over a display case, examining an assortment of rubber sex toys. "You can't help admiring the ingenuity of whoever manufactures those things," he said, really more to himself than to Underdog, on the way back to the car. "And the fine tolerances they achieve!" he added, slipping behind the steering wheel. Underdog slammed his door shut and hit the lock button with his elbow, wishing he could so simply lock out the troubling thoughts that whirligigged around his ears.

"What a load," said Underdog, a little bit light-headed if truth be told.

"Think of the ramifications if word got out in Jasper," said Reid, smoothly merging onto the four-lane, limited-access highway home.

"It's like ammo that's been dropped in my lap," said Underdog, whose mood transformed from shock to triumph when he ascertained the extent of his newfound power. Then he went "KABOOM!" into cupped hands, simulating an explosion.

"For sure, it could blow the whole town apart," Reid agreed. "But you've got to be very careful how you play it. Save it, like an Ace up your sleeve."

Ten minutes south of Sally's, they approached a convenience store called Jake's, renowned in Jasper for never checking birthdates on driver's licenses of the many underage drinkers who carpooled it there on Friday and Saturday nights. "Pull in here," Underdog urged; Reid made a sharp left turn and parked in the gravel lot out front. Underdog ran inside and two minutes later trotted back out to the car, carrying a brown paper bag. They got underway again, and Reid asked what they had stopped for.

"These," said Underdog, pulling out of the bag and unwrapping two cigars, one of which he handed to Reid. He leaned over to light Reid's cigar with a disposable lighter from his pocket; seeing that Reid had a good, solid flame going, he lit his own.

"News of this will blow apart Race and Ione," gloated Underdog, drawing hard on the cigar and making contented sucking sounds when releasing his lips to blow out smoke.

TEN

On the Sunday morning after his trip with Reid to Sally Valentine's Adult Book Store, Underdog awoke to a frantic knocking on the door to his room. After carefully wrapping the top sheet around himself toga-fashion, he opened up. Among the kaleidoscopic shards of a dream that was interrupted, he made out Mona Baine standing in the hall, wearing a pink, button-down robe and brown and white slippers shaped like beagles' heads, complete with floppy ears, whiskers and rolling eyes. "There's a policeman downstairs that wants to talk to you," she whispered. Underdog nodded. He shut the door and threw on a tee shirt and gym shorts, all the while wondering what the hell a cop would want to see him for.

Cataloguing all his actions during the past week, he came up with nothing that might attract the police. He remembered a little further back in time and thought of only one potential thing: slamming Race Fletcher on the basketball court a few weeks before. Suffering a momentary panic that electrified his fingertips and toes, he relaxed again, deciding that there shouldn't be a problem with that, because the police would be hard-pressed to prove anything, since to everyone the incident looked like an accident.

Meeting him on the bottom landing of the stairway was a gaunt, dishwater blonde woman wearing painted-on blue jeans and a white tank top baring shoulders as worn and wrinkled as two old baseball mitts. Faint maroon circles atop her breasts indicated she wore no bra. Her craggy face suggested an age of about forty; Underdog figured that over the years a lot of grit had blown in and out of its cracks. Aside from her gun holster and the silver badge pinned on her hip, in no way did she fit his conception of what a police officer looked like.

When he thought "cop," an image of Ziggy sprang to mind. Ziggy was the campus cop stationed with a phone and little else in a closet-turned-office underneath the central staircase of Castle Hall. All day long he paraded up and down the wide, echoing halls of the Castle, past all the W.P.A. grain elevator and railroad station murals peopled with musclebound men of a bygone era, pointing his finger like a pistol and going "Pow," to greet passers by. Clanking from a wide, leather belt slung low on his bulbous hips were a gun holster, billy club, handcuffs and two-way radio. When he moved, his belly jiggled like a tub of jelly that bakers filled doughnuts with.

"Officer Sheila Flanagin, Jasper Police Department," the woman groused by way of introduction. "Are you the person known as Underdog?"

"Yes," he responded.

"What is your real name?" she asked, poised to write in a small vinyl notebook that she whipped out of her back pocket.

"Thomas Emmendorfer. Why are you here?"

"I'm from the Gender Crimes Unit of the Jasper Police Department. I investigate rapes and domestic violence. Basically any crime where women are victims based on their sex."

"I'm not sure I understand what you want from me," he said. Glancing upstairs, he noticed Mona Baine peeking around the corner of the second floor landing and tilting her ear downward like a satellite dish in order to tune in their conversation. He figured that the floppy ears on her beagle slippers were perked up, too.

"You've been named as a possible suspect in a stalking case," Officer Flanagin answered.

"Excuse me?" he asked, panic surging again through his fingertips, the voltage setting switched higher than before.

"Do you know an Ione Twayblade?"

"Yeah, but I haven't seen her in almost a month. And I certainly haven't been stalking her," he said, with complete and utter confidence that he goddamn told the absolute truth.

"Then what about this?" Officer Flanagin asked, unfurling a sheet of paper she took from between the pages of her notebook.

He read aloud, "STAY AWAY FROM HIM!"

"It's a photocopy of a note found last week," she explained. "It was stabbed into Ms. Twayblade's back door with a kitchen knife. That jagged, grayish mark at the top is where the knife punctured the paper."

"I had nothing to do with leaving Ione this calling card," he said, annoyed at the audacity of her allegations. He loved Ione, he wouldn't want to do her any harm. He backed away from her, as if to dismiss her, and headed up the stairs.

"Do you have any information as to who might be stalking Ms. Twayblade?" she asked after him.

"No, I don't," he answered without turning, less from disrespect than from a desire to hide the expression on his face. For it would give away that he knew the identity of the true culprit: Judy Baine, who apparently had gone whacko and was warning Ione to stay away from Underdog. It was not, as Officer Flanagin suspected, Underdog telling Ione to stay away from Race Fletcher.

"Stalking is a serious crime," continued Officer Flanagin, louder. "You let me know if you have any information on this case."

On the second floor landing, back still turned on his questioner, he promised he would. Rounding the corner, he brushed Mona Baine's fuzzy, pink sleeve with his bare arm and received a carpet shock. As he tramped up the final flight of stairs, he overheard Mona defend him while escorting Officer Flanagin out the door. "I'm positive it's not Underdog you're looking for," she was saying. "He's really a nice, quiet boy." Knowledge that Mona believed him innocent caused a feeling of warmth to pool in Underdog's chest, like he just swallowed a shot of whiskey.

But inside his room, the calm, liquidy feeling quickly left him again. Sitting on the unmade bed, he spent a few moments anxiously drumming on his knee. Then he reached over and picked up from the desk one of his few personal possessions, a bust of Abraham Lincoln. He often handled it when troubled, holding it up in the air, tilting it this way and that, rolling it between his hands, generally treating it like a totem that enabled him to face the injustices of life. It was something he owned since childhood; he made it when he was nine at one of those arts and crafts places where you paint plaster of paris figurines with enamel paint, then bake them in an oven so they harden into ceramic showpieces. This particular piece had the appearance of a heavy copper heirloom, the result of first painting it copper, then applying specks of green which melted over it, giving it that oxidized look.

Staring Lincoln in the face, Underdog mainly dwelled on what his dad said to him once in a moment of fatherly advice: "The truth can never hurt you." It was a statement that Underdog had tried all his life to believe in and live up to. Most times, his father was right — the times when Underdog had not told the truth he was penalized. It happened in grade school, for example, when his principal, Mr. Smith, asked him who broke the back window of a car parked in the teacher's lot. Although he witnessed his friend Tony Warner throw a rock at a group of girls with cooties and strike the car instead, he chose not to tell. As punishment, Mr. Smith made him stand in the hallway during a whole week of recesses.

Listening to his dad's bromides — and what should be expected? antacids were what his sour stomach responded to best, so he thought everyone was soothed by them — Underdog was harkened back to the late 1950s, the time of his dad's youth. Was the world really simpler, with the right answers and the wrong ones divided up so neatly? After a childhood of watching reruns of *Father Knows Best* or *Leave it to Beaver*, Underdog was convinced he had personal memories of the black-and-white time before he was born. Sometimes, Underdog caught himself asking who really was grounded for two weeks for flying a balsa wood airplane in the house and crashing it into Mom's favorite vase — Theodore Cleaver or himself?

Underdog considered the consequences of lying to the lady cop. Maybe it would leave Judy free to direct her wrath at him. Awaiting him might be a fate similar to that of the man living on the other side of the state, about whom he read in the *Jasper Weekly Shopper*. The man announced to his wife that he wanted to divorce her. She persuaded him to have sex with her one last time. Afterward, as he slept, she snipped off his penis with a pair of sewing scissors.

He set the Lincoln bust back down and saw the burden was on him to set matters right. As he saw it, there were two actions he had to take right away: first, he needed to get Ione to call off her dogs; he obviously couldn't allow her false accusations to snap at his heels. Second, and even trickier, he needed to get Judy to stop bothering Ione, plus he needed to keep her at bay on the home front — parked elsewhere than in his lap and camped elsewhere than in his room.

Underdog put on his denim jacket and set out for Ione's house in Trailerville, using slimy, rain-slickened, leaf-spattered sidewalks (for it was daylight, and not dark, when he normally cut through yards). Church bells pealed, proclaiming another day of worship to Jasper's residents: Bells in the steeple of the Lutheran Church rang out the anthem "A Mighty Fortress is Our God." In a different key, the martial "Onward, Christian Soldiers" issued from the belfry of the Catholic Church. In still another key, tape recorded chimes played the homespun "What a Friend We Have in Jesus," broadcast over the Baptist Church's P.A. system. All clashed in a huge cacophony that spread over flat, uninterrupted prairie; the dissonance rivaled an event of two years before, when the college's Music Department performed the artsy, post-modern "Concerto for Two Orchestras and Concert Band" on the green in front of Castle Hall. In no mood for listening to the cheery melodies he sang in his boyhood, when forced by his parents to attend church services every Sunday, he wondered if he could sue the local churches for ringing their bells and invading his privacy. At least you could slam the door in the faces of Jehovah Witnesses who came to proselytize.

Upon arriving in Trailerville, Underdog braced for what he might find at Ione's trailer. For courage, he gulped down a tremendous amount of air, which expanded in his lungs as if little fingers were pushing putty into every corner. Threading his way through the development, he hoped at the very least that she didn't slam the door in his face, and at the very most that she didn't sic Officer Flanagin on him. Outside Unit E-9, he noted that Ione's yellow Volkswagen was parked out front, and he was relieved to find that neither of Race Fletcher's vehicles was present. The coast evidently clear, he exhaled voluminously, cracked his knuckles and knocked on the white aluminum door, which opened a moment later.

For the first time in a month, Underdog beheld Ione. She was wearing an oversized tee shirt, on which was emblazoned "Feed Your Head at St. Mark's Book Store, NYC," and no other clothes, except, he figured, underwear. Her hair, normally gelled and combed straight back, was dry and fluffed at odd angles. Looking into her eyes, he saw suspicion and fright, like she just won the lottery and a serial killer was calling to award her her prize. To signal his honorable intentions and to deflate the tension with a pin prick of humor, he pulled out a white handkerchief and waved it, saying, "I come in peace."

She chewed on her lower lip, deliberating, then she opened the door wider and nodded him into her house. Entering, he noticed a new addition to her living room: on a white, three-foot-tall pedestal stood a cylindrical gray vase covered with red and yellow squiggles; it had a jagged rim, like one of those crazy New York sculptors took a few bites out of it for art's sake. Noticing him notice her vase, Ione said, "I bought that in New York. From a gallery in Soho. Late one night about two weeks ago, Race and I snuck into the Art Building and stole the pedestal."

"That's illegal," he said.

"Not any more illegal than stalking is," she responded, taking her seat on the couch. Her shirt hiked up a few inches, confirming that she indeed wore off-white cotton panties underneath. Distractedly, she started to peel the skin off her thumb tip.

"If I was guilty of anything, would I have come to visit?" he asked.

"How do you explain the knife stuck in my door last week?" she wanted to know. "Or the dead squirrel inside my car? Or my windows getting smeared with dog shit on Halloween?" Her finger-picking escalated to a rapid corn-shucking pace.

"I sympathize," he said, marveling at the gross things that Judy Baine was capable of pulling. "But, believe me, I'm not the one harassing you. I'm crazy about you. Don't you know that?"

"Then you admit being crazy," she accused.

"ABOUT you. I'm crazy ABOUT you," he shouted.

"Well, that's different," she said, ceasing with her fingers. If she were a porcupine, her quills would have lain down.

Obsequiously, Underdog dropped to his knee and kissed the top of her bony left foot, which rested on the trunk serving as a coffee table. "I like you much better when you act worshipful," she said, then giggled nervously.

He sat down on the couch next to her, leaning comfortably back, clasping his hands behind his head, and resting his feet on the trunk next to hers. Playfully, he bumped her naked right foot with his sneakered left foot. "You know, I had quite a rude awakening this morning on account of you," he said. "I thought Officer Flanagin came to arrest me for whacking Race Fletcher when I played basketball with him a couple of weeks ago. I never dreamt it was for stalking you."

BOING! Her porcupine quills went vertical again.

"You ARE stalking me!" she howled, flinching from him. "You're trying to get to me through Race!" She whirled off the couch and landed across the room, crouching defensively with her forearms crossed in front of her face.

"It was an accident. Honest it was!" he pleaded, amazed at how quickly she had been reduced from the proud leopardess he met a few months before to what he presently saw: a skittish porcupine frozen in the road, staring into the high beams of a car bearing toward it.

"Race told me it was an accident, too," she said. "But if I had known you were involved, I would've suspected otherwise. You know, he went to the emergency room at Jasper Hospital, and they kept him overnight, afraid of a concussion. In fact, the whole episode delayed our trip to New York."

Underdog felt his face flush red, all the while hoping that Ione would not misread this reflex for guilt; rather, he was proud that his little stunt took something away from Race Fletcher, at least briefly. "I'm sorry," he said, "But none of us knew it was so serious. He didn't tell you it was me?"

"He probably doesn't even know who you are."

The news that Race Fletcher might not know who Underdog was slammed against the wall of his abdomen, like a load of cargo against the hull of a listing boat. Impossible! he thought. Unless what he heard ever since moving off-campus was true: that townies were invisible to college people.

"Please believe me," he begged. "Fouling Race so hard was an accident. And, for the last time, I'm not stalking you!" Tears of frustration welled up in his eyes. He wondered if she noticed — after all, clear liquid flowing down transparent townie cheeks would not be visible.

"I believe you," she said, uncramping her tautened muscles and sighing a passenger balloon-full of adrenaline into the room. "But now I'm back to square one — somebody is stalking me, and I don't have a clue who it is."

"You'll get to the bottom of it," he assured her, unsure himself whether he could prevail upon Judy to lay off Ione. He patted the couch cushion next to him, inviting her to sit back down, which she did.

"I see that Race's injury didn't prevent you from going to New York," he said, eyeing the front of her St. Mark's Book Store tee shirt. Acknowledging this fact pierced his pride worse than an incident in junior high school, when a girl he was teasing for having big boobs tackled him in the hallway, then stabbed him in the butt with a pencil.

"Actually, I visited New York three times last month."

"Three times!" Underdog exclaimed. "Are you going every weekend now?"

"I don't plan on going again until Christmas-time. Last month was special, because Race had some business to attend to with his publisher, and he had to be introduced around at a couple of *Strobe Magazine* parties. I met Patti Smith at one party and Chuck D from the rap group Public Enemy at another!"

"How exciting."

"Best of all, I met Liza — in the flesh! We watched her give a surprise, impromptu performance at the Algonquin Hotel. Liza herself gave me that picture," she said proudly, pointing behind her at a new photograph of Liza Minnelli hanging on the wall. It was a publicity photo of a somewhat pudgy, middle-aged Liza, dressed in a flashy black pants suit. Written with a red marker was the message "To Ione. With best wishes, Liza."

"Impressive," said Underdog.

During the uncomfortable half-hour that followed, Underdog seethed as every one of Ione's sentences began with "New York this" or "New York that." He heard about the bizarre nightclub where Ione saw a woman wearing nothing but a five-foot boa constrictor. Accompanying her was a man — or woman, she couldn't tell which — who was wrapped in a clear plastic sheet smeared with motor oil. He heard about a yowling performance artist who shoved a yam up her ass during the show Ione attended. He heard about a six-foot-seven bald transvestite singer, such a curiosity that he packed the house every night, even though, she confided, he sang like he gargled with beer can tabs. And he heard about a troupe of mimes wearing white smocks and blue make-up who spit multicolored goop all over each other, becoming, she explained, "human art objects."

To Underdog, New York City sounded like the planet Mars. Yet, in spite of his derision, he was jealous that he wasn't there with Ione, participating in the many fun things she described, the same types of things copiously covered by the *Village Voice*, a newspaper he had picked up a few times at the student union. In every single article he read in that publication there was the sniggering assurance that New York City was the best of all possible worlds; as well, there was the underlying suggestion, an insulting one when he thought about it, that if you didn't live there, you simply weren't cool. Underdog felt he had news for the *Voice*: there were cool, right-thinking people everywhere, even in the middle of nowhere like Jasper, where he knew people who were every bit as cool as people in New York — genuine people unimpressed by the shock value of your clothes, or by all the money you flash, or by media-driven outrageousness. To him, it just appeared that New Yorkers were cooler, because the New York media flooded the world with TV images and print stories spotlighting famous assholes who, anywhere else, would be plain, ordinary assholes. He wanted to ask Ione whom she thought was more real — him, or somebody with purple hair and pierced everything who lived in a warehouse upstairs from trendy gourmet cookie shops and leather sock boutiques.

More, he wanted to ask her why she hadn't caught onto Race Fletcher's game. He jetted off to New York regularly, ostensibly to meet with his agent and publisher, but in truth he wanted to soak in the neon, to hear drum beats rebound off the walls of fashionable night spots, and, most of all, to lord it over townies, whom he professed to admire. But the irony was lost upon him, like it was on his *Green Acres* book subject, Oliver Douglas, who, in Race Fletcher's own words, never fit in, who belonged to the city wholly, despite his pro-farmer speeches and attempts to farm the old Haney Place.

Obviously, Race Fletcher had completely blurred Ione's perception with a swirl of activity. Like a tilt-a-whirl ride at the county fair, the two of them cut across Manhattan in looping figure eights. That he had charmed the pants off Ione was evident when she described to Underdog his capacity to freeze a motor vehicle in its tracks. With a look that she said bordered on the supernatural, cars, taxis, trucks and buses all screeched to a halt when fixed by Race Fletcher's gaze. All he had to do was glare through the windshield at the driver, who would slam on the brakes, no matter how busy the intersection, and allow them to cross the street. She doubted that he was the *brujo* that one taxi driver called him; this phenomenon was probably due to his well-exercised street smarts. Underdog didn't doubt it at all, however. After hearing all her stories, he felt more convinced than ever that Race Fletcher had cast a spell on Ione.

At the end of his visit, he lingered on her cement block doorstep, once more imploring her to get the cops off his back. He was sorely tempted to inform her of Race Fletcher's adult film career, still more evidence of his counterfeit character. So tempted was he, it seemed like gravity from the lopsided, gibbous moon he saw floating in the bright blue afternoon sky was pulling at the knowledge dissolved in the clean, clear water that made up ninety-seven percent of his body weight. Choosing to buck the tide for now, however, he merely said, "Till later," with several fingers and a couple of toes crossed that she understood he wasn't giving up on her yet.

ELEVEN

It was the Friday after Thanksgiving, which Underdog spent at his parents' home in Peru. He ate a traditional turkey dinner with all the trimmings, fine except his mother could never manage to break up all the lumps floating like marbles in her gravy. He also watched on television what his dad called the "Dog Bowl," annually featuring the lame-footed Lions of Detroit playing football against somebody equally bad, this year the Tampa Bay Buccaneers. Already sick of his parents and Peru after spending only one day (GOD! it bugged him how they pronounced it "PEE-roo"), he made his dad drive him back to Jasper first thing the next morning, claiming he had to work Friday at the print shop, even though he really didn't. Taking the back roads, they drove past harvested fields, many not yet plowed under, where corn stalks tangled and bunched from the tramp of hunters, peck of birds and slap of storms. The whole route home, his dad chided him for lighting out so soon. "Why can't you ever stay with your mother the full four days?" he asked, and Underdog retorted, "Don't YOU have to get back and work today, too?" to which his dad couldn't answer, because he always worked at the insurance office on the Friday after Thanksgiving, bringing with him a leftover turkey leg for lunch. That his dad had never attended college himself helped Underdog's cause, because he didn't know most colleges shooed the kids home and locked the whole place up for the entire weekend.

As they turned onto Elm Street, Underdog ended the conversation by reminding his dad that the yellowish, puke-colored boarding house — which looked closer to gold to him as they pulled up — was home now, not the three-bedroom ranch house he left back in Peru. He bid his dad a hasty so long, then hopped out of the car. For the rest of the morning, he straightened and restraightened the blue-lacquered furniture in his room. First, he dragged the bed into the center and pushed his desk in the corner; next, he pushed the desk in the middle and put his bed in the corner. Eventually, he returned everything to where it was when he started: bed and desk pushed against opposite walls, leaving a nice, empty aisle of cobalt-blue carpeting where he could pace and think hard about things.

Paced-out by afternoon, he found himself feeling lonely with nothing to do. Thankfully, around three o'clock Reid called, inviting Underdog to smoke dope and drive around the surrounding countryside. In explaining his presence over Thanksgiving weekend, Reid said he didn't want to drive all the way to Iowa where his family lived; he didn't think his car would make it — its dying battery had given him scares twice earlier that fall, almost stranding him in the middle of the night on the pitch-black roads running from Jasper to Sally Valentine's. Underdog asked Reid what was to stop his car from killing while they drove around. Reid answered that he wouldn't stop the car, they would just drive the whole time, sticking close to town. Hanging up the phone, Underdog wondered where the sociological field work at Sally Valentine's ended and Reid's own sex life started, but opted not to pry into what was probably a fulfilled auto-erotic life — not celibate, maybe a little kinky, but certainly consistent with the chaste attitude he watched Reid normally take with women.

After retrieving Underdog, Reid drove them through Jasper's business district on Highway 17, the quickest way out of town. For weeks already, the Jasper Chamber of Commerce had installed Christmas decorations. Silver garland swagged across the street every half-block, the words "Merry Christmas" or "Season's Greetings" hanging below, each letter on separate square cards alternating with over-sized green and red ornamental balls. Red and white stocking caps were perched atop traffic light and street sign poles. Strings of festive white electrical lights enlivened the dead branches of trees lining the street. Within a week of Halloween, all vestiges of that holiday — the black and orange crepe, the electric jack-o'-lanterns, the Indian corn arrangements — were replaced with a sparkling Christmas display. Each year it happened slightly sooner than the previous, making Underdog wonder if within a few years all the tinsel and nativity scenes would be remounted the day after Christmas, along with signs saying "Only 364 more shopping days till Christmas."

When they passed the abandoned gravel pit on the western edge of town, site of at least one drowning every summer, they entered the country proper. Given the dry, sunny, if somewhat chilly afternoon, a handful of farmers had seized the chance to plow their fields; as they drove outside town, Underdog and Reid saw them riding their tractors back and forth through long fall shadows created by fence lines, telephone poles and trees clustered along creek beds. Upturned were clods of what was reputed to be among the richest, blackest dirt in the whole United States. Underdog thought it was probably a wonderful life, driving around all day high above the ground in your John Deere tractor, shut inside a roomy, soundproof, climate-controlled cab, listening to a tape deck blast your favorite tunes.

For the first few miles of their trip, Reid and Underdog shot the bull — they talked about the declining fortunes of the college's football team, the unusually mild fall weather, and the recent rise in the state's liquor tax — then the subject turned to Underdog and Ione. "I make deliveries to her office once every week or so," said Underdog. "Mainly, I get caught up on her life with Race Fletcher.

"Like, for example, one afternoon last week. She told me she spent her lunch hour posing nude at the Art Department, like usual. Normally, she takes a sterile, clinical approach to posing. She 'becomes a statue,' she says. But on this occasion she got to feeling so horny for Race that she couldn't stay still. She kept squirming around and making the teacher mad because it was fouling up his students' drawings. When the hour was finally up, she rushed over to Jackdaw Hall and made him screw her on his desk, right spank in the middle of the work day. Like I want to hear about her sex escapades with Race Fletcher!" Enraged, he kicked the dashboard, leaving a dusty tennis shoe print and causing a bundle of wires to fall down from behind the dash and dangle freely like a blue and yellow scrotal sac.

"She's toying with you," suggested Reid, eyeing the wires uneasily, as if he didn't have enough trouble with his car's electrical system.

"Right then she was," Underdog said, nodding. "But on some days, she acts completely victimized by life. A few days ago, I come into her office, greet her with a 'What's shaking,' and she screams back, 'Don't bother me, I'm concentrating!' I shut up, take my scolding in silence. While I'm thumbing through the printed matter in my box, looking for her damn account transfer forms, she's busy cussing under her breath and smacking her computer monitor like she's slapping the cheeks of somebody who insulted her. I offer to help — I know a little bit about computers from my job; the main thing I know is you don't hit them — but she yells at me 'It's none of your business!' and 'Get the hell out of here, you're bugging me!' Like it's my fault she's ignorant about computers."

"So did you get the hell out of there?" asked Reid.

"No, I vaulted over the counter and grabbed her wrists to stop her from beating her poor computer monitor to death. Then I talked her through a pretty common formatting command in her word processing program."

"What set her off?" asked Reid.

"She told me she was writing a letter to her dead husband. Sure enough, when I looked at the computer screen, it started off 'Dear Geoffrey.' I was exactly like him, she said. 'You both would drop everything and do anything for me, no matter how unreasonable or impossible I was being.' After that, she started to sob and wouldn't stop till I hugged her."

"Writing a letter to her dead husband," Reid said, mulling the situation. "Must be some kind of coping strategy."

"When I finally left, I walked away thinking it was all so unfair that Race Fletcher gets to have all the fun with Ione, while I get all of the grief."

"He takes care of Ione's animal needs, you're stuck looking after her emotional needs," Reid assessed.

"Through it all, I continue to see a bright side, though," Underdog said. "She can see I'm steadfast. I figure I've got the firm, but gentle, character she requires. Only I wish she'd hurry up and recognize that I've got a firmer character than Race Fletcher does."

"You've got to act like her dead husband to win her away from Race Fletcher," observed Reid.

"Exactly!" agreed Underdog. "I figure I can save the news about Race's porn career, hold it till my options run out, like a doomsday device. Then, with Race out of the way, I have to be more like her dead husband than he was, to win her away from him. That's the ultimate, long-term strategy: to lift her over the hump of her dead husband's grave."

For a few seconds, Reid didn't have anything to say; he was moved to speechlessness by Underdog's poetic utterance. It struck him that Underdog possessed a gift similar to the English Romantic poets, who conveyed their supreme, if melancholy, devotion in a way most sublime. (Also he hoped that his friend didn't go so far overboard as a couple of those poets, literally, by rowing out into the middle of Jasper College Pond and diving off the back of his boat with a cinder block tied to his leg.) "Why don't you call her tonight, when you get back home?" he asked, regaining the ability to speak. "Maybe she stayed in town for the holiday."

"No, she left town Wednesday night. When I asked her what her plans were for the weekend, she said that she and Race Fletcher were going to Chicago. Told me he and a whole flock of other deconstruction professors from Duke and Yale were invited to a conference at the University of Chicago."

"And Jasper College fits right up there on that list of school names," Reid huffed, directing Underdog's attention to a bit of notable scenery on the left side of the road. Together, they craned their necks to take in the "Pink Farm," so named for its centerpiece, a clapboard shack absurdly painted hot pink. A local landmark, it was owned by a couple of old, crotchety men who over the years had collected a large array of rusty farm implements; surrounding the pink house were antiquated tractors, outmoded reapers, blade-less plows, broken-down combines, flat-stricken pick-ups, beached hay-balers, and even a grounded crop-duster. With a barnyard reaching up to the very doors of the farm house — convention and sanitation be damned — cows and pigs lay against the porous pink walls, and geese and chickens fluttered about the front porch. Overall, the place appeared a cross between a wrecking pound and a petting zoo.

The Pink Farm fading in the rear view mirror, Underdog continued where their conversation left off. "I didn't want to ask Ione this question, because I didn't want to sound stupid — I'm not a college man, you know. But what's this deconstruction jazz anyhow?" he asked.

"To be honest, I don't think I can explain it much more than saying it's like reading between the lines," answered Reid.

Underdog gave him the same "So what?" look he would give somebody who could toss a buffalo chip fifty yards.

"Maybe this will help," Reid said, reaching behind him and retrieving a tightly wadded piece of paper from a backseat that contained a dumpster-load of fast-food bags and burger wrappers. He handed it to Underdog, who began unraveling it like a slaughtered baseball.

"That's my take on deconstruction," he explained. "It's a report for my convocation class. You have to go to five public lectures per semester and write a short report about each one. Everybody in the liberal arts grad program is stuck doing it — for a measly one credit hour.

"Anyway, as you'll see, it's about a lecture I had the misfortune of seeing where this dorky assistant professor spoke on deconstruction theory."

Wishing he had a steam iron to smooth the crinkled paper, Underdog took his eyes off the roadside scenery and read.

"This deconstruction business sounds like a lot of tail-chasing to me," commented Underdog, shaking his head as he finished.

"There's a good term for it," said Reid. "You should've seen everyone at the reception afterwards. All the faculty acted fascinated, but you could tell from their strained looks that deep-down they were reminded of their worst fear: that they truly taught at a buttfuck college far away from the intellectual centers up and down the east coast. And on the faces of grad students was the dumbstruck look of hayseeds seeing an airplane for the first time." Clearly agitated, Reid fished a joint from the glove compartment, stuck it onto his lower lip, lit it with a disposable lighter, and slammed the glove compartment door shut as he began to puff away like a fog machine at a rock concert.

After they passed the joint back and forth a few times, Reid steered the car off the blacktop road and onto a rutted gravel path leading to a familiar site, the coaling tower bridging the railroad tracks about two miles west of town. Abandoned since the age of steam locomotives, which paused there and were refueled before highballing another two-hundred miles to the next stop, the coaling tower was a magnet for high school- and college-age townie kids looking for privacy to drink, smoke, fornicate and vandalize. Looming behind a large stand of oak trees, it called to mind ancient ruins situated in the jungles of a Central American country, say, Guatemala. Underdog pondered what future archeologists might think of the civilization that worshipped at the foot of the eroding, reinforced concrete colossus. Sifting through the soil, they would find such artifacts as drained beer cans, empty Boone's Farm bottles, cigarette butts, used prophylactics, shotgun shell casings, assorted paper litter, and tin cans of Spaghetti O's licked clean by coons or dogs. Around the base of the structure, scrawled like cave drawings, were cryptic messages and pictograms spray-painted for posterity by young people who had no personal memories of the coaling tower's original purpose. As he studied the quiet, unpeopled scene, Underdog figured a fairly decadent picture would emerge, once all the jigsaw pieces were examined and fitted together.

They rolled to a stop beside a large fire ring, recently blackened by an autumn-tide bonfire. Reid yanked up the emergency brake lever, shifted the gearshift mechanism to Park, and left the motor running. After sitting a moment or two in reflective silence, marijuana humming like gnats at the edges of their vision, Reid asked, "How's things on the home front?"

"Radically changed," Underdog said. "I don't think I've talked to you since Judy and I, uh, have become an item."

"Way to go!" shouted Reid. Then he went "YES!" and shook his fist in the same exclamatory fashion as a guy cheering his favorite team for hitting a homer or kicking a crucial field goal. "When and how did this come about?" he asked expectantly.

"A couple of Tuesday nights ago. I decided I needed to have it out with her, you know, persuade her to leave Ione alone. To work up the nerve, I went to Roger's Bar for a few hours."

"How many hours?"

"Four. Anyhow, it was after dark when I got back home via a few choice back yards. I knocked on her window a few times, but she didn't answer. So I went into the house and up to my room. When I turned on the light, I couldn't believe my eyes: Judy was lying asleep on my bed, spread-eagle and completely naked, tied to the bed with ropes around her wrists and ankles."

"You're joking!"

"It gets better. Taped on the inside of her thigh is a rubber. 'How long have you been expecting me?' I ask. 'A couple of hours,' she says, all groggy. 'How did you get inside my room?' I ask. 'Mom's key chain. My girlfriend Frieda tied me up like this.' 'Did you have a little fun with her first?' I ask. 'Oh, no,' she says, 'She's just a good friend helping me with my plan.' 'Which is?' I ask. 'To let you have your way with me,' she says."

"What a scenario!" said Reid, incredulous.

"I proceed to tell her that Ione is just a friend, that she's dating Race Fletcher, that she isn't interested in me, and PLEASE would she stop harassing her. I tell her not to deny she was; I knew it was her causing all the trouble. And worst of all, an innocent party, namely myself, was being questioned by the police about it. Of course, I didn't tell her I was holding a torch for Ione still."

"You can't let that slip out," cautioned Reid.

"No I can't," Underdog agreed. "Then I tell her I'm not going to untie her till she promises to leave Ione alone. She agrees, so I take out my pocket knife and cut the rope. She sits up, begins rubbing her calves, and I rub her shoulders to help get the stiffness out."

"I'll bet you were stiff!" Reid surmised.

"Actually, no, I think I had too much to drink. Never mind, because Judy's little stunt was getting to me right here," he said, jabbing his thumb into his solar plexus. "She was really knocking herself out on my account. What can I say? I was flattered by her attention — who wouldn't be?"

"Judy's a show-stopper. But she's also a salt-of-the-earth type, like you. By comparison, Ione's a psycho woman with thighs of ice."

"I'm beginning to agree with you. Judy's like a work horse, I guess you could say, one that's big and strong and loyal, without an ounce of mulishness. And to top off everything, she kicks and bucks real good during sex." He coughed in a deadpan manner, for emphasis.

"Still and all," he continued more thoughtfully, "it's like a situation I remember from my high school band days. Now, I confess we all were very immature and shallow back then, but you still got a little prestige out of dating the first-chair player. Ione's like that first-chair clarinet or flute player you always wanted to date. Although, I admit, landing the second-chair player wasn't too shabby, either."

"You still get the cream of the crop," Reid piped in encouragingly. "Skim it, I say."

"I have. Last Friday, for the first time we went out together on an official date. To a movie at the Triple Slam Theaters at the mall. We shared a box of popcorn, I put my arm around her, we held hands, everything."

"Like a real girlfriend."

"Yep. One problem remains, however: hiding our little rendezvous from Mona. I'm sure she suspects already that we're sneaking around upstairs, doing it. But she looks the other way, I think, because all fall-long she's been dropping hints that I should ask her daughter out."

"It's all for the best," opined Reid. "I'm convinced the time will come when you believe so, too." With a note of finality, he threw the car into Reverse, steered the wheel sharply to the left and stomped on the gas; the right rear tire spun, spitting out gravel like a mouthful of teeth. Rear bumper backed into the slope leading up to the train tracks, he shifted into Drive; moving forward again, they made a wide pass around the fire ring, saw glints of late afternoon sun reflecting off a few scorched bottles among the ashes. Then they tested the car's suspension the whole way up the bumpy lane and exited left onto Highway 17 and headed back into town. But first, before returning to their respective homes in Jasper's student ghetto, they stopped at the convenience store, where they stocked up on a myriad of items, including Twinkies, beef jerky, deviled ham, pretzels, Fritos, bean dip, Coca Cola, gummi worms, dill pickles and ice cream sandwiches to feed their very sudden, very substantial hunger.

TWELVE

Throughout the first half of December, Jasperites busied themselves with swapping gossip about a big event on the horizon, a holiday party for alumni benefactors and community leaders to be held at Jasper College President Milton Flaghorn's house. The party promised to be the social event of the year, especially for the scattered townie invitees, who were rarely fêted in a style higher than the occasional wedding reception at the beer-scented, knotty pine-paneled Elks Club or inside the banquet room of Pasta Casa, where chipped, bronze-colored plaster cherubim poured chlorinated water out of pitchers into the round, rusty base of an indoor fountain.

All month, anticipation clung inside Underdog's nose like the smell of cinnamon buns with only another minute's baking time. Because, happily, he was one of the elect, invited to the party by Judy, herself invited by the Flaghorns, for three years faithful clients of her lawn care business. Underdog's buddy Reid finagled an invitation on behalf of the Graduate Student Union, for which he served as Treasurer. Ione — "naturally!" she crowed to Underdog — planned on attending with Race Fletcher, the most well-traveled professor at Jasper College, an updated version of the sea-faring author and raconteur like Melville or Conrad, whom the Flaghorns figured to entertain with tales from his New York society adventures (and through his presence maybe get some national press coverage).

Next to celebrating the festive, end-of-the-year atmosphere, reflected everywhere in fast-forwarded packets of occasions and personalities — banners hung, trinkets exchanged, corks popped in honor of Christmas, Hanukkah, Kwanzaa, the New Year — there was another reason for throwing the party: the grand gala opening of the newly renovated President's Home.

Originally a low, long ranch affair built in the late fifties of alabaster brick, with a black-shingled roof that reflected sun like obsidian, the Home overlooked the western sections of town from a hill graded steeper than raw prairie would naturally dictate. Around the lot's perimeter grew tallish, gangly trees, mostly poplars planted in the 1970s; in their teenage years now, they spurted up one foot one year, four feet the next. Bordering the cement walks and blacktop driveway were two-inch-wide drainage troughs, a super-deluxe touch Judy Baine reserved for her favorite customers. She carefully measured and lovingly dug them to a uniform depth, from a distance making the lawn look outlined in pencil, then colored in with a wash of green acrylic. Parked out front of the Home's three-car garage sat a couple of college-owned vehicles — identified by the college crest stenciled on their front doors — a cardinal mini-van and a black sedan. Underneath the American flag that flapped vigorously from a flagpole flew an equally large, jock-influenced pennant emblazoned with the words "Go Jasper! Yeah, Redbirds!" sewn in white letters on a field of brilliant red.

Fourteen months before, Flaghorn, Jasper College's eleventh president and present occupier of the President's Home, impelled by ego and his wife and fellow empty-nester Daliah, decided to exercise his presidential prerogative and build himself a fitting legacy. He announced that he would redecorate the house into a showplace for hosting academic lectures, donor parties, chamber concerts, sports banquets and guest receptions. Within a week the Board of Trustees approved the proposal, and construction crews began to erect a new addition to the back of the house. Drawings reproduced in the *Jasper Weekly Shopper* and the *Jasper College Chronicler* pictured a multipurpose design that would convert from lecture hall and art gallery to formal dining room and ballroom. Roadside onlookers saw a high vertex emerge from behind the four-bedroom house; then the triangular openings for windows; followed by a layer of white brick, the closest shade available to the color of the main portion. Topping the structure, installed in dramatic fashion by a sky-sweeping crane, was a peaked, mirror-polished bronze cap visible on a clear day all the way to the interstate, fifteen miles north. During the coming spring thaw, Flaghorn planned to use the remaining back yard space by surrounding the jutting addition with a flagstone patio and modern sculpture garden.

On December seventeenth, with clipboard in gloved hand and party thoughts heating up his skull, Underdog embarked on a frigid trek to every single photocopy machine on the Jasper College campus. The air was bitter cold as only air can get swirling overnight on the empty, wind-flattened prairie hundreds of miles from any warming body of water like ocean, gulf or Great Lake. "Expect the temperature to climb four degrees to a high of twenty-two," predicted a chipper student disc jockey on the campus radio station. It would be five o'clock until it got that warm, however, he warned, whereupon the temperature would drop down to a low of ten or twelve above. The students Underdog passed, cinched inside hooded coats and snorting steam through woolen scarves, huddled in packs as they walked between classes, unconsciously giving into the survival instinct by ducking behind the windbreak lead member. Unlucky for Underdog, his monthly chore of recording paper usage happened to fall on the coldest winter day so far.

The task took all day, so Underdog could not defer it to the warmer hours of late afternoon. Despite his policy of never drinking before noon — except on the infrequent progressive beer day at Roger's Bar, when he steered headlong into a morning-till-night alcohol fog — he stashed a half-pint of whiskey in his inner coat pocket and sipped from it whenever a gust of Arctic wind wheeled around a corner and knocked into him like a wrecking ball. He felt he needed strong drink to oppose the devastating clockwise cold shiver with a counterclockwise whiskey shudder.

One consolation, to collect meter readings from photocopiers was a solitary pursuit. With no more than a "Hi" or "Hey" or nod of the head required to go through social motions, he maneuvered through mazes of desks, filing cabinets and ferns, then squished himself inside cramped storage rooms seeking out the hidden beasts. Familiar clerical staff and work study students generally ignored him, but he faced one or two confrontations every meter-reading day, provoked by newly hired secretaries or watchdog security guards. He simply nudged aside the former and interrupted their copying, sternly telling them to "Relax, this will only take a moment." To shut up the latter, beefy townies with tiny brains, he usually said, "I bet you wish you were a real cop," a statement none so far could respond to, since in every case it was true, so they let him pass.

Once the machine was located, Underdog opened up a side compartment, thus exposing paper feeders, toner cartridges and other mechanical guts, and took note of the five- or six-digit number he read off a small counter lit with his pen light. He penciled this number into the appropriate space on the form clamped onto his clip board. Upon returning from his rounds, he entered these numbers into a computer, which ported the data over to the Central Computing Center, where the figures ultimately were buried in some instantly forgotten corner of the campus computer system, only to face the light again if college deans or department chairs quibbled over reproduction budgets for the coming fiscal year.

After a long pull on the whiskey bottle, designed to put him in a jocular mood and make him more sociable, he opened the door to the

Jasper College *Chronicler*, located in the sub-basement bowels of the Student Union, next door to the boiler room. Getting down there reminded Underdog of crawling through the lower decks of a navy ship; the steep, winding stair cases and battleship gray HVAC pipes lining the walls heightened this effect. A low roar coming from the boilers caused the floor to rumble steadily, making one fear the place might explode any second, either alone or as part of a chain reaction set off when a bomb was dropped down their smoke stack or they took a torpedo hit in their belly.

Underdog caught the startled Chuck, his student newspaper buddy, take a beer bottle away from his mouth, hide it behind his back and set it out of sight on the floor under his desk. "Oh, it's you," said Chuck, reaching down and retrieving his beer and returning it to his lips.

Underdog took off his wool stocking cap in a crackle of static electricity, unzipped his coat and drew from his pocket his own bottle. He unscrewed the cap, reached over the counter, clinked it against Chuck's beer bottle and toasted him, saying "Happy Holidays."

"Likewise," said Chuck, and they glug-glug-glugged their respective beverages, Adam's apples jumping like frisky gerbils in their throats, until Chuck finally gagged on beer foam and Underdog groaned, feeling the whiskey hit his pipes like drain opener.

"Munchies?" offered Chuck, pointing to opened potato chip bags and chocolate chip cookie packages on a folding table beside a miniature Christmas tree decorated with sticky, half-eaten candy canes, empty prophylactic wrappers, and cut-out magazine photos of one-name celebrities like Madonna, Sting or Cher safety-pinned to its branches. A pleasing smell of pine crossed with peppermint surrounded the tree. "The real treats are in the store room," Chuck added. "A few of our radical editorial writers are celebrating the end of the semester by smoking pot back there. Feel free to join in."

"I'll pass," said Underdog. "I've got to visit every Xerox machine on campus today to see how much paper everybody wasted in the past month."

"Quite a lot of dead trees on account of our office, I bet," Chuck said, laughing. "What with everybody Xeroxing their butts." He referred Underdog to a corkboard above the photocopier on which were tacked about a dozen copies of butts of various dimensions, each with a legend scrawled beneath identifying the owner by position: Chief Editor, Sports Editor, Features Editor, and, most fitting, Ass. Editor. Underdog snickered as he opened the photocopier, knelt to read the meter, wrote "455,996" on his log sheet under the

"Chronicler" heading, then closed the machine back up again. Finished with business, he stepped over to the snack table and reached inside the potato chip bag, whose oily contents made the cellophane feel wet and slippery, like an animal's mouth swallowing his hand. He scooped out a handful of chips and nodded appreciatively to Chuck, then he popped them into his mouth.

"What's the latest news?" Underdog asked, clapping crumbs off his hands.

"The big party tomorrow night, what else?" answered Chuck.

"You going, or are you heading home for the holidays?"

"I'm staying in town one extra night to go to the party. A few of us on the paper scored press credentials." He paused a moment to see if Underdog looked impressed. "It's curious that old Blowhorn gave them out to us," he continued. "So far, his office has stonewalled every reporter who's requested budgets having to do with the addition to his house."

"Smells fishy," commented Underdog, scrunching up his nose like he was sniffing haddock gone bad.

"Exactly," said Chuck. "Especially since the college traditionally releases its budgetary information to the public."

"Getting invited almost sounds like a bribe."

"Almost? It is a bribe," said Chuck, almost shouting. "Blowhorn knows we don't publish again till January. That's why he scheduled the party after school was out — he thinks we'll forget about the whole thing. Then to divert our attention even more, he plans to load us up with food and drink." Chuck's eyes burned brighter, like hot coals somebody blew on. "I guarantee you that nobody in this office will let the matter drop," he declared. "Come next semester we'll hound him till we uncover what he's trying to hide."

In a heroic effort to challenge the low temperature outside, the furnace next door to the newspaper office kicked on high. Stronger vibrations from the raw cement floor spiraled upward through their shoes and made their shins buzz. Given Chuck's indignant breast-beating, Underdog wondered if the rumbling presaged like tremors some earthquake of a scandal that the *Chronicler* staff would expose in the near future. He already could see headlines referring to "Flaghorngate."

"Now that you mention it, nothing has come my way discussing the President's Home," said Underdog. "It's strange, because we photocopy financial reports pretty regularly."

"That's right!" Chuck exclaimed, snapping his fingers like he just remembered the formula to solve a complicated math problem. "You work at the print shop, so you're privy to all kinds of confidential information. Ever think about doing a little spy work for your old pal Chuck?"

"I could just about retire on all the money I've been offered to pilfer exams for frat boys and the football team. The opportunity is always there, but I guess I'm too honest. It's like shoplifting food at the Piggly Wiggly: I know I can get away with it, only I choose not to."

"We're not talking about stealing hamburger meat from a basically honest, hard-working merchant. We're talking about thieving from thieves — in service to a higher ideal, namely truth. With a capital 'T.'" He spoke so fervently he shook.

Stirred by his friend's speech (and emboldened from whiskey), Underdog became convinced that his civic duty lay in ferreting out corruption, wherever it faced him. "Long live a free and independent press!" he burbled, raising his bottle in a toast, mimicking a character wearing a powdered wig and tri-cornered hat whom he saw recently in a public television documentary about the drafting of the Constitution. After promising to forward copies of any paperwork discussing the renovation of the President's Home that perchance he picked up, he exited with a stack of three cookies clamped between his teeth.

* * *

For the next day and a half, Underdog worried. He worried over the ethics of divulging information people trusted him to keep confidential. He worried over how and where he would hide the materials if he obtained them. He worried over what might happen to him if he were caught passing along college secrets. The longer he worried, the tighter the tightness in his chest and stomach became. It felt as though nuts and bolts fastening his innards together were being wrenched ever more tight.

"Maybe I'll hide the evidence there," he thought, glancing down Judy's cleavage, squinting to make out freckles hidden in the dark between her breasts. Creating a virtual cave, so black inside it would take a high-wattage lamp to see anything, were Judy's low-cut cocktail dress and push-up bra, the first purchases using her new credit card, acquired with great effort due to her self-employed status. "What do you think?" she asked, turning first to the left, then to the right, skirt aswirl. "My mom took me to Monique's Boutique and helped me pick out this dress."

"You have impeccable taste," he said, then hastily added, "Your mom, too," when he saw Mona enter the living room — it always helped to butter up your girlfriend's parents. All three stood together by the fireplace fumbling in unison: Mona working to snap a flash cube into her Instamatic camera dangling from a strap around her wrist, Judy fussing with the rolling waistband to her panty hose, and Underdog straightening the twisted cummerbund to his rented tuxedo. So frustrated was Underdog that he felt like laying the cummerbund out on the hearth, grabbing one of the andirons, and beating the kinks out of it.

Once everyone got themselves situated, Mona had Judy and Underdog pose by the fireplace, flame-less because Mona couldn't "see perfectly good gas heat go up my chimney." She photographed them, flash cube bursting not just once, but twice, to make sure she caught good expressions on their faces. "No winking eyes or sourpuss mouths allowed," she said. For the next several minutes, massive purple amoebas swam before Underdog, making it even harder to negotiate the icy front steps with a teetering, spike-heeled Judy hanging from his arm as they headed for Reid's car, which meantime had parked out front. Reid emerged and opened both passenger-side doors; from the back seat floor he scooped out onto the snowy pavement several wadded-up paper sacks, mementos from several trips to drive-through windows of fast food restaurants.

As Reid tidied up the back seat, Underdog studied the phlegmy exhaust that Reid's wheezing, pneumonic car was coughing up. "Is your car going to hold up for a return trip home?" Underdog asked. "Last time I rode with you, you couldn't even shut the damn thing off for fear you couldn't get it started again. Remember, we've got a lady with us tonight."

"A lady in heels," Judy corrected.

"No problem!" Reid promised, ushering Judy into the back seat. Then he walked around to the rear of the car and raised the trunk lid, which made a creaking sound not unlike doors to haunted houses in horror films. "I can cut the engine without worry tonight," he boasted, holding up a series of car maintenance products stowed in his trunk. "Here's a jug of antifreeze, a can of Heet, deluxe jumper cables and, if worse comes to worst, a blanket for covering up."

"Comfy," said Underdog.

Reid closed the trunk, and he and Underdog slipped into the front seat.

They took the northern route to the west side of town, past the massive cylindrical grain elevators comprising the seed and feed operation built on a spur along the railroad tracks, the foremost reason Jasper grew originally in the middle 1800s, a venture predating barbed wire by close to thirty years. In their latest manifestation a series of seven elevators built of corrugated tin, each over a hundred feet tall, the tallest structures in Jasper, not counting the high-rise dorms at the school, they loomed over the prairie town like the single thing you could collectively count on to always be there.

They turned left at the barbed wire company offices, a three-story modern concrete building banded horizontally in black glass and white cement. Out front was an office park setting, where carefully, almost cynically, situated trees ruled over a grove-like environment, including a waterfall and reflecting pool, now in early winter turned off, drained and covered with a khaki tarp. Despite this pleasing façade that the barbed wire company turned toward society, Underdog always felt unnerved around it, for in back forbidding faceless structures that he presumed contained the production facilities were surrounded by a high chain link fence topped not with barbed wire but with the company's latest product, razor wire. "I've always gone way around that place," said Underdog turning his head and speaking to Judy. "When I walk places, I mean. Climbing fences is the easiest thing in the world for me. But I won't touch that place's fence. No way, no how."

"It's creepy," Judy agreed. "And you know, they hire a franchised operation out of Ohio to spray their lawn and tend their grounds."

"Environmentally incorrect," chimed in Reid.

"This is all pretty incorrect," said Underdog, looking around, as they approached the President's Home, located on a block where keeping up with the Joneses consisted of out-doing your neighbor, at least in the case of Christmas, by installing a holiday display more elaborate than the last: they passed a home where the owner exhibited a twenty-character nativity scene; another where a life-sized Santa Claus, sleigh and reindeer were teamed on the roof; and still another where multicolored lights spelled out "Peace on Earth" and "Merry X-Mas!"

Sighs and oh!s emanated from Reid's car as they turned at the direction of a red-jacketed valet into the Flaghorns' driveway. Spotlights illuminated four ice sculptures spread across the sloping front yard — a seal, bear, swan and snail — which glowed with a quiet luster, like opals. Adding to the subtle show of light were not-so-subtle sparks from Reid's bumper scraping the cement, his gas hog car too long for the steep incline. The car skidded to a halt, and the trunk popped open by itself. The valet, a high school kid who needed to shave his fuzz, rolled his eyes, let Judy out, then handed Underdog a claim check. After Reid tied down his trunk lid again, he joined arms with Underdog and Judy; in unison they took deep breaths and marched lockstep up the driveway to the front door.

At a massive oak table inside the foyer, a frumpy girl wearing an ill-fitting blue corduroy dress, whom Underdog estimated to be a sophomore at the college, checked them off her guest list, then ushered them into an anteroom where they hung their coats on a coat rack the size of a jungle gym. "Do I tip her?" Underdog asked Reid, who shrugged his shoulders. She directed them down a hall that appeared to perfectly bisect the house, until the time they all had madly anticipated finally arrived, and they made their entrance into the party.

A svelte woman, sleekly dressed in a long, black, satiny gown, with a strand of pearls swinging around her neck, greeted them, introducing herself as Daliah Flaghorn. "Judy, darling!" she gushed, leaning forward and kissing Judy on the left cheek. Underdog saw that her pointy chin extended very far, stretching her skin, drawing her lips back and baring eternally clenched teeth; he felt a cigarette holder or something similar was needed to help divert attention from her flawed mouth and jaw. Judy presented Underdog and Reid to Mrs. Flaghorn. Upon learning their names and discovering that neither was anyone she wanted to schmooze, she pointed them in the direction of the bar and abruptly excused herself, whisking Judy away to discuss plans for spring flower planting. Reid spotted one of his sociology professors in the sea of heads, a spike-haired, bucktoothed woman in men's horned-rim glasses, and made his way across the room to say hello.

Left alone, Underdog explored the room. His first stop was the bar, an opening framed by two sliding doors that led into the kitchen. Pouring drinks inside was an older bald man, dressed in a white shirt, bow tie and black vest, whom he recognized as a waiter from the Black Angus Restaurant, which a little sign on the wall identified as the evening's caterers. His taste for whiskey continuing from the day before, Underdog ordered straight bourbon and proceeded on his tour.

His first stop was a series of glass and aluminum display cases along the wall. Inside were animal skulls arranged by species: in the first case he saw reptiles — two varieties of turtles with powerful-looking lower jaws; three types of snakes, including a rattler with huge fangs; and a gila monster. The next display case contained small mammals: several species of exotic South American monkeys and a number of more familiar animals like foxes, rabbits and squirrels. On view in the last two cases were larger mammals. Here Underdog looked at the horned skulls of a deer and antelope; the sleek, elongated skulls of a dolphin and seal; and the snaggle-toothed skulls of a wolf, tiger and panther. Underdog didn't need a sign to tell him the source of the exhibit, but there it hung anyway, mounted on the wall in the center of it all:

From the Private Collection
of Professor William Fletcher

Nearly a week had passed since the last time Underdog gave Race Fletcher a thought; it was only a short synaptic bridge to thoughts of Ione. Apropos the situation, he recalled a poem assigned in his high school English class where the speaker, attempting to seduce a woman who was holding out on him, tells her that they should seize their opportunity, because they would soon grow old and die, and worms would eat away their flesh, leaving nothing behind but bones and regrets.

Underdog perambulated, following a tin carpet guard demarcating purple rug running along the wall from redwood flooring laid diagonally across the room's center. Gray, hump-backed sofas with heavy-duty hides like bus depot furniture lined the walls; punctuating these were blocky, triangular end tables littered with lipstick-stained wine glasses and paper plates containing the picked-apart remains of shrimp or chicken. The back wall was comprised wholly of windows, two stories'-worth. Beyond the redwood deck outside a broad, smooth expanse of snow glittered; behind that, squat evergreen trees were clothed in snow, looking as white, fat and lumpy as naked monks. For a moment he gazed at the scene, soaking in the tranquillity, and then a heated discussion behind him intruded. One professor sounded the siren that Christian fundamentalists were slowly taking over the government; the other professor told him he needn't be so alarmed, they were a minority numerically — he knew because he personally measured their numbers.

"Measure this," said Underdog under his breath, annoyed his reverie was interrupted. He walked over to the room's focal point, a fourteen-foot Christmas tree that blinkered like a Las Vegas casino sign. Relief of relief, Judy returned to his side, threaded her arm through his and stood with him for a moment in front of the monstrous electrified pine.

"It's such a pretty tree," said Judy. "So colorful."

"It clashes with the placid backyard scene I was enjoying a minute ago," he said.

"Hush, Grinch," she said, pinching his left butt cheek through his tuxedo pants. About that time, the general hubbub edged up a notch or two. Underdog and Judy turned around to locate the source of the rise in noise level, finding that clusters of people were coalescing across the room. Curious, they joined the throng, and Underdog telescoped on tip-toes to see. "It's just Race Fletcher," he said, retracting.

"Is the skinny, flat-chested bitch with no ass with him?" she asked, suddenly pricklier than all of the needles on the Christmas tree combined.

"Uh, yes."

"Let's go say hello." She grabbed Underdog's hand and dragged him through a patchwork of laughers, huggers and hand-shakers to the crowd's locus. There they ran headlong into Ione, who stood back-to-back with Race Fletcher, busy with acknowledging all who stopped to wish him happy holidays or to congratulate him on his latest *Strobe Magazine* article. Ione looked resplendent in a loose-fitting black jacket trimmed with narrow bands of gold under which she wore a black silk blouse and black slacks. On her feet were platform shoes with soles that rivaled truck tire treads.

"Underdog!" she purred. "So good to see you."

"Judy, Ione. Ione, Judy," was all he could muster by way of introduction, afraid that the cat fight he kept watch for all night long would commence any second now.

"Charmed," Judy said, her nose puckering like she smelled barnyard in the breeze.

Ione curtsied condescendingly to Judy. "I saw you noticing my platform shoes," she said, lifting her cuffs for a better view. "I picked them up at a cute little shop in Greenwich Village called Sassy's."

"Cute," said Judy. When Ione went to get Race's attention, Judy leaned over and whispered into Underdog's ear that it looked like Ione bought her shoes at a Goodyear store.

"JU-deeee!" Race Fletcher oozed over his looped, red string tie, completing an ensemble of brown tuxedo, ruffled white shirt and green vest, making him look like some character from a Dickens novel. "Judy Judy Judy," he cooed, arms spread to hug her. That loose shock of hair, always that hair over his eye, cock crest to all women around, thought Underdog.

"Hulloh, Race," she said, receiving his embrace. In return, she kissed his cheek politely.

"Come tend my garden next year, too," he urged, winking. "You're lucky to know Judy," was all he said in addressing Underdog, interaction over before he knew it. Then, without skipping a beat, eyes like bing-bing-bing follow-the-bouncing-ball, Race picked up another conversation in a different quarter of the room and was gone, along with him the crowd orbiting Jasper's brightest star.

Left lingering by the seafood bar, Judy and Underdog were soon accosted by Chuck, Underdog's friend from the student paper. "The shrimp is tits," he announced, talking with his mouth full of a white mash of chewed shrimp, plate in one hand, champagne glass in the other. Then he drunkenly blathered something more that Underdog couldn't make out. Underdog looked Chuck over and felt mild disgust; nonetheless, he credited him with the most original bow tie and cummerbund of the night, a loud Dick Tracy comic design. Everyone in the vicinity agreed, the shrimp looked inviting, like fleshy pink ornaments decking green shrimp trees foresting the table. Also recommended by those who had acquired a taste for snotty, highfalutin food were oysters served on the half-shell. The Acapulco crab dip was consensus favorite, however, to die for when spread across Melba Toast. Underdog slurped some oysters, crunched a few crab dip crackers and downed a half-dozen shrimp doused in cocktail sauce; beside him Judy sipped her wine, glancing everywhere but at Chuck, who tottered beside them, nodding and mumbling things into his chest.

"And how 'bout old lady Flaghorn's hairdo?" erupted Chuck again, emerging momentarily from his semiconscious world. "That braid of hers coiling up like chocolate soft-serve at the Dairy Dreem! Or like a turd!" he yowled.

From across the room Reid saw that Judy and Underdog needed rescuing, so he joined them at the seafood bar. Saying they were searching for champagne, they promptly removed themselves, quite content to let Chuck rant and rave by himself. Still, Underdog sympathized; he had found himself in the same intoxicated state before, helplessly adrift in the static between locked-in radio signals. The trio settled beside a table dedicated to glassware, where rows of punch cups were lined up and pyramids of champagne flutes were stacked. Prompted by the sound of flowing liquid circulating through a sterling silver punch fountain, Judy excused herself to visit the ladies' room.

"How you holding up?" asked Reid.

"Hanging in there. And you?"

"Great night so far. I won a research fellowship for next semester. A free ride. All I had to do to qualify was fetch a gin and tonic for the

Sociology chair. They're right: it's not who you know, it's who you blow."

"Congrats."

"Why so dejected?"

"Women, what else?"

"Ione do something?"

"Judy."

"What could Judy have possibly done?"

"Actually, she's been very good. She hasn't thrown her drink on Ione. Or started one of those kicking, screaming girls' fights straight out of grade school."

"What then?"

"I'm pretty certain she slept with Race Fletcher."

"NO! When?"

"Probably in the summer when she did yard work for him."

"Well, I hope you put a stop to that shit next summer."

"I can't ask her to give up a good customer. Even him." Despite this declaration against his meddling in Judy's business affairs, Underdog looked upward, mentally dividing the blank white ceiling into pro and con columns.

"It all happened before you and Judy got together. You can't hold her responsible for something prior to then."

"I wouldn't normally. I view myself as the latest in a long string of boarders she's been screwing since she was seventeen. But I don't resent any of those guys, only Race Fletcher."

"There are plenty of reasons to resent Race Fletcher besides sexual ones."

Underdog looked around him at the glitzy display, seeking the perfect image to convey his feelings on the subject. Then, viewing the sweets table, he seized it: "The world is like one big dessert table, see? and Race Fletcher's at the head of the line, sticking his fingers into each piece of cake and every slice of pie. And here I am, at the tail end of the line forced to eat my dessert with his fingerprints in the frosting."

Reid sipped his gin and swallowed reflectively. Then he shooshed Underdog when he glimpsed Judy winding her way back through a crowd of hoary-headed men and their dye-enhanced wives. Underdog thought she looked ravishing and so real compared to the other women at the party, with her genuinely blonde hair that had soaked up so much sunlight in summer that it continued to shine in winter, like some glow-in-the-dark object removed from under a lamp. Judy had one hand hidden behind her back; she took Underdog's hand in the other and jerked him toward her, blow cushioned by her breasts. From behind her back she pulled a sprig of mistletoe, raised it above their heads, and kissed Underdog good and wet and long, her tongue sweeping across his teeth like a finger on piano keys.

"Merry Christmas!" she said, lips purpled from the pressure.

"Whew!" he said, catching his breath. He couldn't admit to her, of course, that his breathlessness had less to do with her kiss, which rivaled a Ball jar vacuum seal, but more with the sensation that she had knocked the wind out of him.

Judy proceeded to introduce him around to several clients of her lawn care business, all of whom were doctors, lawyers, bankers or other high society types. The sudden change in his opinion of her was completely lost on Judy, but it was consuming Underdog for the duration of the party. He saw it reflected in her eyes, whose languorous lids now made her look dumb and lazy rather than sexy and dreamy. He also could feel it in her hand, which felt cooler to the touch than he remembered and as stiff and unfamiliar as a mannequin's. Finally, he sensed it inside his nostrils, where her scent failed to register. Only two hours before, he would have recognized her smell anywhere, even in a crowded room, so familiar was he with nosing her cleavage, its ultimate source. Now her smell escaped him, as inscrutable as the vapors given off by ancient Greek oracles.

THIRTEEN

Upon learning of Judy's infidelity — what Underdog called infidelity, what she called exercising her rights as a liberated woman, playing the field, everything but what it was, treachery — Underdog decided to distance himself from life in Jasper by spending the holidays elsewhere. Taking full advantage of the shutdown at the college as an excuse to be apart from Judy, he left town on December twenty-second, spent Christmas and the week after at his parents' house in Peru chatting with his mom and bickering with his dad, then accepted Reid's timely invitation to spend New Year's Eve in New Orleans. To get there, they drove straight through in Reid's hulking, behemoth of a car. Stretching comfortably inside its ballroom-sized front seat, they gorged themselves en route with potato chips, warm dip in vacuum-sealed cans, Doritos, beef jerky, pickles, Cokes, ice cream sandwiches and half-pound bags of M&Ms.

"Augh!" bellowed Underdog not far into their trip.

"What happened?" asked Reid.

"Damn Dorito went perpendicular and poked me in the roof of my mouth."

"I knew a guy once who died that way," said Reid. "A Dorito razorbladed through the roof of his mouth and into his brain."

"You've got to be joshing me."

"You're right. But it could happen."

They picked up Interstate 55 in southern Illinois and proceeded due south. As they came upon Memphis, Reid switched off the classic rock radio station, one in a long sequence that they tuned into, picking up their signals forty miles apart, each with what sounded like the same deep-voiced announcer doing station breaks in between Who, Zeppelin or Stones. He popped in an Elvis cassette, the only one he owned owing to his head-banger tastes, believing it irreligious not to include in one's music collection at least one tape by the King of Rock and Roll. As they listened to smash hits like "Jailhouse Rock" and "Hound Dog," they punched the dashboard and kicked the floorboard to the unsubtle rockabilly beat. This then was their tribute to Memphis's most famous resident.

Before they left the bridge crossing the river into Arkansas, they noticed a speed limit sign, along with a smaller sign beneath, which threatened "No Tolerance."

"My dad was pulled over in Alabama when I was a kid, for going ninety in a seventy mile-an-hour zone," commented Underdog. "He was driving an old, beat-up Rambler that would never in a million years reach ninety, even if you floored it."

"Speed traps are the South's biggest industry," said Reid. "Even bigger than agriculture." Not wanting to risk landing in some redneck jail, he let up on the gas and cruised at about sixty-three miles per hour. As he drove, watching cars with Arkansas and Tennessee plates whizzing past, he wished that he could throttle up his boat and race it through the surrounding sea of cotton, too.

After a short hitch through Arkansas they entered Mississippi. Suddenly, flat bottom land gave way to rolling, wooded country. Thirty miles later, they saw the first of several signs that informed motorists a rest area was ahead. On the same sign post, below, was another sign which said "No Facilities." When Reid and Underdog passed by the so-called rest stop, all they saw was a turn-off that led to a trash can with a couple of parking spaces beside it.

"That's the first time I ever saw a rest stop without a toilet," said Underdog.

"Kind of defeats the whole purpose of having a rest stop," said Reid.

"What a crappy, broken-down state Mississippi is," Underdog harrumphed. Like many other northerners, he had inherited from his parents a prejudice towards the South, an impression coming from somewhere deep, as if manufactured in his bone marrow, that southerners were slow, that they were behind the times.

Winding through densely planted, seemingly endless piney woods, glimpsing in peripheral vision glints of dinnertime sun refracted in trees, their bladders full and bellies empty, they pulled off the interstate and entered a small town where just about every fast food chain was represented. They opted for the drive-through of Burger King first, so Reid could order a Whopper, and Taco Bell second, so Underdog could order a Burrito Supreme. For variety's sake, they parked in the parking lot outside McDonalds, where they gulped down their food; when they finished their meal, they entered McDonalds, used the washroom, and bought hot fudge sundaes for the road.

Driving off, it struck both Reid and Underdog that they were not in the thick of a large pine forest like being on the road suggested; only a narrow strip of trees lined the highway, comprising a two hundred-mile-long camouflage curtain. Behind these trees lay the red clay farm land of Mississippi, looking to them like all it could grow were stones and weeds, quite a departure from the rich black dirt of Jasper County. "They must have planted trees to keep outsiders' eyes off their business," said Reid, merging back onto the interstate.

"They probably planted trees to keep everybody from seeing what a crummy state this is," answered Underdog.

* * *

It was well past dark when the duo entered Louisiana. By Reid's calculation, they only had another hour till they reached New Orleans. The traffic speeded up even further; they saw red tail lights pass, then zip up and over the horizon. "I know it's chicken-hearted to latch onto somebody who's speeding, because most likely they'll get busted before you, but what the hell," said Reid, as he stomped on the gas and steered his car behind another which was part of the swift current.

After awhile, Underdog noticed that things had gotten moist; it felt like an invisible clammy hand reached down from the sky to glue his bangs onto his forehead and smooth down the hairs on his arms. The smell changed, too, curiously reminding him of Judy Baine — a sweet and sour mixture of vinegary perspiration and grassy chlorophyll. Molecules of romance, sex and intoxication crowded the air, joining and separating in a nonstop series of infinite combinations, making Underdog respect the quiet volatility of the climate along the southern coast. This obviously was what weathermen back home spoke of, humid gulf air that cymbal-crashed with cold Canadian air in the skies above midwestern towns like Jasper, stirring up trouble in the form of thunderstorms and tornadoes.

Suddenly, the ride got bumpy, like a three-foot wad of gum adhered itself to one of Reid's back tires. Reid steered off the road and onto the shoulder, where the car rolled to a halt beside a guard rail. "Damn flat tire," he said. "And us only a half-hour outside New Orleans." He held up his hands six inches apart to illustrate how close they were to their destination.

After Reid and Underdog stepped out of the car to inspect the damage, they simultaneously paused to look over the guard rail at exotic, unfamiliar sights: moonlit cypress trees with their water-bloated trunks, reminding Underdog of one-tree desert islands he had seen in cartoons, and fog wisping across the brackish water, like smoke exhaled by cigar-smoking alligators prowling below the surface. They groped their way along the car until they reached the rear end, whereupon they gave each back tire a kick to determine which was flat.

Finding the right rear tire a chewed-up blob, they set themselves to the task of changing it. Reid opened the trunk and felt around amongst vinyl travel bags, emergency car care products and yellowed newspapers he meant to take to the recycling center six months before, finally fishing out his jack. "I'll do the changing, but you'll have to produce some light," he said to Underdog.

"Is there a flashlight in there?" asked Underdog, pointing inside the trunk.

"There could be. But even if you found one, I bet the batteries are sulphured over," he said, jerking out the spare and bouncing it on the pavement.

"It's a good thing I smoke," said Underdog, pulling his lighter out of his pants pocket. "And they say it's bad for you." He flicked it on, casting weak light on the blown tire.

"I'd say this is an example of one of smoking's benefits," said Reid, yanking the wrench upwards to unfasten the first lug nut.

Thus the two worked together, on the side of the road in the middle of a Louisiana swamp at one-thirty in the morning, wrestling with a flat tire during a night so black and slippery you probably could extract oil from the air.

After finishing a half-hour later, during which time Reid grew skillful in changing a tire by feel due to Underdog's lighter running out of butane five minutes into the process, the two discussed the next leg of their trip.

"I guess we'll get to town too late to meet your friend at the café," said Underdog.

"Afraid so. He said it closed at two o'clock, and that's what time it is now," said Reid.

"So we'll go straight to his house."

"I don't have his address."

"We'll call him from a pay phone then."

"Um, he doesn't have a telephone. I always call him at the café."

"You mean we can't reach him till tomorrow?"

"That's about the size of it. Maybe we could rent a cheap hotel room."

"In the middle of a swamp? It'd be like *Psycho* meets *Deliverance*."

"No, in New Orleans."

"Without a reservation during Sugar Bowl week? Yeah, that'll happen."

"There's always the car," said Reid. "We'll catch some Zs in the car, then wash up at a gas station in the morning and meet up with Brent later."

"Sleep where?"

"In the car."

"I heard that. I mean, pulled off to the side of the road here?"

"Why not? As long as we're on the interstate, we ought to be okay. The thing we don't want to do is get off at an exit and get lost. Then it truly will be like doing a cameo part in *Deliverance*."

"This sucks!" said Underdog, throwing his lighter as far as he could into the swamp. A second later they heard it go "kerplunk" in the water.

"Don't blame me, blame Uniroyal," said Reid.

"All right. But if we get eaten by alligators, I'm never, ever going to speak to you again," snapped Underdog, opening the rear door, slipping off his shoes and lying across the back seat. Reid shrugged, opened up the driver's door, and reclined in the front seat. Within a few minutes, each fell asleep listening to a million-member cricket choir sing "Uhr-upp uhr-upp uhr-upp" in a capella fugue.

* * *

Neither Reid nor Underdog had anything planned for their visit to New Orleans much beyond kicking around, drinking beer on Bourbon Street, and sleeping on the floor of Brent, a high school friend of Reid's, whom they met the next morning in the café he worked at on St. Charles Avenue. Reid and Brent embraced, then all three sipped their coffees at a filthy wrought iron table underneath a canvas umbrella shielding them from a southern latitude sun that showered their skin with piercing light particles. Upon meeting again after so many years, Reid and Brent immediately began recounting all that had happened to each since they parted at graduation.

Underdog's attention to the conversation slipped in and out; he knew all of Reid's old stories, and he didn't know Brent well enough to care about his. As he sat, he examined his surroundings. The café boasted a flagstone patio enclosed by potted palms, closely spaced so their fronds intertwined like a wicker fence. Small white flowers bloomed on ivy corkscrewing around phone wires that ran parallel to the property line. Beyond, the tops of great magnolia trees loomed over Uptown boulevards, looking grandiose as the archways in photographs of European cathedrals Underdog had seen. Spanish moss creeping over every branch according to its own elaborate design added to the Baroque feel. Most of all, Underdog, blinking, couldn't get over how potent the colors were, how the vegetation shone almost phosphorescently.

Holding his cigarette palm up, pinched between two fingers, the very image of Peter Lorre smoking, Brent spoke: "The week I moved here, some people I met took me to a see Beausoleil, a Cajun band. Everybody was up on their feet, dancing their heads off. And I thought, 'You simply don't see this in Iowa.' So, no, I don't regret leaving behind small town life at all."

Though he missed the build-up, Underdog saw his point; probably gay, Brent was unlikely to mix with men appraising pigs at a county fair or families playing bingo at the grange hall. Not that there weren't like-minded men in small towns — Underdog knew there were. Just none of them would appear in the guise of a gentleman caller Underdog could see Brent, with his cultivated espresso cup manners, attracting.

"Underdog and me are unreconstructed townies, I guess," Reid responded. "Like to visit, but wouldn't want to live there."

"Speak for yourself. I'd rather sit on a porch here and see a palm tree than sit at home and look up at a rusty old grain elevator," said Underdog, wishing that Reid would shut up about his townie ways for the weekend. Brent, turning down Reid's invitation to party on Bourbon Street because he had to work, gave them copies of keys to his apartment and told them the address on Prytania Street, describing it as a "modest two-room affair." With his round-the-clock holiday work schedule, it turned out that Reid and Underdog saw very little of Brent, except for late in the afternoon on New Year's Day, when they bumped into him in a suddenly all-male mob on the eastern end of Decatur Street, at the periphery of the French Quarter, where a veritable fog of cologne rested overhead, as men on the street exchanged propositions with shirtless men perched above on iron grillwork balconies.

* * *

One local custom Reid and Underdog took to right away was this business of taking your beer with you when you walked out of a bar. Usually, they would forget and have to be reminded to "take your beer" as they got up to leave. They also drove around town while drinking beer, nothing drunk or reckless, but simply because it was legal and they were allowed. "Ah, civilization," sighed Reid, offering a toast to this freedom as he sat back from the steering wheel and swigged from his cup of Dixie Beer while waiting for a red light to change.

"I get a kick out of the street names down here. Like this one," said Underdog, directing Reid's attention to a street sign mounted on an antique-looking street light meant to resemble an old gas lamp. "'Tchoupitoulas,'" he read. "Much more personality than 'Quarry Road,' wouldn't you say? Or how about 'Esplanade?' More grandiose than 'Base Line Road.' Or 'Elysian Fields.' Which has got a ring of poetry to it. Unlike 'Airport Road,'" he said, pinching his nose and pronouncing the word as nasally as possible to prove his point.

They were heading from Brent's Uptown residence to the French Quarter in order to hang around and later view the fireworks display ushering in the New Year. Lining the street were squat wooden houses, several you could term shanties when applying Jasper standards, each painted in tropical shades of yellow, blue, pink and aquamarine. Grime and paint blisters detracted from the otherwise cheery effect, however. Small homes soon gave way to stucco mansions with the same garish paint jobs, and the closer they got to their destination, the more noticeable became the transition to French and Spanish colonial architecture, signaled by intricately woven wrought iron railings enclosing upper floor balconies. Finding a parking space elusive at first, given the hordes that had begun to assemble, Reid finally found a spot on Chartres Street after circling around the block for half an hour.

Their plan was simply to spend the evening crisscrossing the French Quarter, people-watching, window-shopping and beer-guzzling. Immediately upon exiting their car, they ordered beers at a nearby daiquiri bar, a novel experience for those accustomed to such walk-up windows dispensing ice cream cones, malted milk shakes and other frozen, non-alcoholic treats. Milling about the narrow streets were thousands of college football boosters in town for the Sugar Bowl. The school colors of the favored team were black and gold; garbed in black baseball caps and yellow sweatshirts, its cocky fans resembled giant bees. The underdog school's colors were much more flattering — white and crimson, the color that prognosticators said the faces of its players would turn after their embarrassing defeat in the big game. Bourbon Street was especially clogged with revelers who paused below balconies to exchange expressions of school pride with those who stood above waving banners and cups of beer. The whole spectacle seemed completely juvenile to Underdog and Reid, like the corniest high school pep rally; nonetheless, Underdog felt a pang of regret that he never attended a large university fielding nationally ranked football teams invited every year to big-time bowl games.

Near the corner of Bourbon and St. Louis, their attention was drawn to an establishment where live Cajun music was being performed. Peering inside its open shuttered windows, they saw people eating Cajun specialties like jumbalaya or red beans and rice. Sweaty couples packed the tiny dance floor, feet shuffling to the rollicking rhythm. The beat infected Underdog's feet, too, and he commenced a little jig on the sidewalk while Reid pushed his way inside to retrieve more beer. After finishing the song with a great big "Aye-EEE," the accordionist introduced the next song, what he called the "Cajun National Anthem," whose title translated to "Pretty Blonde." Underdog listened carefully to the hard-sawn fiddle, the snare drum brushwork combing out a waltz beat, and the honky tonk piano cascading lightly in the background, and especially he paid attention to the lyrics, sung in the clumsy rhythms of Acadian French translated into English, but sounding more heartfelt for that, like the song were hacked out of pine, not sculpted from hard wood:

> Jole Blon, little flower,
> you're my darling, you're my sunshine.
> You know I want you, adore you, forever I love you,
> and I promise to always be true to you.
>
> In the evening, in the shadows,
> I'll be waiting in Louisiana.
> When I hear your sweet voice, I rejoice I'm so happy,
> and I'm saving all my kisses for you.

On the surface a pleasant love song, the doleful wails and yelps coming out of the singer's throat belied the song's upbeat façade. Underdog thought he recognized the true emotion being communicated: that of profound sadness over the capriciousness of women. When thoughts arose of Judy, his own pretty blonde, a tear drop rolled down his cheek.

"What's the matter? Did a piece of confetti land in your eye?" asked Reid, extending to Underdog a cup of beer.

"The music was reminding me of Judy," said Underdog, wiping his eyes.

"Hey! You came here to forget about Judy!"

"I did forget about her. Until now. I bet this place is unbelievably romantic when you've got someone to share it with."

"It's clear we've got to get you into one of the strip joints they've got down here. That'll take your mind off Judy."

"I'd put Judy's body up against a stripper's anytime, anywhere," Underdog declared. Typical of Reid, he thought, that he wanted to attend a strip show with hundreds of single women hovering around, several of whom they saw pull up their shirts when invited by men on balconies to "Show your tits."

"Let's start heading over to the fireworks then," suggested Reid. "I'm getting real claustrophobic here."

Underdog acquiesced, and they began moving riverward. As they walked, Underdog wished it were Judy who accompanied him instead of Reid. They would hold hands, taking turns squeezing a little harder to call attention to sundry sights: shop windows containing pewter Confederate soldiers or crudely painted coconuts, people with outrageously made-up faces or frat letters painted across their bare chests. They would listen to the scrape of their shoes and the knock-knock-knock of horse-drawn carriages on cobblestone. They would look appreciatively into each other's eyes, warmly lit from dim orange gaslamps. Then, as the clock struck midnight, they would veer into a private courtyard to embrace underneath a palm tree and kiss passionately in celebration of the New Year. Such were the wondrous images encased in mental amber that Underdog planned to share with Judy when he returned to Jasper.

Several sights he didn't intend on sharing, because they spoiled the otherwise inviting atmosphere of New Orleans, included vomit puddles in gutters, the result of amateur drinkers not respecting the high rum content of hurricanes or daiquiris, instead treating each swallow like just another fruit-flavored Life Saver. He also objected to the garbage bags piled on the sidewalks which attracted fat clouds of flies, the first he ever saw in the month of December. "Look at that mess, will you?" he said to Reid, pointing to an especially large, sprawling waste pile. Comprised of splintered picture frames, backless kitchen chairs and waterlogged cardboard boxes, among other things, it looked like someone had decided to enter the new year with a clean slate, unburdened by possessions evidently removed from his attic or spare bedroom. Nevertheless, Underdog was drawn to the pile, appraising it with eyes well-trained from browsing resale shops back in Jasper.

In particular, his eyes zeroed in on a small brown and beige, leather and canvas suitcase. Attracted by its two-toned look, despite frayed threads around the edges and a broken latch, he picked it up, intending on appropriating it if the inside was reasonably intact. He laid it on the sidewalk, and he and Reid examined it with as much anticipation as someone kneeling before a treasure chest recently dredged up from the sea. Then, after a deep breath, Underdog unfastened the surviving latch and opened it up. Inside, among faded and balding blue velvet, there rested a silver cornet. Looking it over, he noticed that all three mother-of-pearl fingerpads were missing from its valves, and the cork sealing the spit valve shut had all but disintegrated. Still, the valves retained their spring, and he suspected that only a few minor repairs would restore it to a playable condition. Returning the cornet to its place and tucking the ragged case under his arm, he said to Reid, "Who knows? Maybe it once belonged to Jelly Roll Morton."

"I'd say it's a suitable souvenir from New Orleans," Reid responded.

When approaching the river, they saw that quite a crowd had gathered. To their left loomed the Jax Brewery, which hadn't brewed beer in ages, but rather served up a multistoried myriad of shops selling homemade pralines, tee shirts linking New Orleans with drinking, and other assorted tourist trinkets. To their right stood the Hard Rock Café along with an adjoining tent where rock and roll bands played in terrible acoustical conditions. "Imagine amplified music ricocheting off tent fabric," said Reid doubtfully after poking his head inside the entrance. They opted to join the drunken, cheering throng atop the levee and claimed their ground, which amounted to little more than the area taken up by a floor tile.

When midnight rolled around, the crowd, like every other crowd in the Central Time Zone, counted down the last ten seconds, then erupted in a thunderous "Happy New Year!" This was followed by a barrage of fireworks that splayed across the nighttime sky; with each explosion red, blue, gold and silver washed across Underdog's face, each color feeling slightly different in temperature, red being the warmest, blue the coolest. Simultaneously, the steamboat Natchez, a paddle wheeler once counted among the Queen class of riverboats, blew her horn mightily, expelling a guttural tone so low in frequency that the ground pulsated. It had to be the loudest sound Underdog had heard in his entire life, far surpassing in volume and power the diesel locomotives that rolled through Jasper, which sounded like coughing ducks by comparison.

After a short fireworks display — a chintzy one thought Underdog, although this didn't seem to faze anyone in the hooting and hollering crush of people — the Natchez broke into song, tooting the traditional "Auld Lang Syne." Still incredibly loud, the sound rose in pitch, now sounding like a choir of huffing flutes. It suddenly hit Underdog: they were hearing a calliope, that's what the thing making all the racket was called; he vaguely remembered listening to one at the county fair when he was a small child. A bittersweet song anyway, "Auld Lang Syne" sounded especially sad this time to him. Or perhaps it was the sight of so many merry couples hugging and kissing and groping each other, which made him yearn for Judy.

The calliope kicked into circus music next. Normally, circus songs were the brightest, cheeriest songs imaginable — and from his high school band experience, a blast to play — but, again, he was left feeling sad. Then he figured out why: the calliope was out of tune, with certain notes so flat that minor chords resulted. Hands down, it was the saddest sound he ever heard. Not noticing, those around him continued shaking their beer cans and spraying their neighbors. Even Reid, in his beer-soaked Mardi Gras tee shirt bought out of season, seemed oblivious.

Underdog ignored the mob and privately mused. Over Judy and his feelings of betrayal. Over Ione and his feelings of resentment. Over Race Fletcher and his feelings of jealousy. Over Milton Flaghorn, embodiment of the school that had screwed him over, and his feelings of vengeance spurred by Chuck at the *Chronicler*. Over lust for Judy, longing for Ione, friendship with Reid. Over his attachment to the city of New Orleans, parish of Orleans, state of Louisiana, and his feelings of regret for having to leave soon.

Accompanied by the sort of sentimental music that causes you to smile as you cry, this latter wave of more beneficent feelings finally overrode the negativity dished out from everyone everywhere, especially when he saw how easily the overwhelming majority of characters whooping it up around him forgave and forgot all the troubling folks in their lives and eagerly welcomed the start of a brand-new year, another rhythm, a different phase, better times ahead. This idea was what Underdog celebrated when he brought the cornet to his lips and with great resolve trumpeted as loud and forcefully as an elephant, letting loose a massive clarion call of hope for himself and a curse against his enemies.

FOURTEEN

Underdog stumbled into work promptly at eight o'clock on Wednesday, January fourth, his head still whirring from the weekend spent in New Orleans followed by a grueling fourteen-hour return trip. The morning had been slow, what he expected on the first day back from the ten-day holiday shutdown. Finding neither a backlog of photocopying nor any leftover bindery work, he puttered around the first forty-five minutes, going for coffee twice, visiting the men's room once, and getting a drink from the ceramic water fountain in the hall three different times. Against his better judgment he finally asked his boss Ron Sullivan what he should do, in the process interrupting a debate over who was more hungover, Ron or Fred Leary, Castle Hall's janitor. Ron pulled the last doughnut from a box somebody brought in, set it spinning across the counter and said to Underdog, "Why don't you take a flying fuck at a rolling doughnut!" Immediately, he and Fred broke out in hysterics, spraying everything inside a three-foot radius with spit and shaking so violently from laughing that their shoulders knocked together. Then they clapped their aching foreheads and settled into complaining of hangover some more.

Lacking any meaningful guidance, Underdog decided he would explore a rarely-opened closet and throw out crap they didn't need any more. To reach the closet door, he had to move aside a stack of heavy paper cartons; upon entering the closet, the decades-old smell of sweat, canvas tennis shoes and leather basketballs nearly overcame him. Given the closet's location, underneath what used to be the visiting bleachers, he expected to find old-time athletic equipment like medicine balls and juggling pins. Surprisingly, he found no such thing, only metal filing cabinets stuffed with computer keypunch cards dating back to the 1970s and some blank cards bound in reams of about two hundred scattered around the floor. Even though nowadays the print shop's records were kept on a personal computer in the business office upstairs, Ron elected to leave the cards alone "in case they're ever needed." Underdog considered volunteering to remove them anyway, knowing their use to be extremely unlikely, but he caught on that Ron was feeling too lazy to supervise, so he let the matter drop.

Around eleven Underdog left on his messenger rounds, empty-handed due to no outgoing deliveries. There were only two stops on the agenda, psychology and the president's office. The thirty-something secretary in psychology, whose laid-back outlook and lost moon of Pluto aspect implied she did plenty of drugs in her off-hours, gave him a booklet that contained a list of questions regarding alcohol abuse. Pausing in the hall next to a tile mosaic of Indians portaging a canoe past a waterfall, he mentally answered a few, concluding that he must be an alcoholic, for the wording of the questions steered him to one of two conclusions: if he denied he had a drinking problem he was hiding it, and if he admitted he had a drinking problem he was acknowledging it. "Talk about trick questions!" he mumbled as he walked to the sociology offices down the hall. There he found Reid, moving into a tiny office that he was to share with four other graduate students in the coming spring semester.

"We have staggered office hours so there'll never be more than one person in here at a time," explained Reid, arranging some books on three narrow shelves he laid claim to. "Look! Shelves all to myself! My own private drawer in a desk that I get to share with four other people! A room so intimate that visitors will have to sit on my lap! This is my reward for winning a fellowship."

"Reward or sentence?" asked Underdog. On the red-lacquered desk were a brass ashtray overflowing with cigarette butts, bottle caps and marijuana seeds; a dying spider plant with brown shoots radiating everywhere seeking water, light, any nourishment it could find; and piles of yellowed multiple-choice exams Underdog remembered photocopying for some grad assistant about a year before.

"It does resemble a jail cell, doesn't it?"

"More like those hot boxes that misbehaving prisoners are sent to."

"Check this out," said Reid, unrolling a poster onto the desktop. "It's a Christmas present from my sister who's at school in Lawrence, Kansas." Titled "Penises of the Animal Kingdom," the poster featured scientific-looking drawings of the reproductive organs from a dozen animals, including a mouse, cat, dog, pig, horse, deer, elephant, giraffe, whale and man.

"Educational. You think your officemates will approve?"

"Guess they'll have to," Reid answered, raising the poster onto a bare portion of wall and thumb-tacking its corners, "because up it goes. By the way, speaking of penises, how was your reunion with Judy last night? Did you make her damn glad you were home?"

"I'll tell you, Reid, it was like she hauled off and hit me across the face with a snow shovel. Can't you see the imprint on my forehead?"

"That good, huh?"

"Good? It was *bad*. Remember I told you about the conversation she and I had before we left for New Orleans? About how I needed a little time away to sort things out in light of the news that she and Race Fletcher slept together? Well, she took it to mean I was breaking up with her." Underdog proceeded to recount for Reid all that had happened recently on the Judy front.

When Reid dropped him off at the puke-colored boarding house two nights before, Underdog went straight to his room, duffel bag dragging behind him going clonk clonk clonk as he climbed the stairs. It was past eleven o'clock in the evening, and all he wanted to do was sleep, so he postponed his reunion with Judy till the next morning. All night long he tossed and turned, unable to sleep on his stomach, his accustomed position, due to an erection lifting his midsection off the bottomsheet like a jack.

He rose from bed at ten-thirty the next morning with a mild craving for alcohol stimulated by a week of drinking breakfast beers in New Orleans. Fending off the urge, he showered, shaved and shat, a more proper start to his day now that he was returned from hurly burly land to the staid Jasper. Next he dressed, throwing on blue jeans and a ragged green sweater, a favorite of his, although stretched and nearly ruined the first time he placed the wool garment in a washing machine with all of his other double knits. He hung onto the misshapen sweater nonetheless, believing it gave him a certain disheveled charm. Hot sauce from a diet of po' boy sandwiches and shrimp creole still made his mouth water; to solve the problem he decided to fight fire with fire, meaning a trip to Mott's Diner for the house specialty, huevos rancheros.

Not coincidentally, Mott's was a favorite hangout of Judy's, especially in the flush times of summer when mowing and mulching jobs abounded, the only eatery in town open at five a.m. She ate her breakfast there every morning before daybreak, allotting herself the coolest hours of daylight for her labors. While farmers and other early risers like home builders and road crews lapped up cholesterol-laden bacon and eggs, she nibbled on a recent addition to the menu, the lo-cal breakfast, consisting of granola with milk, grapefruit juice and toasted wheat bread lite, substituting diet Coke for coffee. Underdog felt that taking Judy to Mott's would create the right tone for their reconciliation. And who knew? if Mona had afternoon errands to run, maybe a roll in the hay was in his future.

When Judy opened the door Underdog stepped in and threw his arms around her and hung on like she were a life rock. "Hey, you're squeezing the stuffings out of me," she said, then wormed her way out of his embrace and backed away from him. He followed her into the kitchen, looking around to see if Mona hovered nearby, an explanation for Judy's curious modesty. Everything appeared the same as he remembered, though it looked like Mona made out well for Christmas, as her collection of ceramic bells with different North American birds for handles had grown noticeably, taking up two full shelves of her china hutch now.

"Mom's not here," said Judy. "She's at the Wal-Mart picking up cleaning supplies for next week's student invasion."

Often, under similar circumstances, she had ushered him to her four-poster bed for a quickie. Once, they did it slipping and sliding on her mother's kitchen table; lying on its slick formica surface afterwards cooled them down as effectively as a block of ice. Today, however, for whatever reason, she was not making any such overtures. "I was thinking," he said, "that if you want, we could maybe go out for breakfast. To Mott's."

"Okay," she shrugged, leaving the room to track down a coat to throw over her purple sweater.

On the way to Mott's, they walked in silence doubly muffled on account of a soundproofing layer of new snow that fell in his absence. Where negligent, probably hillbilly, neighbors did not shovel their sidewalks, he held her hand as they perilously crossed brief stretches of snow trampled into slippery slush. At the diner, she insisted they wait a few minutes for a booth, even though four tables were vacant. "More privacy," she explained.

Once settled in their seats — only a cigarette-long wait, thought Underdog, not bad — they stared into their menus. Underdog knew what he wanted to eat as soon as he got out of bed, so he used the time screened behind the menu to silently compose his apology speech. He wondered if she was doing something similar behind her menu, because he never knew her to order anything but the lo-cal breakfast. "I've got something I want to say," he began, putting down his menu. "I took the news of your affair with Race Fletcher pretty hard. It really changed how I felt about you, at least in the short run. That's why I ran away. For the long run, I want to be with you. I came to that conclusion when I was gone."

"I have something to say, too," she said, looking him square in the face for the first time that day. "I didn't even know you when I messed around with Race, and I really resent that you're punishing me for something that happened almost a year ago."

"You're right, I'm sorry." He sank into his chair, felt himself shrinking in stature like cartoon characters when they got chewed out.

"That's only part of it," she continued. "You see, when you were gone, I met somebody. Last Friday morning after it quit snowing, there was a knock at the front door. It was some college guy trying to earn a little extra money by shoveling our driveway. I told him sorry, that was my job, and that as soon as I got dressed I was heading outside to shovel it myself."

"As soon as you got dressed . . . ?"

"Yeah, I was wearing my heavy terry-cloth robe."

Underdog had seen her wear that robe a dozen times. The blue color of swimming pool water, it begged the viewer to leap into her cleavage and gladly drown there. "Anyway, I invited him inside to warm up, we drank some herbal tea, one thing led to another, and, um, well, I seduced him."

In shock, Underdog spent a minute moving the ketchup, mustard, sugar bowl, napkin holder, and salt and pepper shakers around the checkered table cloth like chess pieces. Then he picked up the menu, turned his attention to the beverage portion, and read the juice selections over and over until he committed them to memory: orange, grapefruit, apple, tomato; orange, grapefruit, apple, tomato. Next, he held up eating utensils into the light, carefully examining them for dishwasher spots and specks of food.

"The usual for you two lovebirds?" a waitress asked, snapping him out of his distracted state.

"Yes," answered Judy, who quickly ended her story. "He took me out to dinner at the Black Angus for New Year's Eve, and I'm going out with him on another date this coming Friday night."

"I can't believe you boinked another guy when I was away. Not only that, but a college guy. What ever happened to your preference for townie guys?"

"It's not just about sex, Underdog. If that was all I wanted, I'd call on you, because you're the absolute best. But you lack vision. You need to set your sights on something. I have a dream to own the biggest landscaping business in the county. Brad is a physics major who dreams of becoming an inventor someday. He's already applied for a patent on a poultry feeder he designed. Tell me, what's your vision?"

As he deliberated his answer, the food came. Suddenly unhungry, his stomach feeling like a blender whose blades were at war with a tin can, he sent his food back, saying he suddenly felt ill. "I guess my ultimate quest is to win back Ione," he admitted.

"The skinny, flat-chested bitch with no ass? My woman's intuition told me so. When we ran into her at the Flaghorn's Christmas party you looked at her like she was some priceless painting you wished you could afford."

"And you know, Reid," Underdog said, bringing them back into the present, "Judy was right about my thing for Ione. I respond to the angular body and multiple personalities like you find in those paintings by Picasso."

"Know what I think? Given the luck you've had with women lately, I'd say one of your New Year's resolutions ought to be to stay away for awhile."

"I'm not sure what I'm going to do next," confessed Underdog. "It seems like I've got to think myself up a pursuit."

He excused himself and headed for the president's office, considering his plight as he walked. A quiet, thinking atmosphere prevailed, for the campus was nearly deserted, sparsely populated by townie staffers and completely devoid of snot-nosed students. Adding to the ghost town feel was a cardboard box rolling across his path like a tumble weed, blown by a sharp gust of January wind. Seeking relief, he darted halfway up a gang way, a windbreak and shortcut that he took frequently, and paused to smoke in the warm crack between buildings. From either end came a howling sound, a king-sized version of blowing on a pop bottle and hearing a whistle.

Warmer now, smoking deliberately and unhurriedly, he marveled at how fast Fortune could deliver something, then snatch it away. Three months before, he was intimate with not just one but two desirable women. Drawing with his finger on the brick wall next to him, he tried to chart where everything stood: Underdog wanted Ione, who wanted her dead husband. Race Fletcher also wanted Ione, who wanted Race, who at one time wanted Judy. Judy wanted Underdog, but now she wanted some guy named Brad. When he was finished, he rubbed his hand across the brick to erase the messy diagram, frustrated that he had no clue how to proceed since it wasn't a flow chart. Nonetheless, he felt he had learned a valuable lesson from the exercise: that Fortune, which all but nullified a person's own free will, was mainly a collection of other people flexing their individual wills, often at cross-purposes. He thought natural forces like weather and gravity were ingredients, too, but determined while crushing out his cigarette that he would explore that possibility another day.

Underdog dug the leather smell that bopped him in the face like a full sack of wine every time he entered the president's office. Originating in the waiting room from two Italian leather sofas that were pumped-up like weight lifters or body guards, the intoxicating aroma bespoke authority and the largesse which came as its tribute. Even brawnier than the sofas was the president's secretary, Sharon, who presided over a desk covered with stacks of paper, writing pads, folders, three-ring binders and phone message slips lined up as straight as parade columns. "You're late," she groused, picking up a manila envelope and shoving it towards him.

Underdog really wanted to yell "Eat me!" in return, but thinking better of it, he said "Happy New Year" over his shoulder as he exited. Looking over the reusable interdepartmental delivery envelope addressed to the print shop, he saw in big bold letters the word "CONFIDENTIAL." He had to laugh, because anyone could unravel the string on the back of the envelope, pull out the contents, read them and return everything without being detected. Mindful of his promise to alert Chuck to any documents having to do with the renovation of the president's home, he headed over to the Music Building for a peek.

Consistently amazed at the lack of locked doors anywhere on the Jasper College Campus, he strolled past the Music Department office and into the practice room area of the building where he selected a soundproof room. Taking a deep breath, he pulled from the envelope a two-page memo from Milton Flaghorn to the college's Board of Trustees. The "Re" line stating "Improvements to the President's Home" indicated he had struck paydirt. After skimming a page-and-a-half, he put his finger on the long-sought-after explanation of how the renovation was to be paid for:

> Given the unpopularity among students of the most recent rise in tuition and fees, during the Fall 1991 semester, I strongly urge that principal and interest on the loan be paid from the capital budget until a suitable interval has passed, whereupon the College shall raise tuition by a percentage equal to that required to offset mortgage payments made from the capital fund.

The sneaky bastards planned to pass the hat the students' way to pay for old Blowhorn's private rumpus room! If knowledge of Race Fletcher's career in pornographic films packed the power of dynamite, then this little tidbit had the potential to unlock the atom bomb. He became short of breath as his brain galloped back and forth between ideas of how next to proceed.

He rejected option one, photocopying an extra set of minutes for the *Chronicler* bunch, because it would be too easy to trace his involvement: every time he ran a photocopy job, he had to enter into a log the starting and ending numbers from a counter attached to the machine that kept a running total of copies made. He also rejected the second option, taking the memo directly to the *Chronicler* and letting them photocopy it — too many potential witnesses. So he settled for option three, copying by hand the relevant passage on a piece of scratch paper, then later secretly forwarding it to Chuck. Finding himself without paper, he looked up and down the hall for a wastebasket or other source. As luck would have it, Jerry Battle, janitor for the Music and Science Buildings, was dragging a trash barrel across the tile and creating a terrible screeching noise. Being deaf, Jerry was oblivious, but it caused the wincing Underdog to feel like someone was puncturing his ear drums with knitting needles. He signaled for Jerry to stop and let him look over the trash.

Making up its bulk was a cello inserted neck-first into the barrel. Jerry nodded, giving Underdog permission to lift it out. Underdog saw that the cello was missing three of its four strings, plus a number of nicks and gouges marred its faded rosewood finish. Otherwise, the cello still possessed all of its tuning pegs and looked serviceable enough with a little work, so Underdog decided to keep it. He also remembered to grab a piece of discarded staff paper to complete his spy work. Saluting Jerry, who continued again on his screeching trail, Underdog considered how Fortune had reared her head another time. She had given Jerry the hulking build and bearded visage of a grizzly bear, yet he could neither make nor hear the squeak of a mouse. (Underdog thought this might be a blessing in disguise, for Jerry was spared listening to the very imperfect music made in his work environment.) As for himself, Fortune had dispensed a second musical instrument; he couldn't figure out why so far, but he knew it was no simple coincidence.

Underdog again shut himself inside the practice room. He propped his cello in the corner and hastily copied choice passages from the memo on the wrinkled staff paper. This he folded in half a bunch of times until it was a tiny square that wouldn't fold anymore, and he pocketed it. With a defiant jauntiness in his step, he went back to the print shop, fingering the paper inside his pocket with a disbelieving smirk on his face like he just walked off with Aladdin's fabled lamp. During lunch, he planned to return and fetch home the cello, meantime trusting that nobody would abscond with his other prize.

FIFTEEN

Underdog couldn't have been more pleased with the snowball he set to rolling. Gray-colored, full of stones and twigs and dog piss, it was already too great to melt in hell; correctly, he predicted that, with a proper shove, it would grow larger and tawdrier than hell could ever muster heat against. So he had no fear when striking his devil's bargain by mailing to Chuck a more polished copy of juicy bits from Blowhorn's stick-it-to-'em memo, made in the privacy of his room at Mona Baine's using a typewriter borrowed from his roommate Ndeka in order to avoid incriminating himself with his handwriting.

Under a headline screaming "Flaghorn In Plot to Defraud Students, Raise Tuition," a damning article — so damning it was signed collectively by the whole *Chronicler* staff, who pledged to stand or fall as a group rather than reveal the individual author's identity — appeared in late January on the first day of the new spring semester. Quoting from "certain documents leaked to the *Chronicler*," plus "unidentified sources" and "parties who requested anonymity," the article accused Jasper College President Milton Flaghorn of masterminding a scheme to pay for the addition to his home by using money raised from future tuition increases. Adding further embarrassment, a sidebar to the main article described an investigation into what social functions had been planned for the space in the upcoming semester. *Chronicler* reporters discovered that exactly zero were college-sanctioned events. The list included meetings of the Jasper Lawn and Garden Club on the second Tuesday of each month, several Board of Trustees poker and billiard nights, regular luncheons/slide shows with Japanese executives from the auto plant, and a family get-together on Easter Sunday where the Flaghorns' niece from the Chicago Lyric Opera chorus was slated to sing. Sullying Flaghorn's reputation further was an editorial splattered across the bottom of the front page that referred to him as a "modern-day Robin Hood" who "robs from the poor student and gives to the rich benefactor."

Challenged by the *Chronicler* to explain his side of the story, Flaghorn acted swiftly and decisively to quell the unrest created among financially overburdened students and morally outraged townies, all of whom were inflamed at the thought of private parties with short guest lists and big bankrolls. Within one day of the article's appearance, he scheduled an assembly in the school's gymnasium to address the issue publicly, inviting Jasper College students and faculty as well as community leaders and ordinary townies. At the appointed late-afternoon time a large crowd entered the gym, flowing through turnstiles to the sounds of bells dinging like an orchestra of pinball machines. Among the swarms of people were Underdog and Reid, who wouldn't miss the occasion for all the oil in Iraq.

As they took their seats in the visitors' bleachers, Underdog saw that a virtual circus atmosphere prevailed. Clusters of students clapped their hands, drummed their feet on wooden planking, chanted rude slogans. A group of fraternity brothers to their right side were dressed in burlap bags symbolizing the poverty a tuition increase would sink them into. Distributed everywhere throughout the gym were mouthy radicals holding up placards that echoed sentiments expressed in the *Chronicler*: that Milton Flaghorn was a cheat, a fraud, an elitist asshole. Underdog hated to admit it — tiresome as propaganda spouted by ex-hippies was to him — but the scene resembled footage he saw in TV documentaries of student disturbances in the 1960s.

It had been nearly two years since Underdog witnessed such rousing, boisterous behavior, at a fall shindig that took place on a fallow corner of Osa Wallace's farm. All afternoon long a rock band played on a flatbed trailer in the middle of a pasture while all kinds of hell was raised — underage drinking and marijuana smoking, multiple brawls between students and townies, and an all-day sex orgy inside a tent somebody set up for the purpose. At dusk, floodlights that Osa installed along a fence line switched on, and the party culminated in a demolition derby Jasper's underground talked up for weeks ahead of time and planned for by purchasing junker cars from local scrap yards. For twenty-five minutes after Osa whistled them to start, old abandoned Chryslers, Chevies and Fords revved up and crashed together in a cavalcade of caved-in doors, crumpled bumpers, crinkled fenders and cracked engine blocks. The motor to a single car, a battered white Granada, could be heard misfiring though still running as the cloud of dust rising above the trammeled furrows cleared. Its driver, a teenage boy from Trailerville, received a cash prize of a hundred dollars ceremoniously awarded by Osa himself. The festivities took their toll, however: one injured driver who had to go to the hospital with a sprained shoulder, one date rape accusation, four cases of crabs and seven drunk and disorderly arrests, the result of numerous complaints by neighbors who spent all day phoning sheriff's deputies to come out and settle things down.

The focus of the afternoon's events would be underneath the pep band loft, a balcony draped with red and white bunting and a sign saying "The Red Birds are Taking Flight" along with a caricature of Joseph "Mo" Momboto, a six-foot-eleven ringer imported from Nigeria, who so far in the basketball season had succeeded in dunking to death every single team in Jasper's conference. On the dais sat several key individuals: Milton Flaghorn, whose defiant gaze slowly swept the audience; Flaghorn's secretary Sharon, who perfectly fit the minutes-taking, sergeant-at-arms task assigned her, right down to a navy blue blouse decorated with epaulets; several pinstripe-suited board members, who looked bothered and annoyed to be called away from their plastic molding factories, farm implement dealerships and fast-food franchises; Chuck and other representatives from the *Chronicler*, comical in their efforts to display a united front by squeezing onto their corner of the dais a total of eleven people; and, finally, the math professor ombudswoman who kept cleaning her glasses by sucking on the lenses and wiping them off with a handkerchief.

Looking around, Underdog spotted the faces of people he knew, tiny dots in a pointillistic haze of heads: Race Fletcher and Ione sitting in the front row of bleachers, immediately to the right of the dais (Flaghorn loyalists?); Judy alongside some toothy college guy whom Underdog couldn't tell was her new boyfriend or not; even Mona Baine, who looked fabulously entertained by the nearby Rotten Fingertips, dressed in his tie-died tee shirt, probably an original from the sixties, who angrily shouted and waved a protest sign that read "Milton Flaghorn — Pig at the Tuition Trough."

Flaghorn rapped his gavel, and the inquisition proceeded. "I have called this meeting to address certain accusations scurrilously, and I might add libelously, leveled at me," he intoned into the microphone, a portentous and godlike thundering high among the rafters. "You, members of the *Chronicler* staff," he said, pointing preacherly and accusatorily, "from whose ranks, incidentally, the network news anchorman Vic Elroy was drawn, have wantonly slandered me and my reputation, carelessly, recklessly and cavalierly dispensing with all pretense of responsible journalism . . . mumble mumble mumble . . . mumble mumble mumble . . . mumble mumble mumble."

Underdog leaned forward to make out words drowned out by the echo rising thickly in the barn-like structure like cake in a baking pan. But then Flaghorn slowed his cadence dramatically and concluded with a clearly enunciated, heavily resounding "I say to you now, where is your proof?"

The *Chronicler* bunch huddled in the manner and number of a football team. Next, the Editor-in-Chief, a woman Underdog knew slightly, who had a penchant for low-cut sweaters that revealed a constellation of zits across her chest, came forward and raised a sheet of paper into the air. "Here's your proof, Dr. Flaghorn," she said triumphantly into the microphone. "A letter received at the *Chronicler*'s offices two weeks ago quoting portions of a confidential memo from you to the college's Board of Trustees." In a gesture Underdog had seen a hundred times before, coming from girls when he was a boy and women now when he was a young man, she placed her hand on her hip and smugly nodded once, as if to say "Told you, smarty-pants."

"Is the memorandum you possess an original or a copy?" Flaghorn demanded, his eyebrows arching steeply, almost satanically.

"A copy."

"Then I ask who is your source? With a copy of an important document, you must have someone attesting to its authenticity."

"Maybe you should ask the board members sitting beside you. They're the ones you were addressing in the memo." The board members lowered their heads in unison, and they stared at their wing tips, shaking their heads doubtfully.

"Was this memo allegedly written by me leaked to the *Chronicler* by a member of our esteemed Board of Trustees?"

"I can't say."

"You cannot say. Then who on your staff authored the article making these ridiculous accusations? Perhaps he or she will reveal the source."

Again, the *Chronicler* gang put their heads together, murmuring among themselves; after thirty seconds they broke apart, nodding their mutual agreement at something. "No one individual wrote the story," the editor declared. "It was a joint effort by all of us you see here."

Next, the ombudswoman approached the microphone and spoke, her voice tinny, letter Ps and Bs popping like kernels of corn inside the speaker cabinets. "Pah-resident Flaghorn has demanded that you pah-roove your accusations. As om-bahudsman, I order you to identify your source. If you cannot, you must pah-rint a retraction."

The editor stood erect and proud, similar to Nathan Hale in schoolbook illustrations Underdog had seen of that hero's final moments. "We stand by our story and will do everything we can to protect the confidentiality of our sources. To do otherwise would dishonor the journalistic profession." Deafening applause broke out in every quadrant of the gym, temporarily halting the batting around of a few beach balls that had been going on during the speeches.

Flaghorn glared at the loudly demonstrating audience, looking individual members in the face like he was recollecting their names and social security numbers for a future audit of grade-point averages or financial aid eligibility. "Let us not ignore the truth by substituting high-sounding rhetoric," he said as the applause died down again.

"It's not only rhetoric. We published the most truthful account possible. But a debate over sources misses the real issue here, which is to explain the financial improprieties you appear to have engaged in." A giant "Sssssss!" filled the gym, a reaction normally reserved for moments in a basketball game when the player with a hot hand sank a three-point shot.

"It is my opinion that the *Chronicler* has been the subject of a practical joke of monstrous proportions." Like a soldier furiously swinging his sword to back his enemy up against the edge of a precipice, Flaghorn pressed forward. "You have no material evidence of any conspiracy, nor do you have a credible witness. In sum, you have no concrete proof of any wrongdoing on my part — absolutely none — so you have no choice but to print a retraction." A thousand throats gulped at once as everyone awaited the editor's backwards tumble into the chasm.

But she hung tough, counter-whacked. "I must again respectfully refuse. The *Chronicler* stands firmly behind the story, and each of us on the *Chronicler* staff is prepared to accept the consequences of that decision." Wild cheering erupted like the ghost of President John F. Kennedy walked into the gym and reprised his "Ich Ein Berliner" speech. Underdog might have felt more choked up if he believed that lofty moral principles motivated the students to such a loud demonstration, rather than fear of empty wallets or checking accounts due to higher tuition.

Like storm clouds gathering, Flaghorn's bushy gray eyebrows joined together, and his hairline scrunched downward. The crowd was frightened into silence by his angry countenance. Then he spoke, a fearsome Zeus-like presence for those in the crowd taken with Greek mythology, looking as though he could have pointed his finger and delivered a lightning bolt to any spot in the gym, immolating anyone who got quarrelsome. "Consequences you shall receive," he boomed. "First thing tomorrow morning I am ordering that funds to the *Chronicler* be cut off until such time as it issues a public retraction of the article and an apology to me personally. I shall also direct the ombudswoman to initiate a libel lawsuit against you and the other members of your staff present here today. You forget, Miss Mantua, that judges often incarcerate journalists for withholding information in the name of confidentiality. Give a prayer of thanks that I am only acting to silence you and that you did not land in jail. At least not yet."

A voluminous BOOO! cut him off, jarring the ceiling, making the bleachers rattle and the floor undulate. This was followed by everyone hurling insults, giving the raspberry, yelling out obscene places where Flaghorn could stick his microphone. In response, Flaghorn hammered his gavel repeatedly to no effect, like he was trying to kill a cockroach too stubborn to die. Then a spokesperson for the pissed-off mob stepped into the limelight ringing the dais, and the gym gradually silenced. Readying himself to rally the mob was Race Fletcher, nodding knowingly with pursed, insulted lips. A thousand ears moved closer to hear him speak un-miked.

"That's censorship!" he accused, assented to by the crowd's windy "YEAHHH!" which drowned out the rest of what he said and threatened to blow the gym walls clean out from under the roof.

Flaghorn banged his gavel some more, then gave up trying to quiet the crowd. He sidled over to the microphone and uttered something barely audible with all the noise, though Underdog heard the word "adjourned" pretty clearly. Nobody was budging, however; instead, a thousand-voice-strong chorus began to chant "Flaghorn sucks! Flaghorn sucks! Flaghorn sucks!" Another chant quickly evolved in counterpoint to the first: "Fuck Flaghorn! Fuck Flaghorn! Fuck Flaghorn!" until the word "fuck" gradually supplanted "sucks" on everyone's lips, including Underdog and Reid's.

Amidst the pandemonium, few people beside Underdog noticed the figure emerging from the shadows and slithering past the crowd to the dais. Underdog recognized him right away; it was Ned Casey, a college-age, mentally ill townie whose bizarre antics were familiar to all who resided in Jasper. Often he could be seen sitting in fast-food restaurants, chewing the fat for hours at a time with imaginary companions across the table from him. Curiously, his mouth moved and he gesticulated with great emphasis, but no voice was ever heard. Apparently, Ned reserved his pantomime act for Wendy's and KFC, because the police had picked him up numerous times over the years for riding his bike through Jasper in the middle of the night, baying dementedly like a dog at the moon and shaking people out of bed from one end of town to the other. And, although never arrested, Ned was the primary suspect in the infamous train track greasing incident of the year before, when persons unknown spread axle grease on a stretch of rail and caused a switch engine to slide on locked wheels into a string of auto carriers, in the process destroying forty-odd automobiles just off the Jupiter assembly line.

If Ned's unbalanced behavior were not enough to handicap him, he retardedly held white supremacist views, indicated by his army-surplus olive-drab clothing, skinhead haircut and green swastika tattooed on his forehead. Numerous times during his messenger runs, Underdog had seen him skateboard across campus in a racist slalom, classifying each student he passed by shouting out his or her ethnicity. When he really got to cooking, you could hear a goose-step rhythm inside the string of epithets:

> White, white, white,
> Nigger, white.
>
> Jap, white, white,
> Nigger, Jap, white.
>
> White, nigger, Jap,
> White, Jap, Jew.

As with the village idiot of olden times, most folks claimed to feel sorry for Ned, while at the same time they complained of the nuisance he raised. For himself, Underdog shared the opinion of a few progressives in town, in particular members of the Black Student Union and the Hillel Foundation, who believed Ned to be dangerous, going so far as to denounce him on fake wanted posters tacked up around the college.

Thus, Ned's prior brouhahas made his actions in the gym almost anti-climactic to some who watched the drama unfold as if in the fluid slow motion of murder scenes from movies. Feeling helpless, Underdog saw Ned ascend the stairs, coolly walk across the platform, raise his arm, and carefully take aim at Flaghorn's head with a pistol he gripped in his hand. When he fired, chanting gave way to screams of horror as Flaghorn, face a bloody blot, swiveled round and dropped to the floor, where he lay motionless. Ned looked over his handiwork a moment, then threw his head back and laughed maniacally until security guards, stationed at either side of the dais, wrested the pistol from him and tackled him about the knees, dumping him onto the floor beside the prone Flaghorn. The crowd was shocked into silence, everyone except for a few isolated co-eds who were crying hysterically into the shoulders of boys beside them. Underdog and Reid stared at one another, stunned as if sucker-punched.

Flaghorn's body was surrounded now by many people attempting to revive him, including Race Fletcher, who dramatically leaped onto the dais like he was Errol Flynn and pushed his way into the ring. A few moments later, Race stood before the microphone, grinning from ear to ear, rather inappropriately thought Underdog, given the tragedy. "Ladies and Gentleman," he began, then snickered into his lapel, "Dr. Flaghorn is fine, he's completely uninjured by the incident you just witnessed. It seems that the assailant here" — he pointed at the handcuffed Ned — "was packing a squirt gun, not a real gun. All the blood you thought you saw was red food coloring mixed with water."

Next, Flaghorn himself staggered forward, mopping stage blood off his face with a handkerchief. His heavily starched white dress shirt was streaked in red; along with his navy blue suit it looked like he was wrapped in a flag — a mock Old Glory, defeated, weak and above all funny as hell to the vast majority present, who all laughed as one, a thousand spastic bellies heaving forth laugh on top of guffaw while the pale and dazed Flaghorn was led down the steps and out a side exit, looking as though tweety birds circled his aching head. After a few more minutes of hooting and hollering, even more triumphant than the week before, when Jasper finally beat State in basketball after eleven tries, the crowd began to disperse, congratulating itself for putting Flaghorn on the defensive — adding up to a very sixties scenario, thought Underdog, who fell in behind a jubilant Rotten Fingertips.

SIXTEEN

Underdog gave up hoping for a quiet day when he saw from the stack of phone messages taken off the answering machine in the print shop office that Ione had called for a pick-up. Without actually hearing her voice and determining her mood, visiting Ione was like taking a boat out to sea without knowing if it was supposed to storm or shine. He knew it was sexist and cliché to think of a woman, but he thought so anyhow: she was every bit as unpredictable as the weather. Experience had proven that the barometer never held steady at the credit union — everything was either blinding sunrays of confidence or sharp thunderclaps of angst.

Lately, with the whole campus buzzing about Flaghorngate, Underdog avoided his usual mates, afraid of saying something that might incriminate himself. The only person he discussed the subject with was Ione, figuring she would alert him if Flaghorn and his cronies began tracing their troubles back to him. He knew her information was reliable, because she obtained it through proximity to Race Fletcher, who was investigating the scandal for an upcoming *Strobe Magazine* article. Privately, Underdog questioned why the usual audience for the magazine, trendy types who expected to read the latest news in the rock music world, would want to learn about the troubles of a third-rate college planted in the provinces. Whatever the case, he fully understood Race Fletcher's motivation in writing the piece: standing up to Flaghorn at the assembly and his subsequent efforts on behalf of the *Chronicler* had made him an even more popular figure in Jasper than ever before. Ione in particular applauded his heroism; her idolizing of Race Fletcher lobbed yet more wood on the jealous fires burning in Underdog's stomach.

Upon entering the credit union office he asked, "What's new on the Flaghorn front?" Evidently something big, for he saw that she could barely contain her excitement about something. She sprang out of her chair and practically long-jumped the six or seven feet to the counter where she greeted him. Only her ears prevented the corners of a huge smile from meeting in the back of her head. "Mostly sunny out today," he judged. "With a slight chance of storms."

"It's finally hit the stands," she beamed, slapping a copy of *Strobe Magazine* onto the counter top. "Read read read read READ!" she demanded. While skimming Race Fletcher's column, he sensed beyond the page her agitation: her arms swung back and forth and her hips swiveled from side to side like she danced the twist. She did remarkably well without the help of music, he thought, trying to fight off the distraction.

From the Heartland
by Race Fletcher

Many residents of the Heartland feel supremely grateful for Japanese "Transplants," auto assembly plants owned by Japanese auto companies but operating in the U.S., oftentimes in rural settings where taxes are low, the need for employment high, and the demand for wages modest compared to traditional auto-building centers like Detroit. Taxes are low in these towns, because they don't maintain large, publicly funded bureaucracies. Need for employment is acute because of social dislocation caused by the disappearance of the family farm, which has spawned a labor force ready for work, but with the old reliable source of jobs, farms, vanishing.

Attracting the Jupiter Motor Company to Jasper, where I live, the heartiest town in the Heartland, were a willing, able workforce, a competitive tax and utility package, and inexpensive land on which to build its sprawling assembly operation. What Jasper offered in addition to other similarly situated towns was a fair-sized college that could lend R & D facilities for cheap to the owners of the transplant eventually built. For its part, the college offered research space and free tuition to Japanese executives' children in exchange for dollars to upgrade its classrooms, laboratories and dormitories.

But the more suspicious among us point out the well-documented rise of Japanese corporate imperialism. Ray Morley, who is close to retiring from AgraCorp, a company that develops and markets hybrid seed corn, calls his town "New Manchuria," alluding to the invasion of China by the Japanese army during the years leading up to World War Two. "They're raping Jasper just like they raped Nanking," argues Morley, who has vivid childhood memories of listening to the radio and hearing reports of Japanese atrocities.

Most folks in Jasper take issue with Morley's charges of exploitation, however. They gladly welcome the prosperity the Japanese have bestowed on Jasperites, many of whom labor in the auto plant at wages in upwards of fourteen dollars an hour, plus benefits. But when studying the goings on in this town lately, you question if Morley might be more prophet than patriot prone to hyperbole. For also dipping his hand into the pork (or sushi?) barrel was Milton Flaghorn, president of Jasper College, with designs to renovate his home into a palace suitable for hosting the types of upscale events required to wheedle contributions from well-heeled alumni. Spending an undisclosed sum, Flaghorn built onto his fifties-era suburban ranch house a pyramidal post-modern addition adorned meretriciously with a gleaming bronze roof.

If raising an architectural monstrosity weren't enough, Flaghorn came under fire from the Jasper College *Chronicler*, the student newspaper, which published allegations that Flaghorn planned on raising tuition to fund the project. To quell the campus unrest that understandably followed, Flaghorn subjected the *Chronicler* staff to a show trial that resulted in his revoking their status as a college-funded organization. Flaghorn's move has not silenced his critics, however. "It's been tough, but we're managing to publish two issues a week," gloats Gina Mantua, editor-in-chief of the *Chronicler*.

Credit is due in large part to Kermit Lund, owner of Copython, a twenty-four-hour photocopy shop and sometime meeting space for espousers of left wing causes. Says Lund: "I've lent paper and the use of a Xerox machine. Every other night or so, the kids come over and crank out a thousand copies." The following morning volunteers distribute the *Chronicler-in-Exile*, as the substitute newspaper is known, to every building on campus. "So far it's been a gas," reports Lund, who is forty-something and given to wearing denim overalls and organic cotton peasant blouses. "I'm reliving my own halcyon youth, when I used to publish *BAAAA!*, a hand-lettered, mimeographed rag attacking the Vietnam War."

Meantime, Flaghorn has initiated libel proceedings against eleven members of the *Chronicler* staff. "Without one shred of evidence linking me to any wrongdoing, they have begun a campaign to besmirch my reputation," claims Flaghorn, who resembles Mark Twain, not only in his use of the antiquated word "besmirch" but also in his longish silver hair and whisk broom mustache. Next, I asked him why the *Chronicler* would want to make inaccurate, potentially libelous statements about him. As a student organization the *Chronicler* is fully funded by the school; it clearly is not a gossip paper playing fast and loose with facts in order to boost circulation. "The only motive I can ascribe to them is they are attempting to draw the attention of potential employers by manufacturing the news," he answered. "Upon graduation — if they reach that far — they shall see how such a strategy backfires on them. Newspapers hire people who report facts, not innuendo."

"We certainly are dealing with facts," maintains Mantua. "But Dr. Flaghorn refuses to acknowledge them. We have a copy of a memo that he himself wrote. But he denies writing it. We have in our hands the smoking gun. But the bullets don't seem to faze him."

Adding insult to injury, Flaghorn has yet to host a social function that is college-approved. It appears to many that Flaghorn is treating the space not as a public meeting house, the understood intent, but rather as a private fraternity lodge. Thus far he has held two board of trustees poker parties, one meeting of his wife Dahlia's garden club, and doubtless many one-on-one smokers, where he holds forth on monetary or grade inflation while wearing a robe and slippers, smoking a pipe and clutching a brandy snifter. One can easily imagine the monkey-see, monkey-do handshakes and initiation spanking ceremonies going on behind his walls.

Of particular offense to men like Ray Morley, mainly those of the mechanic class with deep roots in trade unionism and prairie populism, are visits from the Japanese. Flaghorn has received numerous envoys from the Jupiter Motor Company, including local plant managers and even the CEO of the corporation, who flew in via Lear Jet all the way from Kyoto. Each time Flaghorn, or rather Jasper College, has received some major gift, like the soon-to-be-dedicated Takahashi Chapel, named for a Japanese student who last fall committed suicide by jumping in front of a train, and generous amounts of seed money for a new Japan Studies program. "Flaghorn and the Japs are in bed together," says Morley, "and aside from an elite minority, neither one has given the people that were born and raised here diddly squat."

Historically, a racist, xenophobic strain has been a component of Populism. Nowadays, Morley's peers tend to keep their unsettling views to themselves, knowing that it is unacceptable to utter them in polite society, heartfelt though they may be. Occasionally, however, the rabid true believers sprout from among them, in the form of Klansmen or Neo-Nazis. Jasper unfortunately possesses its own freelance skinhead with a long record of race-baiting, Ned Casey, who is presently in police custody for carrying out an assassination attempt against Milton Flaghorn, using a squirt gun loaded with red dye number two. Thankfully, Flaghorn was not injured in the incident, not counting the big exception of his pride. "It wasn't no violent act. It wasn't no act of hate. It was an act of free speech," claimed Casey during his arraignment. "What will happen next to ya'll if my rights are taken away?" he poignantly asked the press contingent as his captors led him back to his cell.

Flaghorn defends his actions by claiming that he is "cultivating good will between different cultures," and he points to the very tangible rewards that have resulted. Not without justification, he accuses his critics of holding "intolerant, politically incorrect views when it comes to the Japanese" — although, with a fawning book about Ronald Reagan's presidency under his belt, Flaghorn himself normally would fall on the right side of the P.C. spectrum. His hypocrisy is best revealed by his ruthless assault on hard-working student journalists who are guilty of nothing more than uncovering his profligate spending habits. Such punitive measures are designed to shut down the free flow of ideas, a chilling fact considering that the college environment should foster dialogue free from commercial influence or political retaliation.

The storyline emerging from the Heartland is that of a Third-World-style dictator selling out the farm to First-World corporations, a figure akin to Manuel Noriega, Ferdinand Marcos, and any of a long string of puppet leaders in Guatemala, Nicaragua, El Salvador, etc. Buddying up to corporate interests, spending lavish sums on a presidential mansion, attempting to squelch the opposition press — all these lead me to believe that Flaghorn is trying to govern Jasper College as if it were a banana republic. Maybe the board of trustees should consider changing his title from "president" to "el presidente."

When he was finished reading, he raised his eyes up to Ione's, which looked at him expectantly in return. "Yes? Yes? Yes?" she asked, then clapped her hands like a trainer coaching her pup to speak.

"Arf," said Underdog, completely deadpan.

"It's a cause célèbre, no?"

He shrugged, not grudging one inch of ground to the Race Fletcher mystique built up in everyone's mind, but most largely in Ione's, where a skyscraper loomed over grain silos. "I think it's good he publicized the situation . . .," he opined, trying to sound disinterested, unlike a participant.

She clapped her hands for more. Clap clap clap.

". . . and I think Flaghorn comes off in the article like the jackass he truly is." He tried to sound as objective and nonpartisan as possible. "But . . ."

"But?"

"There's nothing here nobody didn't know already."

"Race figures there's enough to persuade the FBI to look into the affair." She nudged closer to him, spoke *soto voce*. "Anything questionable in the area of international trade and they're involved."

"I thought it was an in-house thing. Take money from this column, put it into that." He noticed his voice rising in volume and intensity. He admonished himself to go easy; he didn't want to sound too authoritative on the subject.

"Who put up the front money? That's the million dollar question. The tuition collected tomorrow has to pay off a loan made today. When the right papers are found, Race is betting that they'll show the Jupiter Corporation loaned Flaghorn the money."

"Ah," he said, outwardly downplaying his understanding of the scheme and its impact on his life. Inside, he shuddered as if several bogeymen from his personal pantheon clopped their hands onto his shoulder all at once, a group that included monsters beneath his bed, killers inside his closet, demons down the basement stairs, and now FBI spooks behind every tree.

"It's like there's dynamite hidden under Flaghorn's chair," she declared. "And Race has got his hand on the plunger." She stuck her fingers in her ears and shut her eyes, waiting for the explosion.

There was just as much dynamite under Race Fletcher's chair, Underdog thought, and it was connected to a triggering device that he alone possessed. Still, for now, he elected to keep his finger off the red button; Race Fletcher's offense, glomming onto a scandal that Underdog broke, did not warrant its use. But it was not lost on Underdog that it could have been him, standing at attention in a blaze of glory and public acclaim, onto whose chest Ione fastened a gleaming medal, awarded for bravely battling the enemy in spite of impossible odds. How could he have known the scandal's outcome, that someone who seized the moment would emerge a hero? Once again, Underdog had left Race Fletcher an opening, a vacuum he sucked into.

"Changing the subject," she said, "but do any of your buddies down at Roger's Bar need any drums?"

"Huh? I mean, I know a few people. I can ask around. Why do you ask?" Smooth, gentle transitions were not one of her strong suits.

"Race is trying to sell his drum kit."

"Kit?"

"Sotheby's and a few other auction houses in New York turned him down when he offered to sell it. The dumbheads didn't recognize a true collector's item. It used to belong to Tommy Ramone, the original drummer for the Ramones. It's a long story, but the gist of it is that Race inherited Tommy's kit."

"I probably don't know anyone who cares a crap about its collector's value. Though they might be prone to buy it if it's in playable condition." Good, they had turned away from scandal-related red flags and orange warning signs and took a topical detour that he felt more comfortable with.

"He's like, 'Sell it, I haven't got the room' — no room in that humongous mansion of his, sure!"

"How much?"

"I think he'll go as low as a hundred bucks."

"At fifty, I believe he'd have himself a taker."

"Who? You?"

"Might be."

"Marred, blue-sparkle finish?"

"My room is marred and blue. Blend right in."

"It'd drive your landlady daffy."

"Mona's already daffy."

"Do you know how to play?"

"You let me worry about what I do with it."

"I'll submit your bid." Then she presented him with an order to print and pad mortgage loan applications, his signal that he was excused. Normally, Underdog hated the process of creating padded forms; the job of painting the edges of paper stacks with a special red rubbery glue was a messy one, sometimes spoiling pants or shoes. But for Ione and only Ione, a disagreeable chore turned into a labor of love. He foresaw a fun afternoon, licked his chops at the prospect of a return trip later that day.

* * *

Underdog proceeded to his next destination, the Physical Plant. By night, the structure was eerily aglow from spotlights, and muffled, vaguely sinister, industrial sounds could be heard from inside. When approaching, one had the impression it was a mad scientist's castle. By day, in contrast, it looked like a harmless, almost quaint, old-fashioned brick factory, complete with goopy mortar squeezing out between blonde bricks. Rising beside it was a tall smoke stack from which puffy white clouds emerged, coal smoke scrubbed as sterile as cotton balls by a system designed twenty years before by environmental engineers in Minneapolis.

The physical plant was entered by climbing onto a concrete loading dock and rolling aside an enormous sliding door built of steel and connected to a mess of pulleys and counterweights. Gong-like, the sound of this door opening reverberated inside a largely hollow structure lined with two gigantic boilers along either wall, long gray humming tanks that generated steam heat piped into every building on campus except the student center, which had its own furnace. The boilers were fired by coal delivered by rail in hopper cars that dumped their loads into a pit beneath train tracks entering the building through a huge portal. Chutes and conveyers then directed the coal into underground furnaces.

Upon entering the office, Underdog was glad-handed by Burt Moody, physical plant foreman, "the guy that's responsible for getting up in the middle of the night to fix stuff that's broke" as he introduced himself. Burt always welcomed his guests with a crushing handshake and a broad, nearly toothless smile, the result of gum disease brought on from his heavy snuff habit, since abandoned for fear of a certain case of mouth cancer. Summer or winter, Burt was never seen without his filthy Green Bay Packer stocking cap, which made him the object of ribbing from the Vikings and Bears fans among the maintenance staff (Jasper being part of a region with divided football loyalties). "Kept your pecker out of slamming doors?" asked Burt, his standard greeting.

"So far so good," answered Underdog, his rote reply.

"Good. 'Cause I got some receipts for ya' to Xerox in triplicate."

"Be back to you late this afternoon." He took the cluster of invoices and cash register slips, which had turned black from coal dust that settled on them, because the office inexplicably had no ceiling to protect paperwork arranged in neat piles on two enormous wooden desks purchased, according to Burt, from the Pentagon after World War Two. Burt's job promised to be even more tedious than Ione's: dozens of paper scraps of varying dimensions photocopied three times without aid of the automatic feeder.

"It's almost time," said Burt, peeking at his watch.

"Time?"

"For the EBS whistle." He referred to a steam whistle that alerted the county to take cover from tornadoes or missile attacks. To test Jasper's emergency response readiness, the Physical Plant let it roar every Wednesday morning at eleven o'clock. "You want to pull the cord?"

"Could I?"

"C'mon," said Burt, motioning Underdog to follow him outside the office. "I'll count down to zero, which is when you pull. You got to hold it down for two minutes. I'll signal you when you're done. But

I'm warning you. You're gonna' get a little spray of hot water. You'll muss your hair some."

"It'd be worth it."

"That's what I generally think." Burt led Underdog back through the clanging steel door and outside onto the loading platform. They stopped in front of a cluster of pipes and gauges connected to a kid-sized boiler, spawn of the two adults inside. Burt turned a faucet handle to the left until it wouldn't turn any further, and Underdog noticed the needle inside a semicircular gauge heading for the red zone. While they listened to rumblings and gurglings, almost like someone cleared his throat and bronchial tubes before delivering a speech, Burt unraveled a chain and told Underdog to get a firm grip on it. After final glances at the gauge and his watch, Burt shouted "three . . . two . . . one . . . let'er rip!" and Underdog yanked the chain downward. A deafening noise followed, a combination of everything loud he could imagine — truck horns, train whistles, jet engines, police sirens, burglar alarms, lighthouse foghorns, guitar feedback, quarry blasting, riverboat calliopes. But, although tremendously loud itself, the steam whistle had the curious effect of silencing all that clamored inside Underdog's head, from Ione to Judy and from Race Fletcher to Milton Flaghorn. Despite the shock to his ears, Underdog found it soothing to his nerves. Hearing nothing save his own, uncensored inner voice must be why he thought.

When time was up, Burt ran his index finger across his throat, the universal gesture meaning "Cut," and Underdog released the chain. The steam whistle died immediately, and Underdog was jolted back to reality, just like years ago in Peru, when trains rocking his bed and lulling him to sleep finished passing by his parents' house. After each train he awoke with a start, wishing that his favorite railroad lullaby, which silenced every scary noise, didn't have to end.

"That was a blast!" Underdog exclaimed. "Can I come back next week and do it all over again?"

"We'll see," answered Burt. "Meantime, keep your pecker outta' slamming doors," he cautioned.

"So far so good," said the departing Underdog, whose head and shoulders were happily soaked due to condensation dripping from overhead as steam was expelled.

Years later, Underdog could not recollect how he reached the decision to construct his first calliope. Interested persons asked him constantly, but the most he could remember was a deep desire to replicate the comfort he felt when Burt let him toot the EBS horn at the physical plant on that pivotal day.

SEVENTEEN

In order to construct his calliope, Underdog had to secure a workshop, preferably free or close to it, with access to an okay or better tool collection. Taking over the vacant half of Mona's two-car garage would have been the ideal situation, the absolute-most logical and convenient choice. Her car took up only half the garage, leaving a generous amount of room. Another plus, Jack Baine, Mona's deceased husband, had left behind a tolerable set of tools and a sturdy workbench. Underdog and Judy had once tested its mettle by making love on it; as she lay face-down across the plywood top, he drilled her from behind. Hung in several rows along the side of the workbench, wrenches of gradually increasing lengths got to swinging from the rhythm, until they began to clank together during their heaving co-climax, ringing out the news like chimes.

Such incidents were clearly consigned to the past, however, and here was what prevented Underdog from moving into the Baine garage: sharing the space with Judy. For also stowed in the garage were Judy's riding mower, push mower, and other sizable bits of lawn care equipment, including the rotor-tiller he often saw her struggle with, tearing up sod like a farm wife behind her plow horse. If their past together were any indication, sooner or later he was bound to stumble upon Judy and her frat rat beau splayed across Mona's car, acting out a hood ornament fantasy, or, in a sitting position, testing the spring action of her lawn tractor seat. Also loomed the likelihood of bumping into them during a fun-with-tools session on Jack Baine's workbench, where he suspected she'd return, as she appeared to have had a very good time there, slivers in her tits notwithstanding.

More ominous to his cause was Mona, who had turned on him ever since she learned that her daughter had severed ties, making Underdog paranoid that she was waiting for him to misstep so she could banish him from her boarding house. He didn't blame Mona, really; her motive, loyalty, was one he respected. Still, it put a strain on their landlord-tenant relationship. Normally one to sing or whistle while housekeeping, Mona could lately be seen chatting with herself, much in the distracted manner of Judy, in whom he also saw what must have been a genetic trait inherited from a clan of simple-minded chimps. Nowadays, Underdog avoided Mona whenever he could. Making the most recent rent payment, he slipped an envelope containing his check under her back door, whereas always in the past he handed it to her personally, then added a buttery "have a nice day" to stay in good with her. In paying the next month's rent, he considered the extremely impersonal method of mailing his check to her, thereby avoiding her scowls in case she chanced upon him waiting in the stairwell for an opportune moment to deliver his rent and dart away.

When he began irrationally to fear that Mona would create a rule against keeping musical instruments in your room, whether played or not, a misfortune of Reid's roommate metamorphosed into Underdog's gain: the roommate's Ford Escort suffered a fatal breakdown. After the heap was towed away, space in the garage behind Reid's boarding house became available. More convenient, Reid's landlord, Ed D. Parkman, a manly father of three boys who could quote you ancient baseball stats or classic auto specs, possessed an excellent set of tools due to his hobby of restoring a 1966 Chevy Malibu to its original muscle car state. A splendid specimen, almost fully prepped for impending spring and summer drives, to Underdog it symbolized everything male. All told, Underdog looked forward to working alongside Ed D., a regular, flash-you-a-butt-crease-from-bending-over kind of guy who charged him ten bucks a week to rent half of his garage, tossing into the bargain all the tools he could borrow.

Accommodations set, he placed a telephone call to Ione scheduling a time for Race Fletcher to drop off his percussive load. The day they brought the drums to Underdog's new spread, Jasper was enjoying atypically mild springtime weather. The ground had thawed enough to allow a few tulip plants to knife up from the softened earth, dressing up porches and foundations around the neighborhood and coyly promising relief from winter cold. Race backed his Range Rover, which fought and feinted through a mine field of mud puddles, up the gravel driveway. Underdog had never studied it very closely before, believing it a glorified Jeep or Blazer. He discovered he was wrong; in fact, he found himself grudgingly admiring the purr of its Rolls Royce engine, fenders as finely hewn as the haunches of a gazelle, all-terrain tires as sure-footed as a llama in the Andes, and brawny snout complete with space-age teflon bumper and caged-in headlights. He took note that Race had meandered off the driveway at one point, gouging a muddy tire track into Ed D.'s lawn. "If you're going to lay out the money for an expensive car, then learn how to drive the damn thing," he said under his breath while the happy couple decamped.

For what had to be the sixth or seventh time, Ione introduced Underdog to Race. As usual, no look of recognition registered in Race's steely, unreflective eyes; Underdog decided that nobody could be that woefully oblivious to the identity of someone he had repeatedly met — indeed, suffered a conk on the head from — without giving an Oscar-winning acting performance. Did this mean that Underdog had forged a deeper impression than Race outwardly indicated? Maybe the conk on the head Underdog gave him on the basketball court afflicted him with a case of selective amnesia.

Slumming in the student ghetto, Ione wore sweat pants and a tee shirt depicting a colorful stick figure trucking through the city, drawn by artist Keith Haring and seen plastered all over posters, watches, coffee mugs and key chains. Always costumed appropriately for every occasion, in this instance like a moving man, Race wore blue jeans and a "Big Apple Cartage/Est. 1926" sweat shirt. Underdog and Race unloaded the Range Rover's cargo bay in silence, hauling out round black drum cases that looked like over-sized hat boxes, while Ione released some pent-up silliness, like a three-year-old running off crows that landed in Ed D.'s front yard. As he received the items handed out the back hatch by Race, Underdog noticed that the vehicle's dashboard was made of genuine wood. Prominently mounted in the middle of the dash, able to be viewed from anywhere in the vehicle, was an elegant-looking clock, reminding him of the heirloom clock over the fireplace mantel in his parents' living room.

Once they completed unloading the vehicle, Ione halted her pirouettes around Ed D.'s lawn. "Bye!" she said to Underdog abruptly, then opened the passenger door and took her seat. Through the back window he stole a final glimpse of her hair, beautifully illuminated from late afternoon sun refracted in the windshield.

After which came the moment he dreaded: exchanging money with Race Fletcher, to whom he didn't want to pay anything, money, respect, it didn't matter. He suddenly regretted taking part in the transaction, like he predicted he would the very same minute he tendered his bid. Nevertheless, a man of his word in defiance of wiser second thoughts, Underdog pulled from the pocket of his denim jacket a check he had prepared in advance.

Returned now to the driver's seat, wraparound sunglasses on his face, Race lowered his window and leaned out to receive payment, looking as cool and detached as any anti-social anti-hero from the movies — Marlon Brando, James Dean, and all their Mickey Rourke/Harvey Keitel progeny — who acted punchy in the presence of squares. He snatched the check away and handed it to Ione. "Undervalued," he commented to no one in particular as he started the ignition. Watching them pull away in the Range Rover, Underdog wondered if that utterance were meant to play off his name in some insulting way.

*　*　*

Next, Underdog concentrated on the design of his calliope and the organization of its constituent parts. He understood totally the long-term nature of the project, so he leisurely researched the topic by playing hooky from work, supposedly on errands but really inside Inventors Memorial Library, named for the two claimants to the first barbed wire patent. There he listened to dusty mono records of calliope music, and he studied organ design books that contained actual plans of calliopes built during the nineteenth century. The most refined models were German in origin and almost Frankensteinian in scale — ten-foot walnut cabinets enclosing behind glass doors small ensembles of trumpets, trombones, kettle drums, glockenspiels, guitars, even violins, all played by steam-driven mechanical arms or brass tubes feeding air into mouthpieces. Like player pianos, music machines, as they came to be called, played a mixture of classical and popular songs from the Bavarian Hit Parade of 1886. One 1901 model he saw in a book from the Rare Book Room featured a papier mâché blacksmith who hammered along with the "Anvil Chorus" performed by a half-dozen stringed instruments, two trumpets and timpani.

Of heroic proportions, these were the contraptions he contrived to build, their grandiose style what he determined he could achieve by merging the following: pre-fab cabinetry from the Builders Square show room; his budding collection of musical instruments, which now included a dented cornet, a beat-up cello, and drums that once belonged to a punk rocker; an electric motor, whose housing sparked alarmingly when run; an old gas station air pump; and numerous throw-away rods unhitched from printing presses at work, worn down too much for printing tolerances, but close enough for jazz.

What eluded Underdog in his building of the calliope was what drove it. For the cornet, it would have to operate on the same principle as breath — inhale, exhale, inhale, exhale. He had inhalation and exhalation themselves down, of course: the air compressor provided a steady stream of air, from a source deeper than any human diaphragm. Turning on and off the flow of air would be the trick. Having played trombone in grade school and high school, he knew that with horns everything depended on the technique of tonguing. The flow of air had to be turned on and off quickly, eliciting a "Pah!" for each note.

For the drums the trick was up and down, reliant on a wrist-snap motion beating twice per bar for the snare drum and once each for the bass drum and cymbal. The cello had to be plucked, twice per bar, and the finger board required four placements, first in the tonic key for the verse, then in the dominant key for the chorus. Only three well-placed chords were needed, nice and simple for a person who never learned to do more with music arranging than score a few easy melodies. Herein lay the complication: required was a scheme that controlled a system of trips and wires and directed air flow.

Then it hit him one day as he poked through some old printing press parts in the closet underneath the bleachers at the print shop. The nervous system that conveyed instructions to each instrument would entail using the keypunch cards littering the floor of the closet. Remembering back to his freshman math class — which he only attended for two weeks pending his dismissal proceedings, and which only got him as far as binary numbers, but far enough for his present purposes — he remembered that the series of holes in the cards reflected combinations of zero and one: on and off, open and closed, beat and rest. Stringing a number of the cards together would cue correct fingerings and distribute air to wind instruments. Using an old keypunch machine, located for him by a secretary from the computer science department, he assembled a long reel of stapled computer cards that together drove a primitive computer program. Punching holes in four rows, he was able to extract four-part harmony from a Rube Goldberg compendium of unsung musical instruments and printing press entrails. Eventually, he wound the tape-like creation around a common garden hose reel, which turned with the aid of his electric motor.

* * *

Late one evening, in the middle of a block of warm and breezy spring days that put everyone in Jasper in a good mood, Underdog, Reid and Ed D. worked in the garage on their respective projects. Underdog concentrated like an old lady doing needlepoint on marking with a yellow highlighter the holes to be punched in his computer card reel. Reid studied his demographics textbook, scribbling notes on index cards periodically. Ed D. started out the evening monkeying around underneath his Malibu, but later did more beer-drinking than actual work. Mindful of his waist (and bust, thought Underdog), Ed D. guzzled Lite beer, which he shared with his two lessees. After an exaggerated warm-up of grabbing his hip bones to brace himself, Ed D. burped obnoxiously. "Whoa!" he bellowed in the aftermath, like a bear that had surprised itself by giving birth.

"The perforations in the cards really help," said Underdog, in an effort to take the focus off Ed D.'s gross behavior. "They allow you to line up the holes properly, make each instrument play exactly on the beat."

Reid looked up from his book, a quizzical look on his face, unaware of Ed D.'s outburst; like all grad students Underdog had met, Reid had developed the capacity to study anytime, anywhere, even in the loudest hub bub, like Crossroads Cafeteria in the Student Union or in the midst of a rollicking party. "U!" he called from across the garage, where he sat in a bucket seat ripped from one of Ed D.'s earlier projects. "I've been meaning to ask. How are you financing that calliope of yours?"

"I applied for two credit cards. Nobody's ever given me one before, but I think I just about make enough money now. When one or the other comes through, I'll charge the cabinet and some of the more expensive parts."

"How's your credit rating?" Ed D. asked expectantly, always on the lookout for an opportunity to drink a toast to something.

"Good, except for an episode a few years ago, when the college wanted some damn file-closing fee, and I refused to pay. They had just kicked me out. You'd have done the same."

"Fuck'm!" Ed D. responded, a true townie.

"They had a collection agency go after him," said Reid. "Tell Ed D. how you handled that."

"Every week they sent a letter demanding payment. Till finally, they sent me a letter threatening legal process. You know what I did? I took a can of spray paint and sprayed a big, red, runny blob of paint on the reply card and mailed it back. Four years later, I haven't heard anything more from them. It remains the only red mark on my record."

"That's good," Ed D. said, chuckling. "One time at the First Bank of Jasper drive-through, I emptied a whole can of dog food in one of their pneumatic tubes that shoots under the road and up inside the bank. The net reason why was because they pissed me off." All had a good, hearty, male-bonding belly laugh at this.

Then the buoyant mood waned a little, as Ed D. settled into a more sentimental phase of his drunken cycle. "What's that thing-a-ma-doo you're building called again?"

"It's a calliope."

"Callie-who?"

"Calliope."

"Yeah. What makes you wanna' build one of them things? If I was your age again, I'd learn me the electric guitar and have a big-ass Marshall amp out here blowin' off my garage door."

"I'm just inspired, I guess. I have this sense I've been dealt the hand of a lifetime. But I'm nervous about the game I'm in," he confessed, to something bigger than Ed D., Reid or anyone else in Jasper was cognizant. He sipped from his beer for a dose of courage.

"Curious you should use the word 'inspired,'" said Reid. "Because in Greek mythology, Kalliope was one of the muses."

"What's a moose?" asked Ed D.

"They were like a whole family of Tinkerbells that flit around the ancient Greeks inspiring different art forms — poetry, music, whatever. If I remember right, Kalliope was the muse of epic poetry." Reid closed his eyes and began to recite her bloodline. "Daughter of Zeus and Mnemosyne, Mother of Orpheus by Apollo. Sisters Thalia, muse of comedy . . ."

"In my list of muses, the muse of comedy would be Milton Flaghorn, the clown," sneered Underdog, who proceeded to inventory his own family of dysfunctional characters in response to Reid's list.

"Melpomene, muse of tragedy . . ."

"That would be Ione, no question."

"Erato, erotic poetry . . ."

"Definitely Judy."

"That leaves Kalliope," said Reid.

"Race Fletcher. Projected in 3-D on a sixty-foot movie screen, who puts all the motivational speakers on TV to shame."

"Funny you should mention them mooses in a female sense," commented Ed D. "They sound like an ornery lot."

"They're vixens. Sexy but capricious," explained Reid, who then prevailed upon the other two to call it a night. Ed D. shut off all the lights, unplugged the radio, lowered the garage door, and locked the garage behind them. Heading home, Underdog felt oddly sad to leave the conviviality of Ed D.'s auto den.

The following day saw him returned to Inventors Library, where he skimmed through books on Greek mythology to learn more about his muse. Turns out, Kalliope was chief of the muses. Despite a fair amount of further research, he found out little more about them; always, whenever they were mentioned, no personal details were given, like everyone had memorized their names and functions. To ask about them in ancient Greece must have been like asking who Jesus was in modern America. One final piece of info he dug up on Kalliope: she sometimes pulled a double shift as the muse of eloquence. With his pending deal for the TV rights to *The Green Acres Story*, Race Fletcher might win the derby for Ione's attention. Underdog would not surrender without an eloquent plea from his calliope, however.

EIGHTEEN

Because of Ione, Underdog had knocked off work early. She rattled him pretty good during his mid-afternoon stop at her office. Having lost an earring back, she began to act unaccountably hysterical, shrieking to him, "Find it! Find it!" She frantically patted down her lap, checking if it had clung to her spandex pants, while he crawled underneath her desk, nose to the linoleum like a sniffing blood hound. "Look for a clear plastic disc. A CLEAR PLASTIC DISC," she shouted. After a futile five minutes of looking for something impossible to see — an object that was invisible after all — he stood up and confessed he could not find the earring back. "You're no fucking use at all!" she snarled. "Sorry," was all he could think to say, and with legs gone to rubber he staggered out.

As he sat slurping from his glass and wincing at the bitter taste of English ale, Underdog castigated himself for being too quick to bite his lip and receive Ione's rebukes, not normally his first instinct when dealing with difficult people. Yet, even though he resented Ione for her behavior towards him earlier at the credit union, he struggled to forgive her at the same time. Why? Because he loved her too much to risk losing her — standing up for himself might cause her to sever their already tenuous connection. Besides, he had heard many times previously that her dead husband would abandon everything to do whatever she asked, no matter how unreasonable or impossible. She also described how Race Fletcher regularly satisfied her whims, from taking her to the newest dance club in New York City to leading her into a washroom stall for an on-campus quickie. Underdog simply refused to be out-performed by either individual in servicing a very tough customer.

Reid slipped into the bar stool next to Underdog's, then looked around the bar furtively; he seemed to regard a vacant bar as more of a threat than a full one — nobody to hide behind perhaps. "I'm A.W.O.L. right now," Reid whispered into Underdog's ear. "I hope my boss doesn't walk in and find me here, because I falsified my time card."

"My boss will never catch me playing hooky," said Underdog, the single thing he could speak confidently about on a day of uncertainty. "Ron's too cheap to buy his drinks in a bar. He and his buddies split a case of the cheapest beer available and sit around home discussing the camper tops they want to buy for their trucks. That's how they operate. They skimp on beer and spend their money on camping and hunting equipment."

Reid fully understood the species of townie that Underdog described, so he didn't believe it necessary to respond. Instead, he ordered a beer from the bartender, Roger's nephew Kent, another species of the genus *Townie*. Roger and Kent couldn't have been more different. Roger, though middle-aged, retained a youthful, butch demeanor and remained in tip-top physical shape, having broad shoulders built-up from years of lugging beer kegs and liquor cases, plus a trim waist that wedged into his jeans in a way that continued to draw the stares of young women. Kent, in contrast, by age thirty-one had smoked his way to a permanent bronchial infection and had acquired a pot belly from pulling himself and his friends too many complimentary draughts. The women nonetheless went for him, some because they expected him to inherit his uncle's business one day, others because of his reputation for stocking cocaine behind the bar, to which he gave his cute-girl-of-the-week access.

"How's your calliope progressing?" Reid asked.

"Good. Last night I soldered the brass tubing connecting the air pump and the cornet. Tonight, if I recover from the state I'm in, I go to the music store and order parts — new cello bow, cat gut, spit valve spring — and tomorrow at the hardware store I price out proportion air regulators."

"Sounds like your project's under control. But what about the other project, the one you're here recovering from?"

"I'll try to make it as understandable as possible." With his finger he drew a letter "A" on the dark walnut surface of the bar, blackboard where he planned to scrawl complex physics formulae. "Ione." Next, he drew a letter "B." "Race Fletcher."

Before he could draw a "C" to indicate himself, grabbing his attention was a newcomer who had strayed into the bar, a gaunt man of about forty, with rapidly receding brown hair and sunken, ashen eyes, as though gazing into the future while still an optimistic young man he used trick binoculars that inked his eye sockets black. His wardrobe also merited a second, sustained look: he wore a black button-down shirt marked by fanned playing cards above each breast pocket, the hand on the left a Royal Flush made up of clubs, on the right a Royal Flush made up of hearts; black Levi jeans that disappeared into pointy biker boots decorated with buckles, chains and spurs; earrings which dangled from both ears like mini chandeliers; and most strikingly a garnet nose ring, increasingly common among co-eds at the college, but never seen on a guy, and certainly never, ever in Roger's Bar. The stranger had the disoriented look of an out-of-town visitor, like a mom or dad asking directions to their daughter's dorm or a badge-wearing conference goer finding his way back to the student center. If Underdog had to guess his occupation, he would say Aging Rock Star.

He walked up to Kent, pulled out his wallet and showed him a photograph. "You ever seen her in here?" he asked, voice croaking like he chain-smoked straight through since childhood. Indeed, Underdog noticed that after each of his sentences a wisp of smoke was expelled from his mouth.

Kent looked at the photo, then looked appraisingly at the stranger; knowing Kent, he probably was gauging how much money he could earn if he answered "yes."

"I've spent the last hour scoping your town," the stranger continued. "This place is the closest in ambiance to what her tastes are."

"You boys know who this is?" asked Kent, taking the whole wallet away from the stranger and handing it to Reid.

Reid did a spit take, wetting the bar and floor with beer. "I believe my companion is well-acquainted," he said, handing the wallet over to Underdog.

The photo confirmed what Underdog had figured out in the interval. Although the guy was obviously an out-of-towner, Underdog felt like they had met already. Then it hit him, flattened him really, with all the force of hail striking corn: standing there, showing around a picture of Ione was Ione's husband, all in one piece and very much undead. Underdog recognized him from the portrait Ione kept in her living room. He handed the wallet back to its owner. "Geoffrey, right?"

"How did you know?"

"You're Ione's husband."

"Ex-husband. We got divorced last year. I'm trying to find her to ask her to stop mailing me nasty letters and making prank phone calls." He sighed exhaustedly, then gripped the bar to steady himself. If it were true he was married to Ione, it must have been a harrowing experience.

"She told me you were dead."

"I see her fantasy life is as healthy as ever. She used to say that about her first husband."

Underdog came close to peeing his pants; he shut off the spigot in the nick of time, although a few warm drops escaped, quickly went cold soaking into his briefs. "Married . . . ?"

"Twice. She used to tell me her first husband was killed in a car accident, but it turned out he was really alive, even though she could give you this gruesome, heart-wrenching description of his wrecked, dead body. The truth was she killed him off to cope with his absence. She had to kill him off in her mind, so that she could get on with her life. But in the meantime, she acted like the tragic, mourning widow, milking all the sympathy she could manage from every man who got in proximity. That's what originally roped me in." Getting himself situated, looking grateful to unburden his mind, he took a stool, lit an unfiltered Camel and ordered a Bloody Mary.

"I'm Tom, this is Reid."

"I'm Kent," said the bartender, setting in front of Geoffrey the house specialty Super Veggie Bloody Mary, which contained a whole truck farm of vegetables, including celery, zucchini, olives, pearl onions and string beans. Kent returned to his nearby listening post, which, given the sensitive nature of their conversation, seemed to Underdog annoyingly close. He was about to say something regarding how privacy should be respected, but his energy was sapped at present, so he resigned himself to what amounted to one of a bartender's main fringe benefits — eavesdropping.

"Do you date Ione?" Geoffrey asked Underdog. "You seem to know a lot about her."

"I used to date her, but she broke it off early on."

"Did she tell you the story of when she was gang-raped when she was tripping on LSD?"

"Yeah . . ."

"Total fiction. Oh, there's usually some true-life starting point to her stories. For instance, it's true that when she was 16, and she took a hit of acid, she was minorly pawed by her boyfriend, but he stopped when she asked. The story expanded because she freaked out on the acid and saw four or five images of her boyfriend at once." Geoffrey swigged close to half of his Bloody Mary, receiving in the process a snoot-full of leaves and stems. "Did she ever tell you about her abortion?" he asked, wiping his mouth.

"And the guy split?"

"Right. Only she was never pregnant. She thought she was pregnant once, but it was a false alarm. Turned out to be her period was running late, and she was terrified she was going to have to get an abortion. Before she had the facts, she informed the guy of his duty, he bolted, and she felt abandoned in her hour of need."

"Wow," Underdog said, transfixed by the confessions of this total stranger, with whom he shared a lot. He snapped to again; he had to ask about the scar on her belly. "Did she really go to jail and get stabbed in the stomach?"

"Yes and no. She landed in jail with about a hundred other people that the cops rounded up at a protest march. But her family bailed her out, and the charges were dropped. There was never any hard-case woman who stabbed her."

"Then how did she end up with her scar?"

"Self-inflicted. To attract the attention of her rich but out-of-touch North Shore parents, she stabbed herself when she was about fourteen. That occasion marked her first suicide attempt."

"How many of those were there?"

"I know of three. The last time, she OD'd on sleeping pills and champagne. Really put a damper on the post-gig party we were throwing that night. Incidentally, her little episode scared off a record company rep who went away thinking our band was full of druggies."

"How do you explain her?"

"Quite a phenomenon, wouldn't you agree? I've racked my brain every moment of every day — a divorce does that to you, you go through a period obsessed with how things turned out so wrong. My theory is this: Ione has always desired the good life, which means to her the widest possible range of experience. She began to identify with the rich kids she mingled with in school, kids who were sixteen going on forty-five. Kids who ran away from home to places like London on their parents' credit cards.

"Problem is, she personally led a sheltered suburban life. To compensate, she expanded on certain experiences to build a personal myth.

"Why? To make herself more appealing, a woman of experience, which is what she thinks men prefer. I'm sure you've seen her collection of Liza Minnelli pictures. She's enamored of the image of the vamp. She'll find a picture of Sally Bowles at a shop where they sell screen mementos, and she hangs it up on her wall. Then she imitates the image.

"An unfortunate side effect is that she sleeps with every man she takes a shine to. She keeps a running tally of conquered men as a way to quantify her experience."

"I never made it onto her list," Reid boasted, generating a hearty, tension-deflating collective laugh.

"I hope she learns some day that her life is full enough already," sighed Underdog, who joined Geoffrey in shaking heads at their mutual disapproval of Ione's fictions. The sobering mood had resumed.

"I hate to say it, but I think it'll never happen," stated Geoffrey. "She's too mentally ill. Maybe she's outright evil."

"She displays an evil temper sometimes, I'll grant you that," said Underdog. "Like at work this afternoon. She bit my head off for something completely out of my control."

"I ultimately walked out on her in the middle of one of her patented tantrums. I just got plain fed up one day when she was upset that she couldn't find anything to wear that didn't make her look fat. First of all, there were several outfits in her closet that would've worked out fine. Second, she wasn't fat in the least, but when she looked in the mirror she saw herself that way. She's damn quick to perceive imperfections in herself, although no one else is ever allowed. It was really quite comic, thinking back. There I stood, ducking blouses, pants and skirts she pulled out of her closet and threw at me."

"Then there are the times when she acts completely in control," said Underdog.

"And those are the times that she makes you love her dearly," Geoffrey responded.

In testimony to that sentiment, Underdog raised his glass, and toasted Geoffrey and himself. "Here's to being through it all together," he said, swallowing his ale in a troubled gulp that squeezed down his food pipe like a truck tire innertube.

"I just realized," said Geoffrey, "that if you saw Ione today, then you can tell me where I can track her down. I'm afraid she doesn't leave a return address on her letters."

"Right about now, I'd say she's knocking off work. She lives in a trailer park . . ."

"A trailer park?"

". . . outside of town. I'll drive there with you and show you where she lives. But I'll leave you to yourselves for the big reunion."

"Deal," said Geoffrey. Then everyone drank up; Reid announced he was heading back to campus, and Underdog and Geoffrey headed for the latter's car, which turned out to be an early seventies BMW. Outside, the body retained its youthful, rust-free exterior. Inside, foam rubber oozed from upholstery splitting along every seam. During the whole trip, especially on the bumpy backroads outside town, Underdog felt a spring attempting to screw his ass through his pants.

Once inside Trailerville, he instructed Geoffrey to drive slowly and inconspicuously while he kept an eye out for Ione's V.W. Bug. "There's her place," he said, pointing to her spic-and-span homestead. "She's not home yet. And I can't guarantee you when she'll arrive. There's a boyfriend, you see. Race Fletcher. She might be off gallivanting somewhere with him."

"She's dating Race Fletcher right now? The guy who writes that dumb column for *Strobe Magazine*?" He took his hands off the steering wheel and threw them into the air in astonishment; the car swerved off the gravel path. "Well, she always was a social climber of the first caliber," he said, gripping the wheel again and steering back onto the roadway. "You know, I wrote several songs about her," he said, suddenly striking a melancholy minor chord.

"'Red Hair on my Mind,' right? She took a lot of pride in that one. She claimed to be your muse."

"She was. But that was a long time ago."

"It sounds like she was a positive muse for you. I think for me she's a negative muse. I'm inspired more from a need to get even."

"Oh, there was a ton of that in my relationship with her, too," said Geoffrey wistfully as he cut the engine and shifted his car into Park.

"I hated you for a long time, you know," confided Underdog. "You were everything in her mind, and I was nothing. No offense, but now that we've met, and I see that you're a mere mortal like the rest of us, I feel much better."

"I'm glad you've made your peace towards me," said Geoffrey. "Now I'm going to try my hardest to make my peace with Ione. I'll leave you and her to make your own, separate peace. Thanks for bringing me here." He shook Underdog's hand.

"Good luck. You'll need all you can muster," said Underdog, getting out of Geoffrey's car and entering a blustery outdoors that looked like could blow up any minute into a major thunderstorm. He began the trek home. Looking behind him into the car window as he walked away, he saw that Geoffrey had bowed his head and was pinching the bridge of his nose, possibly crying.

* * *

Rather than follow Highway Seventeen, Underdog took off cross-country, traversing freshly plowed farm land. Blown dirt skittered over furrows and flew up into his face. Distant thunder grumbled, and lightning cast its electric web across the sky — instant death if it caught you, as poor Jack Baine discovered less than a mile from where

Underdog walked. When successive sheets of rain began pummeling him, he weighed his options. His only protection from the storm were stands of trees planted along property lines. Yet standing underneath trees in the open prairie was tantamount to inviting lightning to strike. Going back to Trailerville was unwise also; trailer parks were tornado magnets, and this storm looked like it had tornado potential. He decided to take his chances running across open ground in the direction of town and hoping for the best.

Coupled with naked terror from the storm were intensely focused thoughts of the day's events. He decided that Ione's problem lay in lacking any outlet to distinguish herself. Her boyfriend Race Fletcher had his passion for *Green Acres*, his monthly column in *Strobe*, his house, his Corvette, his Range Rover. Her ex-husband had his music career, playing in Chicago nightclubs and recording CDs for a small record label (although to Underdog it looked like his opportunities to strike it big were running out fast). Ione's main rival Judy Baine, classic underachiever that she was, ran her own lawn care business, which, like her sexual escapades, she threw herself into whole-heartedly. Recently, Underdog had acquired himself a project, distinguishing himself from the herd by assembling his calliope.

Ione's outward expressions of self amounted to nothing save stories. Some were true, like the accounts of her trips to New York with Race Fletcher, though he suddenly doubted their veracity, too. Others were exaggerated, like those of her rapes, molestations and abortion. Still others were total fabrications, like that of her husband's death. As he saw it, she traipsed through life writing and re-writing a soap opera storyline, with herself as the star. Each day reaffirmed that for those who have nothing, stories were a revelation, because they were the one thing that could be reliably conjured from nothing. He didn't get why a woman who grew up with every advantage, who obtained a storehouse of social skills, and who possessed natural acting ability, felt so empty. Maybe he didn't understand because he was a townie; he never lived in the suburbs and so never contended with rich people having problems with existence.

A fairly close hit of lightning, immediately followed by a tremendous crack of thunder, indicated that the worst of the storm was upon him. South of the field he was jogging through he saw Lock & Leave, a self-storage facility by the highway. He proceeded in that direction praying he found an unlocked shed where he could take shelter. Three more lightning strikes and attendant thunder concussions exploded in his wake. He suddenly felt like he was charging across a battle field in a scene from a World War Two movie shown on late-night television. A practiced fence climber, he vaulted over the six-foot chain link fence as efficient as John Wayne or Lee Marvin. Then he ran up an aisle between rows of storage units, with eyes peeled for a lock-free garage door. Finding one, he raised it part-way and dove inside the unit like it were a bomb-proof bunker. After a welcome lull in the storm, he was shaken to his core by lightning touching down in the storage complex just a few rows away, a mortar shell landing in a besieged village. Overhead, rain followed by hail the size of shooter marbles pelted the corrugated tin roof. Reverting to the days of his childhood when he sang loudly for confidence when frightened out of his underpants, he murmured like a mantra, "I will survive all of this. I will survive all of this," meaning both the bellicose weather and his buffeted soul.

NINETEEN

A few weeks after the severe thunder storm that almost killed Underdog — which indeed had killed two, when, one county to the east, a tornado flipped over a dump truck containing two occupants and four tons of silica sand as easily as a Tonka truck — he was sitting in the print shop hunched over the saddle stitching machine. With final exams approaching, Ron Sullivan commanded him to step up the pace in binding what was left of ten thousand blue examination booklets that the print shop printed in slack times all spring long. Ordered twice per year, with production costs next to nothing and a built-in market, blue books provided a steady stream of income to an already profitable division of the college.

In fact, it seemed that the print shop would very soon enjoy a further boon: an administrator-wannabe professor was lobbying the college to launch a textbook publishing operation. Like a few private photocopy chains which had similar systems already in place, he and his staff would solicit reading lists from faculty, secure permission to reprint copyrighted material, then edit and print "text booklets" custom-tailored for a professor's precise requirements. Most important, a public/private partnership grant from the state would radically defray expenses, allowing the college to enjoy mark-ups of four to five hundred percent on the text booklets sold to captive student consumers. The scheme seemed like genius to Underdog, as he pondered sopping his biscuit in the gravy train heading round the bend.

Experienced with the task at hand, organized not to waste steps, efficient when he wanted to be, Underdog glided through the process of binding the exam books. First, he took from a paper column rising to the ceiling short stacks of white bond punctuated every four sheets by blue. Next, he fed these stacks into a folding machine that counted to five then folded the bundle in half, thus creating booklets of sixteen lined writing pages plus a cover. Last, he plucked the booklets from the output tray and put two staples in their spines by stomping twice on a foot pedal. While he took a break to re-load the saddle stitcher reel with a new coil of ten-gauge steel wire, lost amid dreams of a better-paying union position, the moment he feared had finally come: he was busted.

Out of the corner of his eye, he saw Ron Sullivan leading two men from the office down the spiral staircase to the shop floor. The former individual was Ziggy, Castle Hall's rotund security guard, the most senior officer on the campus police; the latter was a man Underdog didn't recognize but figured was some sort of plainclothes cop. From the very moment they began their descent, he could feel their officious glares trained on him like laser tracking beams from high-powered rifles. He looked around to see if any red dots appeared on the back of his shirt. Deciding to brave their fire frontally, he turned around to surrender.

"These boys came investigating the print shop regarding our role in Flaghorngate," said Ron. "I told 'em I sure as hell didn't spill the beans. But I bet I knew who did." Ron sure was bringing a lot of enthusiasm to the process. Maybe he was bucking for some reward.

"I've been expecting you," said Underdog, wilting under the heated, accusatory looks directed at him, which converted cold breakfast cereal in his stomach to piping hot Cream of Wheat.

"Are you going to come along peaceable?" asked Ziggy, patting the handcuffs clipped onto his hip, which caused his large, glutinous belly to ripple under his police uniform. It was plain Ziggy wanted a reason to slap the cuffs on him, to put Underdog in his place like them recalcitrant frat boys he took into custody every weekend.

"Yes," said Underdog, irritated that he had to dignify that question with an answer. It was only then that he wanted to punch somebody — motivated more from the insinuation of violence on his part than his actual arrest.

Obviously bored with the proceedings, the stranger — boy, it sure seemed like an awful lot of strangers held his fate in their hands lately — walked about the shop in silent boredom with his hands in the pockets of his khaki trench coat. Every so often he paused to lean over and glance at a test or flyer. Underdog suspected that, to kill time, he played games of pocket pool underneath his coat. "Left testicle in corner pocket," thought Underdog, mocking him silently.

As the group departed, the stranger fell into step behind Underdog, who listened blankly to Ziggy read him his constitutional rights off a card that he pulled from his hat band. "We caught the bugger!" gloated Ron to every person they passed in the hall. "He's the missing link!"

"Just taking him in for routine questioning," countered a stern, business-like Ziggy. "Let's none of us get too excitable," he cautioned the swelling mob of onlookers that began to follow behind the posse and its prisoner marching single-file up the twisting asphalt path that led to President's Hall, housing Flaghorn in his expansive office, plus a flock of lesser functionaries who were kept in offices the size of chicken coops.

Upon entering the outer office, Underdog smelled a strong mixture of hurt and foul perfume. The source was Sharon, whom he could immediately tell felt grievously wounded by his actions. Mindful of her aggressive nature and her three-to-two weight advantage over him, he hoped that his captors would be able to stave off an attack in case she decided to charge. A great relief, she simply stood aside and solemnly announced, "He's expecting you," thankfully keeping her fists out of Underdog's face, but neither blinking nor taking her eyes off him for one millisecond.

Beyond two elaborately carved oaken doors, ceremoniously swung open by Ziggy, there sat a very peeved Milton Flaghorn behind a massive marble-topped desk. Sparsely furnished with a writing blotter and a fancy wood-handled pen stuck into a heavy pewter base, Flaghorn's desk was so big that you could probably land a jet airplane on it. "Sit," he said to the assembled company, directing Underdog and Ron Sullivan into the leather chairs opposite the desk from him and waving the two cops over to a round mahogany conference table that seated six. Underdog took a quick appraisal of the room, noticing in particular a series of signed photographs along one wall that pictured a bleached-out Flaghorn posing beside a freckled Ronald Reagan, a sunburned George Bush, and a deeply tanned Governor Richardson, all of them sporting golf attire.

His responsibilities at an end for the present, Ziggy began staring out the window, most likely at college women who at this time of year broke out the Rollerblades, tube tops and bicycle shorts. As they skated between classes, male members of the college community were treated to quality views of succulent shoulders, untethered breasts, compact rumps and sinewy legs. For his part, the undercover cop reached into a briefcase on the floor and pulled out a writing tablet. So far he hadn't spoken a word; ignoring everyone in the room, he noisily turned over a few pages in his writing pad, read to himself a minute, turned over a few more pages, then began jotting down more notes.

"I believe you are acquainted with Ziggy from Campus Police," said Flaghorn to Underdog, initiating matters. "That," he continued, pointing to the stranger on Ziggy's right, "is Inspector Malberg,

Federal Bureau of Investigation. He's in Jasper as part of a federal probe into the, ahem, difficulties the college is presently experiencing."

The G-man lifted his bald pate a moment, giving Underdog a mental mug shot of his expressionless face, then he lowered his head again and absorbed himself once more in his writing pad. His presence in the room gave Underdog the chills, for he recognized the adult version of a familiar type from his childhood: Malberg used to be one of those kids whom every other grade schooler shunned, because he raised his hand to answer every single question asked during class and because he dropped every single ball thrown to him at recess. In short, Inspector Malberg was exactly like every nerdy kid that Underdog ever knew while growing up; if he decided to avenge his childhood persecution on Underdog, then Underdog would shortly become rotisserie chicken.

"Uh, aren't I entitled to a lawyer?" asked Underdog. "I mean, with the FBI involved . . ."

"You haven't been charged with any crime," Flaghorn informed him. "The FBI is my concern, not yours. Consider this a meeting with your employer."

"Am I arrested or what?" asked Underdog, who felt increasingly concerned about the legality of the goings on. So alarmed was he, his adrenal glands were inducing all manner of shudders, jolts and shocks.

"Ziggy abided by a rule which requires a police escort if there is the slightest threat to college personnel or property. He read you your rights in accordance with legal procedure, but, as I said before, you are not facing any legal charges at present. What you are facing, Emmendorfer, is termination from employment at this college.

"A reporter at the *Chronicler* has confessed to conspiring to obtain and publish the contents of confidential college documents. The party has identified you as his source. In your capacity as college employee, you violated the terms of a confidentiality agreement that you signed upon employment. Mr. Sullivan?"

"Yesssir?" Ron stood at attention, even clicked his heels together, like a suck-up sergeant to his commandant.

"Did Mr. Emmendorfer sign a confidentiality agreement when he was hired four years ago?"

"Yessir, he did. Along with all the other proper forms, like his withholding form, and the form testifying he's a U.S. citizen."

"Then we really need to go no further. These are perfectly valid grounds for dismissal. I'm not even legally bound to listen to your side of the story. However, if you do wish to challenge your firing, I always have Section 27.C of the college by-laws to fall back on, which permits at-will termination of an employee, with or without cause.

"Do you have anything to add, Inspector Malberg?"

"Nope, nothing. He's small fry," said the G-man, without looking up from his note pad.

"And you are a shrimp dick," Underdog thought about retorting, but quickly dropped the idea, considering that it didn't look like he was going to jail or be in serious trouble with the law. And he didn't want to antagonize anybody into changing his mind on that account. More than anything, it appeared that Flaghorn was working damage control, trying his damnedest to sweep the whole tawdry episode under the rug. With the FBI tracking his every move, Flaghorn clearly had much bigger problems in life than Underdog. Underdog had just been ousted from his job, a serious headache to be sure, but Flaghorn's current troubles amounted to brain cancer.

"That's it? I'm fired?" Underdog asked, to be certain of the verdict.

"Yes. And now you're dismissed from this office. Shall I have Ziggy escort you back to the print shop to retrieve your personal possessions, or will you send someone later to pick them up?"

"I'll send my friend Reid," Underdog opted, trying to spare himself further indignity at the college's hands, which had twice now shoved him out the door, never to return.

Flaghorn got up from his chair; everybody else in the office except Malberg rose with him. "Two down, only one to go," Flaghorn sighed in the direction of Malberg. The blast of spent air was a sure indication that Flaghorn's feathers were ruffled, despite the cocksure way in which he dispensed with Underdog. Yet Underdog could foretell his come-uppance; the tighter Flaghorn squeezed his fist, the more slime escaped between his fingers.

Underdog headed towards the door, trying his best to avoid getting his feet stuck in the layers of B.S. that crept up the walls of Flaghorn's office and threatened to bury ex-presidents up to their noses. However, he found himself unable to extricate himself from the ooze, which had grabbed hold of his leg like a giant tentacle. To break free, he decided to light the doomsday stink bomb that he had secretly been carrying around with him these many months.

He turned around, addressed Flaghorn. "What if I shared some scandalous information about Race Fletcher? Could I win my job back?"

Taken aback that Underdog hadn't yielded to his ironclad authority, Flaghorn looked to Ziggy for him to intervene.

"I mean, it's no secret around town that you're pissed off about the article he published in *Strobe Magazine*," he added encouragingly.

"If what you tell me helps rid him from my sight, there could be some favors granted, some quid pro quo arrangements made," Flaghorn said. The scowl dissipated from his face, a favorable sign. He lowered himself back into his fat swivel chair, ordered Underdog to return to his previous seat, then dismissed Ron Sullivan from their midst. Upon realizing that he would miss out on witnessing the scandal unfold in a brand new direction, Ron's mouth wadded into a disappointed pout, and he sullenly left, shutting the door behind him as hushed as he could.

Underdog proceeded to relate his knowledge of how someone he knew from the college thought he had spotted Race Fletcher performing sex acts in a pornographic movie. After seeing the movie with his own eyes, Underdog was prepared to swear that the actor in question was for a fact Race Fletcher. He proceeded to explain that his shamrock tattoo positively identified him. Then he described the particulars of watching the movie at Sally Valentine's, right down to indicating which viewing booth Flaghorn should select if he wanted to see for himself that Underdog spoke the truth. He went so far as to volunteer the services of Reid — whom he hoped forgave him for implicating him in the scandal — in seconding everything that Underdog had said. "Reid's an honor roll grad student. Ask him, if you don't trust the word of a townie."

Flaghorn pondered his possibilities for a moment. Underdog was impressed with how he managed to do all his ciphering in his head, without the assistance of calculator, scratch paper or abacus. "Although he fills an endowed chair, this does not bestow on Fletcher tenure status," Flaghorn began. "We could easily not renew his contract. Invoke a clause from the by-laws prohibiting corrupt or immoral behavior on the part of faculty . . .

"Very well," he said, agreeing to Underdog's terms, "you are reinstated to your previous post. Do I have clearance from the FBI?" he asked Malberg.

"No federal crime has been committed here," the G-man answered.

"Excellent," Flaghorn said, then drew his lips into a smug sphincter of a smile. "But I advise you," he continued, "breathe not a word to anyone about what has transpired in this office. Your job depends on your ability to keep mum."

"Well, in the last minute I've reconsidered my offer," said Underdog, standing up in what he reckoned was a serious breach in decorum — "Nobody gets up before me!" he imagined an appalled Flaghorn saying. "Oh, you can keep the Race Fletcher tip," he continued. "But you can take your job offer and shove it up your ass. Later, gentlemen." Not waiting around for a reaction, he threw open one of the heavy oaken doors and stormed out, slamming the door behind him as hard as he could, in the process straining a ligament in his lower back. A big swoosh of air accompanied him into the outer office, fanning Sharon's nauseating perfume up his nostrils. "Somebody had to, so I'm telling you," he said to a startled, one might even say frightened, Sharon. "That cheap-ass perfume of yours makes it smell like a gas chamber in here."

When he arrived outside, Underdog confronted an unruly mass of people that included students, staff, teachers and even a smattering of townies. Everyone gathered around a cordoned-off area guarded by campus police at the base of the stairs leading into President's Hall. He recognized a dozen or so faces in the crowd of about two hundred, including Reid; Ron Sullivan; Ione; Rotten Fingertips; Gina Mantua, the editor of the *Chronicler*; Chuck, who evidently had sold him out to Flaghorn; Mildred, the grandmotherly secretary from payroll; Errol Watson, top pressman at the print shop; and a few others whose names he could not recall while standing so nakedly in the public spotlight. A great cheer flooded his ears, apparently in his honor, followed by calls of "What happened?" and "What did he say?"

Normally reticent to speak in front of such large numbers, right this moment he felt totally unembarrassed, like he truly had nothing left to lose. His lungs fully limbered and his pipes well-moistened, he hollered as loud as a calliope, "Fucking Flaghorn fired me. For revealing what a fink he is to the *Chronicler*."

The crowd booed Flaghorn initially, then, in a confusing transition of simultaneous boos, cheers and localized claps, the crowd started cheering, clapping and whistling in praise of Underdog's heroic deed.

"Now, if you'll excuse me, I've got some thinking to do." He stepped over the yellow police tape and bludgeoned his way through the crowd. "God is love!" he heard a Campus Christer shout reassuringly.

"God is dead," he shouted back as the full effect of his unemployment began to sink in.

"The sun will come up tomorrow!" sang a giddy female student of about eighteen, no doubt someone with colorful kitten and rainbow posters on her dorm room walls.

"Sunrises set," he informed her, thinking that it was too late today, but first thing tomorrow he needed to visit the unemployment office downtown.

Behind him, he heard through a bull horn the brusque voice of Ziggy saying that the party was over, and it was time for everybody to "disperse peaceable-like." Out of respect to Underdog's need for privacy, no one followed him, which was great, because he hated to lead anybody on a wild goose chase while he located where he was supposed to go and determined what he was supposed to do next.

* * *

At around eight in the evening, Underdog showed up on Ione's doorstep. He had spent the previous three hours roaming through Jasper and the surrounding countryside, first stopping in Civic Park, where he sat awhile watching a bunch of townies play a game of softball. The batting team milled around a beer keg as they waited for their ups; each member of the fielding team had a plastic cup of beer stationed nearby in the grass. Underdog marveled in particular at the skill of the second baseman, who, with a half-full cup of beer held between his teeth, scooped up grounders and threw out runners at first without spilling a drop.

Soon tiring of the game, he continued onward, eventually landing on the train tracks, which he followed for two miles until he reached his second stop, the coaling tower. There he ran across two automobiles parked nose-to-nose on the lane. Inside each car a single male occupant's head was visible through the windows. Approaching closer, he cracked up when he discovered what was occurring: both guys were looking at each other while receiving oral sex from female companions whose bobbing heads Underdog occasionally glimpsed. At first he figured that he stumbled onto frat boys on a double date. This belief was dispelled when he noticed that one car had a Jasper High School sticker in the back window, and the other had a Jasper College parking sticker in the front window, which indicated complete strangers might be sharing a variation on communal sex. Too self-conscious to stick around such goings on, he made his way to the third stop of the night, Trailerville, traveling overland, via pastures thick with brambles and cockleburs, plants with longer growing seasons than corn, which hadn't yet begun to unfurl its leaves in the newly planted fields he traipsed through.

By the time he reached Ione's he was limping, having twisted his ankle on a rock disguised as a dirt clod. The yellow Volkswagen minus the brown Range Rover equaled he had caught her at home absent

Race Fletcher. Waiting for her to open the door, he bent over to pick off the burrs and stickers which had attached themselves to his jeans.

"Well. If it isn't the avenging angel. *Entre-vous*," she said, opening the storm door. She sat on her sofa while he took a quick inventory: more misshapen pottery ("I have an addiction for ceramic pieces," she said), another Liza Minnelli photo ("a still from her upcoming TV special"), and, opposite the sofa, a bean bag chair decorated with about a billion multicolored clothes buttons sewn onto its hide, where she asked him to sit, adding that this chair was "from a loft studio in Tribeca."

Uncertain about how to proceed, he looked into her eyes. Beyond haunted, they looked positively vacant, a vast region of nothingness which allowed Underdog to gaze dozens of light years into empty space. He almost forgot why he came, so lost was he inside her infinite romantic pretense.

"That was quite an escapade you pulled today," she said flatly, relieving him of responsibility for opening the conversation but still leaving him the task of setting the tone of their meeting.

"I think it had its dramatic aspect. I'm a folk hero now, right up there with your precious Race Fletcher," he said. Yes, it was all emerging now; a slow, acidic burn rose in his throat, indicating that the organ soup which had simmered below was finally boiling over. He now realized that all along a crazy woman had control of the knob turning up or down the flame.

"Race left here not too long ago," she said blankly, while reaching up under her black sleeveless blouse with her left hand and matter-of-factly scratching her pale-as-marble stomach. "He told me that you've apparently been singing like a stool pigeon to Flaghorn. Who's not renewing his contract — citing 'moral turpitude' or some such nonsense."

"That bastard Flaghorn. He tells me to keep quiet about things, and here he's blabbing about my involvement to the last person on earth I wanted to know." Underdog shook his head, appalled but on second thought unsurprised that Flaghorn had broken his pledge to keep matters between them confidential — Underdog's insulting him and storming out probably released Flaghorn from all liability.

He looked again at Ione; her lower lip quivered, the first signal that her fantasy world was about to go kerbang. He decided to toss in a few further wads of plastique. "Did Race tell you what Flaghorn found morally objectionable? That he acted in dirty movies? That he fucked on camera? Well, it's true. I'll bet news of this will shock even you," he said, thinking that she would need to make up some awfully weird shit to embellish this portion of her saga for benefit of future husbands and boyfriends.

"That doesn't come as any shock. Race didn't hide his adult film career from me. In fact," she said, while retrieving a manila envelope from the bottom drawer of her china hutch, "he gave me this on our third date." She handed the envelope to Underdog, who opened it and pulled out a black and white publicity photo of a naked couple. Although his head was cropped off, Underdog immediately recognized from his shamrock tattoo that the man in the picture was Race Fletcher. The woman in the picture licked the underside of his erection while staring into the camera with heavily made-up eyes and lolling lids that betrayed more interest in her next cigarette than in the penis on her tongue. In the lower right corner he read,

Little Lost Chastity and Race Fletcher

Starring In *Smokey and the Babe, Part II*

Times Square Enterprises, 212/555-1279

"You want to see a video?" she asked. "I have a collection of Race appearing in seven or eight short clips. There's even a gay scene."

"I think I'll pass."

"Good. Even though I'm a nude model myself, I've decided it upsets me too much to see Race screwing other people. At least I never screwed anyone for profit." She slipped the photo back into the envelope and returned it to the drawer in the china hutch.

"So you knew?"

"Of course, I knew. How do you think Race got his nickname? He selected it because of the racy films he was making."

"How extensive was his, um, career?"

"About fifteen or twenty years ago, after moving to New York for grad school, a male model told him to call an escort service to see about picking up some extra tuition money. Attracted by his wholesome midwestern looks, they brought him into their stable right away. Race ended up studying literature by day and having sex for money by night.

"It's really quite fascinating to hear about. See, the escort service advertised in the yellow pages. Every night, Race got a list of two or three men to visit, mostly out-of-towners staying in midtown hotels.

The agency charged fifty bucks per appointment. His cut was twenty-five, plus tips. Not bad for a half-hour of work, huh?

"Pretty soon he caught on that the real money lay in magazine and film work, so he started posing for porn magazines and making loops for the Times Square movie arcades. Besides better pay, it suited his straight lifestyle better than the agency work, where he was expected to trade blow jobs with the clientele.

"So that's how Race supplemented his grad school stipend — working in the sex industry for a couple of years."

"He's lucky he didn't catch AIDS from the experience," commented Underdog.

"His timing was fortunate. He quit when he got his master's degree in the late seventies, right before the initial outbreak."

"Well, it's a pretty sleazy story, I must say."

"I agree," she sighed. "That's my life: one sleazy story followed by another."

He smirked at this statement, because for once she was telling the truth. Her simple act of honesty revealed to him the surprising fact that she was a lousy actress after all — it was easy to make up total fictions; it was quite difficult to pretend that she felt okay about Race's Fletcher's checkered past.

"Anyway, to get back on track," she said. "Race informed me that he's moving away from Jasper very soon. A TV studio in Hollywood is planning to do a remake of *Green Acres*, and they hired him as a creative consultant — at a minimum of three-hundred thousand dollars, maybe more if a network picks up the show. He's already put his house on the market, although he doubts anyone will buy it at a price anywhere near what he paid. 'My whole Jasper experience has been a losing proposition,' he says." For the first time in Underdog's presence, she peeled some skin off her fingers, expanding on the exposed lower layers visible on several fingertips already, no doubt started during Race Fletcher's visit earlier that evening. The way she induced the purple patches to grow at nearly geometric rates brought to mind the spreading of mold.

"And I've got YOU to thank for taking him away from me," she said, every letter in this utterance spiraling toward him like a tomahawk. "He said that if he wasn't fired from the college, he would've come back to Jasper to teach again in the fall, once the TV show premiered. But now he doesn't have a reason to return."

"Aren't you moving out to Hollywood, too?" he asked, knowing full well that she wasn't, or else she would have begun bragging about it the very first thing. Asking this question was a way to rub salt into her wounds — real wounds this time which visibly pained her.

"I haven't been invited," she answered, then she began to sob. Ouch! That must sting, thought Underdog, watching her dab away tears with her raw fingertips.

After recovering her composure somewhat, she spoke more honestly than he ever had believed her capable of: "Every man I've loved in my life has ended up leaving me."

"I'm not leaving you," he declared, reaching over with his handkerchief to aid her in drying her eyes. He could feel his immunity to her declining, the number of Ione antibodies in his blood plummeting. Perhaps her personality truly was undergoing a reformation, now that her craving for drama had resulted in showing her how life was tragic enough without inviting tragedy. Or making it up.

All of a sudden she slapped his hand away from her face and darted into her bedroom. She emerged a moment later, clutching a stack of letters, lovingly bow-tied with violet gift-wrapping ribbon. She yanked off the ribbon like pulling a rip cord to a parachute, then rifled through them in search of a particular letter. "These are all that remain of my dead husband," she explained.

"Uh huh," said a crestfallen Underdog, chilled to the core like a new set of bones were taken from a freezer and implanted in his body.

"Whenever I feel overly stressed, I dig out these letters and read them."

"Uh huh."

"You know how Christians consult the Bible, matching verses with specific occasions? It's the same way with these letters. They're my equivalent of Psalms or Song of Solomon. Mostly the latter, because several are very erotic."

"And what is the sacred text for today?" he asked.

"From January 29th, 1990." She began to read silently.

"Aren't you going to read it out loud?"

"Oh, no. These are extremely private. No one's allowed to read these letters but me." She continued reading to herself.

"I see," he said, hating her letters with almost religious zeal for being props in her charade. If this were the Middle East, and not the middle west, and he were a Muslim fundamentalist, he could see himself tossing these documents on a bonfire. When people from Iran (or Nazi Germany, for that matter) resorted to this, the goal was always the same: obliterate someone else's history. Underdog felt this type of passion towards Ione and her letters — ever since their first date, he had wanted to erase Ione's past, put her in the here-and-now where he would have a chance with her. Now he understood that she was simply too sick in the head to respond to his attentions. So he reconsidered his tactics: rather than burn her letters like a terrorist, he needed to assume the role of psychological commando — by sneaking up to the perimeter of the mental equivalent of enemy headquarters, chucking a grenade over the fence, and running away before the consequent inferno engulfed him, too.

"Gotten a letter from Geoffrey lately?" he asked, then smiled a smile as wide as angel wings.

Until that time, she was reading a letter from the middle of her stack, lost in fleshing out a fond recollection prompted by the letter. Then she lifted her head and met his gaze with an icy stare, her eyes frosting over like antifreeze meeting its freezing point at well over a hundred degrees below zero. "Is that supposed to be a joke?" she asked.

"Well, no, not really, given the fact I bumped into him a couple of weeks ago at Roger's. Or was that his ghost I bumped into?"

"That's impossible. He's dead." She drew her knees up to her chin, assuming an upright fetal position on the couch.

"Did you know I came out to Trailerville with him, to show him where you lived? I'd say he handled a car pretty well for a dead guy."

"He told me that someone named Tom drove over here with him."

"That would be me. Tom's my real name — Tom Emmendorfer to be exact. I usually only introduce myself as Underdog to cute women."

"You played a nasty trick on me. In fact, you played a nasty trick on nearly everybody I know — on me, Race, Geoffrey, everybody."

"I'll have to admit that the game has gone my way in recent days — like when your pawn reaches the other end of the chess board and you can trade it in for a knight or whatever. But my skills as a trickster pale in comparison to yours. You're the undisputed queen."

She lay sideways, reaching up to a colorful, Indian-looking blanket draped on the sofa back and pulling it over herself. "I got this blanket at a street fair in Chicago a few years ago. It's imported from Peru," she said of the blue, beige and maroon-striped article.

"My victory has come at a heavy price, however," he said. "I quit my job at the college, so I guess I won't be seeing you anymore. Unless we happen to cross each other's path in town." He got up and walked unswervingly towards the door.

"Don't leave me!" she begged from under the blanket, which covered everything but her pleading eyes.

"I'm not leaving you, you're driving me away. Now, if you'll excuse me, I've got a calliope to finish building." With that, he walked out of her trailer and headed back to town, spirits buoyed like helium balloons were pinned to the back of his shirt. In no time at all, he arrived at Ed D.'s garage and set himself to performing one of the final steps in completing his calliope: staining the naked wood cabinet with walnut stain, to be followed with a coat of varnish in a day or two. After that, testing and fine-tuning could begin.

TWENTY

Underdog had little to keep him busy in the weeks after his firing but tinker with his calliope and spend the proceeds from his unemployment checks, so he spent much of his waking time in Roger's Bar. Mornings he started with a screwdriver, made with fresh-squeezed orange juice. Orange pulp suspended in the glass gave him the illusion that his diet was being supplemented with fiber and vitamins. By afternoon, he graduated to beer; for solid food he grazed on the pretzels and Chex party mix that Roger replenished from two o'clock until the end of Happy Hour. For long stretches throughout the day, he studied the intricate grape vine curlicues in the stamped tin ceiling and admired their mock-Roman overtones — "When in Jasper, do as the Romans do," he quipped, stringing out the joke for a whole week.

Mainly he pondered the old adage, "The devil finds work for idle hands." Luckily, the early summer idleness that bedeviled Underdog was broken up by a steady stream of college people filing through the bar and apprising him of the latest campus gossip. His main conduit of information was Janet, the English Department secretary, a firsthand witness to Race Fletcher's activities since his own termination from the college. She came into Roger's every Thursday afternoon, promptly at four-forty, taking precisely ten minutes to travel from campus to bar. While he listened to the perky Janet, Underdog considered making a pass by interrupting her and planting his lips on hers, which were prominent and often rolled into incredulous "Ohs" that punctuated her recountings.

"For the time being, Race is splitting his time between Hollywood and Jasper," Janet explained. "He'd abandon Jasper altogether, but he's having a hard time selling his house. Plus he's got a pending lawsuit against the college for wrongful termination. He's got to return every so often and give depositions or talk with his local counsel." In between breathless sentences, she sucked down her tequila sunrise through a green straw that turned brown when filled with the reddish liquid.

"Nobody really believes he wants his teaching position back," she continued. "One of the professors in the department theorizes that he hopes to settle for a dollar amount equal to how much his house cost. That way, everything turns out even-steven. He's probably got a winnable case. He hasn't done anything illegal — being a porn actor's not a crime. In Race's case, quite the opposite."

She dabbed her forehead and the back of her neck with the damp napkin from underneath her drink. Printed on the napkin was a cartoon of a drunken sailor hitting on a woman who had torpedoes drawn in place of breasts. Underdog couldn't make out the text below, though he had little doubt it was lewd, whatever it said.

"There, I went and admitted it," said Janet. "Like nearly everybody else in town, I went down to Sally Valentine's and took a gander at the skin flick in question. That Race Fletcher was a hot number when he was young, you want my opinion — although, ahem, it appears that he certainly was less than forthcoming when he was hired. In fact, it's plain he tried to hide that aspect of his past," she said, concluding on a feigned note of disapproval.

"I'm surprised my name didn't come up in his lawsuit. After all, I'm responsible for him getting run out of town," said Underdog.

"I've heard he considered it, but then he decided not to, because there wasn't any money to sue you out of."

Race Fletcher eventually won his lawsuit, and the jury awarded him three hundred thousand dollars in damages. Then they trebled this amount for punitive damages, traditional when somebody suffered "gross harm" due to "deliberate and wanton conduct," as the *Jasper County Shopper* termed it in one of their news stories. After paying out one-third of the total in attorneys' fees, Race walked away with a cool six hundred thousand dollars in his pocket, which led him to the decision to convert his Jasper experience into a huge tax write-off. He opted to donate his house to the town, ordaining that it be converted into a museum. He even threw his skull collection into the bargain, thereby forming the basis for a natural history exhibit, which was generously added to by a farmer who immediately donated his collection of Indian arrow heads that he found over the years when the earth coughed them up during plowing season. With the assistance of the college's anthropology faculty and contributions from townies who gave away their collections of blacksmith equipment, campaign buttons, corn cob dolls and Boy Scout memorabilia, the Wallace House evolved into an attraction meriting two paragraphs in the brochure mailed out by the state's department of tourism. Some two thousand visitors were drawn to the site each year.

Unfortunately, Race Fletcher's career in Hollywood came to an abrupt halt, when the pilot for *The New Green Acres Show* bombed miserably in the Nielsen ratings, coming in at ninety-seventh place for the week it aired. The reviewers panned the show also; one critic from *L.A. Weekly* stated that the concept might have been salvaged if members of the original cast appeared in the show. "There is much sociocultural hay to be made," she explained, citing several examples. "Bringing back Alf and Ralph, known to residents of Hooterville as 'the Monroe Brothers,' would call into question gender roles. Bringing back Arnold the talking pig would explore issues concerning the ethical treatment of animals. Bringing back Eb, the Douglas's hired hand, could potentially address the dislocations the farm labor force has suffered in the intervening years." Such script-doctoring was necessary in her opinion "to deconstruct nineties agribusiness reality as successfully as the earlier program deconstructed the sixties' pastoral ideal."

Despite his bad experience with TV, Race Fletcher nevertheless managed to land on his feet when he accepted a teaching job proffered by the TV and Film Studies Department at U.S.C. The scuttlebutt on this development had a notoriously gay film producer pressuring the school to create a job for him. It was said that during his hustling days Race met and serviced him in a Manhattan hotel room; when Race was writing his dissertation on *Green Acres*, the producer, who had taken quite a shine to him, lobbied the studios to allow him privileged access to their archives. The last Underdog heard, Race resided a couple of doors away from the actor Dennis Hopper in a bachelor pad/beach house/literary salon located in Venice, California. Underdog found himself marveling at Race Fletcher's luck in the business of life; he wondered how big a part the four-leaf clover tattooed on his chest played in his continued success.

From his stool in Roger's Bar Underdog likewise heard about Milton Flaghorn's downfall. Never a popular figure in Jasper — Roger referred to him as an "Ivy League powdered asshole," for instance — the scandal that he birthed provided plenty of opportunities for townies to pitchfork his name. During a series of well-publicized court dates, beginning with Flaghorn's indictment in August, everybody who frequented Roger's Bar frankly stated his opinion on what treatment should be accorded such a traitor to the community. Underdog had overheard workers from the barbed wire factory threaten to strangle Flaghorn with a spool of rusty barbed wire — "If he don't choke, the tetanus will surely get 'im," said one member of the group. Farmers discussed the idea of drawing and quartering him by tying his limbs to four tractors that sped off in separate directions. Jupiter Motor Company employees announced they wanted to make Flaghorn their honorary crash test dummy and put him through a series of horrific accidents. And a truck driver from the grain elevator in town advocated disemboweling him, then selling his guts for fertilizer.

The jury that listened to his trial decided against applying any of these cruel and unusual punishments. Instead, for the crimes of embezzlement, fraud and willful breach of his fiduciary duty, Flaghorn was fined eighty thousand dollars and sentenced to sixteen months at a minimum-security prison. There he joined other white collar criminals and witness protection program types in leisurely laps in the pool or rounds of golf on the nine-hole course at a jail facility that differed from a country club only in the lack of bar service and the presence of a high, chain link fence surrounding the property. Like many Jasperites, Underdog felt that the sentence meted out did not match the severity of the crimes Flaghorn committed; his idea of a fitting punishment for Flaghorn entailed throwing him into a medieval dungeon, shackling him to the wall, feeding him nothing but bread and water, searing his flesh with red-hot iron pokers, having a black-hooded guard whip him occasionally, and in general letting him slowly rot from the feet-up in his own waste products. Still and all, Underdog and others found a delicious irony in the fact that the fence imprisoning Flaghorn was topped by razor wire manufactured right in Jasper.

By summer's end, Reid had garnered enough credit hours to be awarded his master's degree in sociology with an emphasis in criminology. He was glad he followed his advisor's advice to complete the writing of his thesis during summer school, even though he felt rushed by the accelerated summer schedule. For, with the majority of students gone for summer vacation, the library shelves were fully stocked with all the materials he needed to perform his research. In the fall or spring semester — especially the spring when several hundred freshman comp students were assigned research papers — he would face stiff competition from seekers of books on gun control, a hackneyed topic in the hands of undergraduates, but in Reid's hands a subject that resulted in a thoughtful, persuasive and original paper unanimously accepted by his committee for fulfillment of his thesis requirement. Weighing the benefits and drawbacks of police spot-searching gun-happy public housing residents' homes for weapons, the piece was later published by the *Journal of Social Trauma* and ultimately led Reid to a job in social work.

Specifically, he was hired by the Polk County (Iowa) Department of Corrections as its Youth Outreach Coordinator. His job entailed getting basketballs or brooms into teenagers' hands in place of switchblade knives or nine millimeter pistols. Most of his charges were current or former street gang members under some kind of court supervision, either on probation or in halfway houses. A couple had actually murdered somebody, usually another gang-banger in disputes over drugs or turf.

The moment Reid departed for Des Moines and entered into his new life was a sad one for Underdog. As the hour of one approached, Roger's nephew Kent, the bartender on duty, started shouting his customary "Bar's closed! Get the fuck out!" Next, he visited every table and delivered to each patron his own personal "Get the fuck out!" message, all the while cracking a wet dish towel like a whip. Still having unfinished business, Reid and Underdog pleaded with Kent to sell them a fifth of Jim Beam to go. Initially, Kent refused, but he finally capitulated when he thought up a ruse to by-pass Jasper's liquor laws: he offered to give them the whiskey as a bon voyage gift to Reid if they bought a bag of corn chips for fifteen dollars.

Their agreement not to call it a night until they finished the bottle forestalled their separation another three hours. As they strolled through Jasper revisiting significant sites in Reid's college career, they took turns gulping whiskey. They concluded their travels on the railroad trestle across Hackberry Creek. A green glow from the nearby signal bridge gave their surroundings a minty flavor; at least that's how Underdog's short-circuited senses, which by four in the morning could taste colors and smell sounds, perceived it. Very drunk, impervious to the sharp taste of whiskey, Reid guzzled the last of the liquor and threw the empty bottle into the creek below. They watched until the bottle floated around a bend in the creek and out of sight, then they proceeded back into the center of town. As they staggered along the train tracks, tears flooded Underdog's eyes and scalded his eyeballs like his tear ducts were distilling whiskey, not too far from reality given that his body was saturated with the stuff.

Approaching his Oldsmobile, Reid broke the silence they had maintained going all the way back to the trestle. "I think I'll make enough money at my new job where I can afford a new car," he said, petting the hood. "And here I thought I was going to own this old heap till I died. I figured I was going to be buried inside of it."

"Put it in your will. No matter where I'm at or what I'm doing, I'll show up at your funeral and insist on it."

With that, Reid got into his car and drove away in a puff of purple pollution, leaving Underdog feeling all choked up inside like he had a grape lozenge caught in his throat.

Thrown out of his job on-campus, Underdog no longer had regular access to Ione. In fact, he saw her only once that summer, in the Piggly Wiggly supermarket. She was pushing around a shopping basket containing only a few items: candy, cookies, ice cream and wine. A steady diet of sweets and alcohol lacked the nutrients to foster strong bones, healthy complexion, glossy hair or good posture, and this was evident in her appearance. Despite the high number of calories in the foods she had thrown in her basket, protruding ribs, collar bone, vertebrae and knee caps indicated that Ione, thin to begin with, had lost a considerable amount of weight; Underdog wondered if she might have turned anorexic or bulimic, for her legs were as skinny as golf clubs.

In the frozen food aisle they nearly had a head-on collision with their shopping carts. He said, "Hello, Ione. Long time no see," in the most neutral tone of voice possible. She swung her cart full around in a hundred and eighty degree arc, meantime knocking over a display of cardboard fruit juice cartons stacked in a pyramid. Amid juice cartons tumbling to the floor, some leaking raspberry juice that swelled around the base of the pyramid like a blood puddle, she rushed down the aisle in the reverse direction and disappeared around the corner. Underdog wheeled his cart around, too, deciding to head her off at the pass. Next commenced a rather comical scene which involved the two warily eyeing each other at opposite ends of every aisle they crossed. Underdog was struck by how it seemed like they glimpsed one another from across a series of uncrossable canyons, a curse to him who wanted to be reunited, a blessing to her who wanted to maintain a healthy distance.

When they reached the last aisle of the store, salad dressings and condiments, actually the first aisle if you took the route the supermarket had designed for shoppers, he saw her speaking with the store's security guard and pointing at him. Realizing that she must be complaining that he was harassing her, he abandoned his shopping basket and hightailed it out the nearby automatic door. Mindful of his run-in with the law during the previous fall for stalking, he chose to pick up a few necessities at the convenience store and pay the inflated prices rather than risk any further legal entanglements. It was the last time he ever laid eyes upon Ione.

Underdog learned later from Janet that Ione had returned to suburban Chicago. "I was as surprised as you are," she said. "I went into the credit union last week to cash a check, and I saw she had been replaced by another girl. When I asked her what the story was, she said she didn't know. But she called her manager out to speak with me, because I told her I wanted to write and see how she was. (Actually, I was just curious. I'm not really going to write a letter to her.)

"So her former boss came out, this guy with so much dandruff it looked like his shoulders were capped with snow. He said that she had left her job without giving two weeks' notice or a forwarding address or anything. All he knew was that she was moving back home. Since that was someplace outside Chicago, I gather that's where she must be living these days. It sounds to me like she split town with her tail between her legs. There must have been too much embarrassment in how Race Fletcher dumped her."

"Or maybe she didn't like reverting to a regular old townie after playing Princess alongside the Prince of Jasper for so many months," Underdog sniffed.

"Wherever she's living now has got to be better than the cockroach-infested rat trap she lived in in Trailerville."

"Roach-infested?"

"Crawling with them. Trailerville's a cockroach farm. They must yield a billion cockroaches per acre."

"Cockroaches dwelling in the creases of her sheets," he muttered, more to himself than to his companion.

It took Underdog about six weeks to learn the humors of the menagerie of musical instruments that comprised his calliope; after that came another week of tuning each horn and string and tightening each drum head according to its own individual temper. Adding time to the length of the project was his mounting frustration, which often prompted him to walk away after only short intervals of work. Although he felt like he had grown up a lot in the previous year, he suspected he hadn't quite outgrown his over-reaction when his patience ran out. In his youth, he chucked model cars or planes against the wall when the glue didn't set right or the parts didn't fit properly. During a spell of humid nights in early August, Underdog was ready to take an ax to the whole enterprise after discovering that he had to re-punch 4,800 holes in a set of 160 computer cards. In essence, his calliope was suffering a total breakdown of its central nervous system, and Underdog was not far behind.

Yet, man conquered machine eventually. By the first week of September, Underdog's calliope was ready for a recital. But when he tried to think of somebody special enough to take part in this momentous occasion, a short list of people turned up; actually a totally blank pad of paper resulted, because Reid, the top, really the only, candidate had moved away to Iowa in early June.

While Underdog sat on a grassy mound at the geographic center of Jasper College, in the so-called "Mall," a network of walking paths, flower beds and park benches stretching between the library and the student center, the obvious audience for his calliope's maiden run came to mind. It was the Friday before Labor Day; the fall semester was scheduled to start the following Tuesday, and the Mall was clogged with hundreds of students milling around folding tables where they spoke to representatives from such student organizations as the *Chronicler*, the Campus Christers, the Gay and Lesbian Union, the Student Council, the Young Republicans, the Beaux Arts Club, the Anti-Intervention Society, the intramural sports teams and, of course, the various fraternities and sororities. Later that evening, the festivities would move a few blocks west to a blocked-off street in Suds City, where the Chamber of Commerce kicked off its annual corn boil to welcome back to town the Jasper College student body, its members' biggest revenue source.

As he watched the display, Underdog regretted summer's passing. It meant that students returning to school after summer break would spoil the peace and quiet Jasper enjoyed in their absence. It meant that the warm weather would soon recede as the northern hemisphere tilted further and further away from the sun. It meant that co-eds would cover up acres and acres of bare skin by putting on sweaters, pants and coats. This was what Underdog regretted most, while his eyes gorged on women who congregated everywhere around: perky blondes in pink polo shirts, purple shorts and virgin white tennis shoes; regal blacks with braided, beaded hair dressed in safari-print pantsuits; grunge chicks with pierced navels, unshaven armpits and dirty legs. When Judy Baine wandered into view, he decided that she was the proper person to hear the first notes from his calliope. Regret immediately gave way to a sense of renewal, the mood that prevailed in the Mall among students who palpably tingled at the fresh possibilities of a new school year.

He waved her over when he saw her notice him. She raised her hand to wave back, then caught herself, remembering that she was supposed to be mad at him. She looked radiant as always; her natural beauty transcended her dumpy outfit, consisting of grass-stained denim overalls under which she wore nothing but a plain white brassiere. Despite the fact that she lived in close proximity to him, she had seldom crossed his path in recent months because of her busy summer schedule. He felt his heart lurch upward in his chest when she sat down next to him on the grass.

"What brings you over to campus?" he asked.

"I'm in between mowing jobs. My client for the afternoon is an art professor who paints all night and never wakes up before two. He won't let me get started till after he's out of bed. Too much noise."

"You're looking good," he said, his gaze directed towards the cornfields to the east.

"So are you," she replied, unable to look him straight in the face either. Instead, she stared at a quartet of shirtless college boys who were kicking around a hackey sack.

"I've got something to show you."

"I'll bet you do. Well, I've seen it. And to be honest, when you've seen one, you've seen them all," she replied.

"No no no, nothing like that. I finished up the project I've been working on over in Ed D. Parkman's garage."

"Project?"

"It's a surprise. I wanted you to be the first person I demonstrate it for."

Feeling flattered, she smiled, though she still looked away. "Okay. But I can't make it till after sundown."

* * *

Come sundown, Underdog was engaged in rubbing steel wool over the varnished calliope cabinet to achieve the smoothest faux walnut surface possible. Around nine o'clock, Judy entered Ed D.'s garage, emerging from a darkness dominated by fireflies that flickered like klieg lights advertising the debut of Underdog's music machine.

"You mean I showered and walked all the way over here just to see a bunch of beat-up musical instruments?" she asked.

"Check this out," he said, reaching around the back of his calliope and flipping a toggle switch. The quiet chug-chug-chug of an air compressor began. Next he flicked another switch and the music commenced, the boom-ding boom-ding of bass drum and cymbal and the plunk-plink plunk-plink of the cello playing the bass line. Following an eight-bar introduction, the cornet joined in blaring the unmistakable melody to the song "Don't Fence Me In."

"Pretty cool, huh?" he said upon the song's conclusion to a clearly delighted Judy who had a most captivating look of wonderment on her face.

"How does it work?" she asked.

"Well, you start with a china cupboard. The mechanism that drives the thing is inside the bottom part, behind those drawers, which are fake, incidentally, glued on. The first sound you heard was the air compressor building up steam. The second switch flicked on the electric generator. It's got a flywheel so it runs smooth. The motor turns a spindle that unwinds a computer tape from a garden hose reel. A rack of sensitive levers lying across the spindle are tripped by holes I punched into the tape. These are connected to a row of rods that lead off to the various instruments. One rod goes to the air compressor and controls the air flow to the cornet. The others raise and lower drumsticks, pluck cello strings and push down cornet valves. The song lasts a minute fifty seconds, and a timer automatically shuts everything off after it runs for two minutes. Then, to restart it, you have to manually rewind the computer tape with this crank handle in the back. (The next one's gonna' have two electric motors and rewind automatically.) It operates on the same principle as the music box. I call it a calliope, though it's more precisely called a 'music machine.'"

"Play it again."

He complied. When the calliope had finished its cycle, he knelt down and pointed to a brass plaque etched with his name, song title and year. "Calliope is the muse of eloquence, you know," he said, then proceeded in becoming ever more eloquent with Judy, telling her that he was sorry they had drifted apart. They belonged together, he believed, and it was imperative that they be married immediately. First he had to sell his calliope. He figured he could get as much as five thousand for it and resolved to contact some antique shops or art galleries in the area to see if anyone might have a customer for such an unusual piece. With the proceeds he could build another calliope, buy her a ring, and rent the reception hall. But first, he said he had some making up to do with her. While he pulled down the garage door, she lifted up her sleeveless white cotton dress that exposed her muscular arms so appealingly, whereupon his face blazed early exploratory trails in the uncivilized light-brown scruff between her legs. This was followed hard upon by penetration of regions further south. One week later, the two were married in a civil wedding ceremony conducted by the Jasper County Justice of the Peace. Mona and Reid attended.

Mona was delighted at the prospect of a union between her daughter and Underdog, so ecstatic that she gave them ten thousand dollars taken from a cashed-in IRA which her late husband Jack bequeathed to her. Connected with all the better families in town, Judy knew exactly whom to speak with about Underdog's calliope, a collector of imported music boxes married to the Provost of Jasper

College. Always the savvy business woman, Judy even bid the woman up to six thousand dollars.

With a total of sixteen thousand dollars in hand, the newlyweds relocated to Ashland, an artsy, historical town full of painters, sculptors and potters who fled the big city to make a new life in an increasingly popular tourist destination. Formerly a frontier boom town in a valley rich with lead mines gone bust, Ashland was a virtual ghost town for almost a century until a multitude of charming shops, fancy boutiques and instructive museums sprouted up, creating a second boom town in place of the first. Paying twelve thousand dollars down, about a third of the total mortgage amount, the couple purchased a two-acre homestead outside of town on which stood an ancient, though well-kept, two-story farm house plus a medium-sized pole barn out back, where Underdog maintains his workshop and Judy parks her tractors and mowers.

Judy presently contributes to the household income by running her lawn care business, which she moved with her from Jasper. In the course of a few months, she stole the accounts of seven buildings on the National Register of Historic Places from a commercial lawn care franchise that used harmful chemical treatments instead of T.L.C. She also won the business of a number of well-to-do townspeople, the local bank, two fancy restaurants, and a sprawling country inn. She is doing so well that she has hired two part-time employees, teenage girls the high school guidance counselor sent, and she is attending classes in agriculture and small business management at the nearby community college. In the future she plans to earn a four-year degree in landscape design at the state university extension one town over from Ashland.

Now considered a "calliope artisan" (that's what he puts under "Occupation" when filing his taxes), Underdog is having difficulty keeping up with the backlog of orders from rich folks eager to purchase his calliopes, not to mention frequent commissions from museums or historical societies who ask him to build replicas of antique European music machines for their collections. A master of casing alleyways on trips to Chicago or the Twin Cities, of rummaging through resale shops in college towns like Jasper or Madison, and of scanning the newspaper classifieds for the phone number of the latest Ashland kid to abandon the idea of music lessons, Underdog acquired a never-ending variety of musical instruments that he bought cheap and sold dear after joining them in an amusing array of configurations. His favorite pieces to date: "Do You Know the Way to San Jose" arranged for a trumpet, tenor sax, French horn and bass drum; "The

Peanut Vendor" played by two banjos, complete with claves and maracas supplying the calypso beat; and, from inside a giant cabinet custom-built by a local furniture maker of note, the seasonal ditty "Winter Wonderland" performed by three old sousaphones the high school band director offered to give free to anyone who hauled them away.

And for the remainder of his life, Underdog tried to follow his townie sense wherever the hell it led.

III Publishing

Pyrexia by Michel Méry
ISBN 1-886625-02-6   192 pages, 5½ x 8½" $10.00
Abelard shares a tiny apartment on Mars with his anima, Kahani. For entertainment he hooks into the GUM (Global Un-Manifested) Station, which has taken him to Pyrexia, the sex-goddess at the beginning of the universe, but usually takes him to late 20th century New York City or Paris. Abelard's problems are multiplying so quickly he should be wondering if he is losing his mind.

The Last Days of Christ the Vampire by J.G. Eccarius
ISBN 1-886625-00-X   192 pages, 5½ x 8½" $10.00
The book that broke the silence about the vampiric nature of Jesus Christ and his fundamentalist zombies. Jesus has set his sights on converting some teenagers in Providence, Rhode Island, but instead they resist and set out to hunt him down before he can release his Apocalypse upon the world. Arguably the best religious satire of the 20th century.

Virgintooth by Mark Ivanhoe
ISBN: 0-9622937-3-3   192 pages, 4.25 x 7" $7.00
Elizabeth has not exactly died: she has been made into a vampire. Now she has not only all the problems she had when alive, but she must also get along with the other vampires. At times terrifying, at times hysterically funny, Virgintooth will horrify and delight you.

Geminga, Sword of the Shining Path by Melvin Litton
ISBN 0-9622937-4-1   5.5 x 8.5", 256 pages $9.95
In a world poised between a superstitious past and a surreal future of bioengineering, virtual reality and artificial consciousness, Geminga surfs on the winds of the present. This bird has been trained since infancy to assassinate the enemies of Peru's Sendero Luminoso. Now she's come with her best friend, Jimmy the Snake, to California Norte.

This'll Kill Ya by Harry Willson
ISBN 0-9622937-2-5   192 pages 4.25 x 7" $6.00
The anti-censorship mystery that will have you laughing out loud and examining your own reactions to materials that surely should be censored. Caution: If you believe that words can be used as weapons to harm people, reading this book may be hazardous to your health.

A.D. by Saab Lofton
ISBN 0-9622937-8-4   5.5 x 8.5", 320 pages $12.00
The future seen through African-American eyes: after decades of anti-utopian racist fascism in the 21st century, revolutionaries create a society based on Libertarian Socialist Democracy. Even then, a menace from the past threatens society. "The price of Liberty is Eternal Vigilance."

The Father, The Son, and The Walkperson by Michel Méry
ISBN 0-9622937-9-2   192 pages, 5½ x 8½" $10.00
A web of fractalled tales mixing science-fictionish absurdity with a quantum-improbability perspective of our information-oriented, reality-denying technoculture. By taking society and intellect as spectacle to new heights, Méry prepares you to be dashed on the rocks of surreality below.

Anarchist Farm by Jane Doe
ISBN 1-886625-01-8   192 pages, 5½ x 8½" $10.00
Pancho the pig is driven off a farm where an animal has been ruined by pigs acting like humans. Raccoons who lead him to the forest defenders, fighting to protect their forest from the Corporation's clear-cuts. At the Apple Farm the animals were free to run their own farm without human supervision. But the Corporation plans to grab the farm and slaughter the animals...

We Should Have Killed the King by J.G. Eccarius
ISBN 0-9622937-1-7   192 pages 4¼ x 7" $5.00
Jack Straw and hundreds of thousands of other English peasants rebelled against their overlords in 1381, killing nobles, lawyers and tax collectors. Ultimately Straw was hung, but his spirit of rebellion is reborn in America in the punk/anarchist movement during the 1980's.

Resurrection 2027 by J.G. Eccarius
ISBN 0-9622937-7-6   192 pages 4¼ x 7" $7.00
Ann Swanson remembers her life as a nurse before the Apocalypse, before she died of The Plague. Resurrected years later by the grace of Mary the Mother of God, she is called to work at the Temple of the Resurrection. A brave new look at religious mind control.

My Journey With Aristotle to the Anarchist Utopia
by Graham Purchase
ISBN 0-9622937-6-8   128 pages 4¼ x 7" $7.00
No government? No taxes? No police? Wouldn't that be anarchy? Tom, is bashed by the police until they leave him for dead. When Tom regains consciousness he finds himself a thousand years in the future where he encounters Aristotle, who leads him down to Bear City where humans live happily without government or bosses of any kind.

Vampires or Gods? by William Meyers [non-fiction]
ISBN 0-9622937-5-X   192 pages, 8.5 x 11" $15.00
Vampires living thousands of years, commanding legions of human wor-shippers? Yes! Every major ancient civilization was associated with a vampire. Egypt had Osiris, who rose from the dead after his body was hacked to pieces. Asia Minor had Cybele, whose followers fed her their blood. Greece had Dionysus, Rome had Quirinus, and the list goes on.

To order direct from III Publishing send check or money order (postage & handling is free for orders of $7.00 or more in the US; otherwise add $2) made out to III Publishing, P.O. Box 1581 Gualala, CA 95445.